JUV
BAE

-99

D0065970

WALK THE DARK STREETS

ALSO BY EDITH BAER

A Frost in the Night

WALK THE DARK STREETS

A Novel by **EDITH BAER**

FRANCES FOSTER BOOKS

FARRAR, STRAUS AND GIROUX   NEW YORK

Walk the Dark Streets is a work of fiction. Thalstadt, the scene of this novel, is not a name on a map. It is a place where memory, story, and history converge to portray a time and those who lived in its shadow.

—E.B.

Sections of this book were begun under a Fellowship Award from the New Jersey State Council on the Arts, for which I wish to express my appreciation.

J'Attendrai by Dino Olivieri & Louis Poterat
Copyright © 1938 by Southern Music Publishing Co. Inc.
Copyright Renewed
International Copyright Secured. Used by Permission

Distributed in Canada by Douglas & McIntyre Ltd.
Printed in the United States of America
Designed by Filomena Tuosto
First edition, 1998

Library of Congress Cataloging-in-Publication Data
Baer, Edith.
     Walk the dark streets / Edith Baer. — 1st ed.
          p.   cm.
     "Frances Foster books."
     Sequel to: A frost in the night.
     Summary: Continues the story of Eva, a young Jewish girl living in
Nazi Germany where she and her parents experience increasing
tensions in daily life while considering possibilities of escape.
     ISBN 0-374-38229-8
     1. Jews—Germany—Juvenile fiction.   2. Germany—History—1933–1945—
Juvenile fiction.   [1. Jews—Germany—Fiction.   2. Germany—History—
1933–1945—Fiction.]   I. Title.
PZ7.B1388Wal   1998
[Fic]—dc21   97-36572

In loving memory of my parents,
and to my children and children's children
in whom they continue.

"... a goodly heritage."
(PSALM 16:6)

■

To Frances Foster, twice my editor,
whose insight, caring, and encouragement
sustained me on this journey

■

And to my husband, Robert,
for having shared it

WALK THE DARK STREETS

ONE JANUARY–MARCH 1933

It had begun at the end of January, with the measles caught from her upstairs cousins, Ella and Uschi. But her illness hung on long afterward, that winter of 1933, her throat flaring red like the Nazi flags she saw flying from the neighboring houses when Anna came in from the kitchen and drew back the bedroom curtains to let in the brief midday sun. The red flags with their black swastikas at the center stung Eva's fever-sore eyes more than the glittering blue brightness that flooded the room. Hitler had been appointed Chancellor, Anna told her in a worried whisper. The Nazis were taking over. In Thalstadt. All over Germany.

Eva was too immersed in her own illness to take it all in. And so, perhaps, were her parents and others in the family who, with mounting apprehension, watched her fever rise and fall while momentous events swept the world beyond her sickroom window. Her father, trying to conceal the anxious look in his eyes, brought her books from his bookstore downstairs. Grandfather poked his head into the room and asked her which was heavier, a pound of feathers or a pound of lead. It was an old game of theirs, one that she was now too grownup, and too miserable, to play. But he ignored her sullen face and told her with forced cheerfulness, "We'll make an Einstein of you yet!" And Aunt Hanni, her father's diminutive sister, would take one look at Eva's eyes, glazed with a sudden spurt of temperature, study the tips of her tiny, high-heeled shoes, and shake her head under its beautifully coiffed cap of white hair. "The tonsils will have to come out, in *my* judgment!" she said archly, calling into question Dr. Pfaender's. Eva's old pediatrician had been called in because he was "so good with throats."

"They *won't* have to come out!" Eva protested hoarsely. "It's just another *cold!*" And her mother, catching the tremor of fear underneath the bravado, said quickly, "Let's give it a little more time."

One morning, her fever having abated for a few days, she insisted on going to school—"at least to get some of the homework I missed from Renate!" She crept back exhausted at the end of the school day, stunned by the atmosphere of excitement in the classroom: Horst Reuter strutting about in his new brown Hitler Youth uniform—"for the parade tonight, when the Führer comes to Thalstadt!" Diete Goetz raising her hand to announce the place and time of Hitler's campaign speech— "My parents say it's a historic occasion to hear the Führer in person—so we're all going!" Frau Ackermann, hiding her discomfort at having politics brought into her classroom under a too-bright smile: "Back to our conjugations, class! The irregular verb 'to speak.' "

"*Sprechen, spricht, sprach, gesprochen . . .*"

"Good! And now for a sentence applying the verb 'to speak' in one of these forms—yes, Klaus?"

Klaus Herzog lowered his waving hand and rose from

his bench. *"Der Führer spricht in Thalstadt!"* he shot back promptly, and there were giggles and even a scattered clapping of hands.

■

"Klaus couldn't care less about Hitler," Renate Reinhardt said on their way to the streetcar stop after school. "He just wants to be on Horst's good side!"

Eva shrugged. "Like Anna's brother-in-law. He told her he'll vote for the Nazis next month, because that's how the wind blows. Now she won't go to her sister's house anymore on her days off."

Renate's eyes searched Eva's face with open concern. "Your parents must be worried about . . . things," she said, as they huddled out of the February wind in the little shelter at the streetcar stop. "*Mine* are. My father told us the things Hitler says and does deny the spirit of God."

Renate's father was a Lutheran pastor who had brought his large family to Thalstadt from the Swabian countryside a few years before. At once they had become friends: Renate, the shy "new girl," whose country ways and dress still set her apart in the city classroom; Eva, who'd been in Buchberg School from first grade on but had always been "different," too—the Jewish girl who was included in everything, yet never quite "belonged."

Eva's Number 7 came down the hill. "Thanks for the homework, Renate!" she called back over her shoulder. They waved to each other through the window; then the streetcar rounded the bend and Eva saw Renate cross the tracks to catch her ride up the hill.

On the Carlottaplatz, where Eva got off, the newspaper kiosk was pasted with huge, garish posters for the parliamentary election to the Reichstag in early March. *Nazi* posters, she noticed on second look; those of the other parties had been torn down or defaced, with just a shred or two left to identify and mock them: the three arrows of the Sozialdemokraten above the slogan "Now More Than Ever: WITH US FOR LIBERTY!" The placard of the Demokratische Partei, proclaiming: "Germany—You Are at the Crossroads!" The Catholic Zentrum's "List 4—the Party for People's Rights and Social Order!"

■

"They are already only *semi*-legal, those coalition parties that defend the Republic," her father said warily, when she asked him about it later. "Their newspapers are suppressed, their leaders are prevented from addressing voters." He shook his head. "Lies, violence, coercion—I fear the election has already been decided."

He managed a small smile. "You've seen and heard enough for one day, Eva. Let the grownup world put itself together again—if there is still a chance. Tell me how things went at school!"

His question caught her off guard. "Oh—fine! Renate gave me my homework. Frau Ackermann said she was glad I was better."

"Well, so am I," her father said. "Let's hope we're over the worst." He gave her hand a little squeeze, but his eyes looked past her into the late afternoon gray beyond the sheer curtains. The sound of heavy boots and raucous voices, muffled but unmistakable, drifted across the rooftops. The Nazis were marching, carrying flaring torches through the streets of Thalstadt.

That evening, her fever shot up again. She perched miserably on the edge of her bed while her mother drew back the sheets and helped her untie the knotted laces of her shoes; the room seemed stuffy and queerly lopsided and it took enormous effort just to bend over and straighten up again. There was no thought of going to school the next morning; nor, for the first time ever, did she want to go. She thought of Diete and Horst, and of the garish Nazi poster on the kiosk she *hadn't* told her father about. The one that showed a huge hammer slamming down on a cringing, hideous cartoon figure with the word JUDE inscribed on its sleeve in fake Hebrew lettering. Her head spun, as if the hammer had already struck its blow. She had no intention of passing the poster again the next day on the way to school. Far better to be at home, with her parents and grandfather and Anna to care for her and shield her from harm.

As for the pains in her ears, piercing, gnawing sensations that made her imagine the wriggling, burrowing motions of tiny worms—Dr. Pfaender dismissed these blandly enough as "merely sympathetic secondary symptoms radiating from the throat, I am happy to assure you, Frau Bentheim. Eva's middle-ear passages are in no wise affected." Nevertheless, to soothe her mother's fears, he warily prescribed drops of heated oil, which her mother administered promptly, one ear at a time, with a small dropper, a slight tremor of her hand, and an anxiously cheerful expression. Then she plugged up the ear with a tuft of cotton and admonished Eva to lie on her side to keep the oil from running out of the unaffected middle-ear passage.

Eva saw no reason to disobey. One could as easily read books lying on one side as on the other. With a surge of anticipation she raised her arm past the soggy cotton already growing cool and lumpy inside her ear. From the night table stacked high with books she selected one and opened it greedily, pausing only for a whiff of the unique fragrance of paper, binding, and print.

There followed a deliciously transposed state of being: a drowsy, fever-lulled time of utter contentment, of blissful self-oblivion and peace. Now and then her mother softly opened the door to fluff up her pillow; to carry a tall glass of stinging hot lemonade, silver spoon faintly clinking, to her bedside; or to temper the flaring furnace of her body with the allotted dosage of aspirin. These interruptions, brief and inevitable, Eva tolerated without protest; they were, she recognized, a kind of unofficial toll to be exacted from the sickroom reader in fair exchange for privileges conferred. Gazing at her mother from remote eyes, she waited for the door to close soundlessly, like the great cover of a secret book, leaving her shut inside a paradise guarded from the changing, troubling world beyond by the flaming sword of her fever.

At last, when her sieges of illness became more frequent and persistent than the brief periods of remission, and when not even Dr. Pfaender—staunch believer in the self-healing propensities of the young organism—could in good conscience advise postponement of a tonsillectomy any longer, she received the announcement with the greatest reluctance.

The next day, her fever fell, and Dr. Pfaender said it was time to "schedule the procedure in earnest."

■

On the first balmy morning in March, just before the elections her father feared were already decided, her mother took her across town to see Dr. Marcus, the throat specialist. Dr. Pfaender had stressed the need for some fresh air and exercise to "build up Eva's constitution," but now the brief walk tired her; her legs felt wooden and wobbly. In the shop windows, a stranger was walking toward her, fragile and pale and elegantly peaked of face, like Monika von Ahlem, her classmate. She had even grown a little, she noted with satisfaction, for her coat barely reached her knees.

At the Toy House Lentz, the window displays had been changed; the last time she had passed them, during Christmas vacation, there had been sleds and skates against the backdrop of a cardboard forest and gingerbread house. In their place now, against a green canvas meadow prematurely sprinkled with bluebells, were roller skates, jump ropes with bright handles, and dolls in pink bonnets sitting upright in lacquered carriages. Spring was almost here.

There was also a bicycle, painted a vivid blue, with silver pedals and large gleaming wheels.

"Come on, Eva," her mother said with a meaningful glance at her watch. "We mustn't keep Dr. Marcus waiting."

Eva shrugged. "I've always wanted a bicycle," she said petulantly, poking her finger against the shop window. "And you and Father kept saying it was too dangerous to ride one in the city—but now you're letting them take out my *tonsils*!"

"Now, Eva . . ." her mother began, but after a look at Eva's pinched, pale face confined herself to a mere headshake and a deep sigh.

In the doctor's waiting room on the fashionable Königstrasse, they sat glumly on the leather sofa and leafed through the magazines. All too soon, Eva was ushered into the doctor's office by a relentlessly cheerful nurse and made to sit in a reclining chair much like a dentist's while Dr. Marcus proceeded to examine her throat under the white glare of a lamp. Sullenly, she did as she was asked: tipping her head back, letting her jaw hang slack, extending her tongue to choke out a desperate *Aaaah.*

The doctor narrowed his eyes.

"A bad winter, Frau Bentheim," he observed over his shoulder. "Influenza—measles—storm troopers taking over the streets, the government . . ."

He shrugged—a rather handsome man, Eva had to admit, looking something the way her cousin Stefan at Heidelberg University might look one day.

With a light, skillful flick of his wrist he depressed her tongue and she gagged, more from a winter-long conditioned reflex than from necessity.

"Good!" Dr. Marcus said, patting her arm. Then he turned to her mother. "The sooner the better, Frau Bentheim. Here or at the hospital, whichever you and Dr. Pfaender prefer."

Her mother looked startled. "The hospital? Dr. Pfaender hadn't mentioned . . . My husband and I took it for granted it would be done at your office."

"I can still offer you the choice," Dr. Marcus said. "Though who knows how much longer I and my Jewish colleagues will retain our operating privileges at the hospitals . . ." He shrugged.

"I don't *want* to go to the hospital!" Eva croaked. Hospitals were scary places; in her books, some people got better in them and others didn't—even died! And though her father had assured her that tonsils meant a minor surgical incision scarcely to be dignified with the name operation, she had only pretended to be convinced.

The doctor, with a half-smile, held out his hand and helped her out of the chair. "Then we'll see you both here the day after tomorrow," he said as casually as if he were arranging an outing for them. "I'm sure Dr. Pfaender agrees that with such youthful patients there's less emotional trauma this way. And the medical risks are equally minimal."

He switched off the lamp at the chair. "No need to take Dr. Pfaender into your confidence regarding the rest of our conversation. I may be too pessimistic—we shall see. Meanwhile, one carries on for one's patients as if one were living in normal times—or gives up one's practice and looks for a country hospitable to foreign Jewish doctors, as Dr. Ullmann is doing. Without any prospects, thus far."

Her mother sighed. "Physicians of Dr. Ullmann's reputation, of yours . . . !" She shook her head.

The doctor walked them to the door. "What flavor of ice cream do you like best, young lady?"

Eva began to tremble. "Ssssstrrrawberry," she forced out between chattering teeth, rushing into the waiting room and pulling her mother behind her by her sleeve.

Suddenly it had all become very real. She probably *wouldn't* die, but her throat would hurt awfully and it would all be quite messy. Her cousin Uschi, she now recalled with a shudder, had been unable to swallow even her ice cream and simply let the stuff drizzle down her chin, like a baby. It had been an altogether ghastly sight, she remembered—quite unlike the fragile heroines in lacy white gowns who bore their sufferings so nobly and enchantingly in her books!

■

Two days later, bundled up snugly against the last vindictive blast of winter, she was delivered to the doctor's office, peeled out of her layers of warmth by the deft hands of the efficient nurse, and strapped into the now familiar surgical chair. In a sequence too swift to be clearly reassembled ever again, a cloth descended over her anxious face, something chill and choking fell from the distant sky, and a voice gently asked her to count to ten. It was a silly request to be made of someone her age, and she began sheepishly, stumbling over her heavy tongue. Before she had counted to three, it seemed to her later, she was back home, lying in her bed; the door opened and her father wheeled into her room a shiny new bicycle painted a brilliant blue, exactly like the one she had admired in the window of the Toy House Lentz.

She reached out her hand to feel the smooth, cool metal.

"For *me*?" Her voice, between a whisper and a croak, came painfully through thicknesses in her throat that made her doubt *anything* could have been taken out.

Her father nodded gravely. "I think you can be trusted with one now, Eva. It's time for you to learn to take care of yourself— time for us to let you," he added with his serious smile.

When she woke up again, it was evening. The bicycle stood in a twilit corner of her room, blue and silver and reassuringly solid. Looking at the bright spokes of the wheels, she began to remember what she had been dreaming, perhaps just a moment ago, perhaps earlier, asleep in the doctor's chair, under the ether.

At first there had been circles: great, whirling circles spinning within themselves, endlessly, blue and red—and suddenly she was with Detta, her old nanny, riding the cog railway up the steep hill toward the wooded peak of the Buchberg. "I am going to *Amerika*, little Eva," Detta said softly, putting her bony arm about Eva's shoulder and holding her close against her starched uniform.

Below them, through the dark window, Eva saw the city: Thalstadt at dusk, with the first violet shadows sinking from the sheltering hills and the first lights flaring in the streets. She saw the tower of the City Hall and the round steeple of the Memorial Church and vainly strained her leaden eyes for Grandfather's house between them—the lighted windows of the living room, behind which her mother might be sitting over her needlework, stitching flowers of subtly shaded blues on the white linen cloth in her hands. Higher and higher they rode, and farther and farther into the darkness receded the city, until it had become no larger than her mother's pincushion, its lights stuck into the velvet black like smooth, bright droplets of glass.

A chill wind swept down from the Buchberg; her throat hurt and her eyes stung with tears. "I want to go *back*, Detta," she heard herself say in the voice of a small child, the child she must have been in the days when Detta had been with them. She burrowed her face in the remembered starched sleeve. "Home, Detta. To Thalstadt."

"But we *are* going back, little Eva," Detta whispered soothingly, her bony hand gently turning Eva's face toward the window. "There—see for yourself!"

She leaned her hot forehead against the glass, staring down the dizzying slope of the hill into the valley, where the bright lights of the city would pierce the dark to meet her.

But there was only the night.

■

" *'Träume sind Schäume!'* " Grandfather would say with a dismissive shrug whenever she tried to tell him one of her dreams over the breakfast table. Dreams, the saying meant, were inconsequential things: evanescent like bubbles, like foam—figments of nocturnal imagination that would dissolve with the clear light of dawn, yielding to reason and reality.

But now the border between sleep and waking no longer seemed so sharply defined, dreams lingering on, pervading the day with the suppressed sense of menace and dislocation peculiar to them. While she had battled fever and infection, the city had been invaded by illness of another kind. Piece by piece, she began to discern the shape of the altered landscape, through her own eyes and ears, or through bits of stories brought to her by others—protectively by her parents, in whispers by Uschi, bluntly and with a touch of self-importance by Ella. It was a place where the Nazi flag now flew not only from houses and apartment buildings but from the City Hall itself, where swastikas on red armbands and pins suddenly erupted like an outbreak of scarlet fever. "And those who don't want to go along with the Nazis—in the City Hall, or in the State Parliament," Ella said, "get beaten up and packed off to the KZ!" "The *what*?" Eva asked, instantly alarmed though hearing the ominous-sounding term for the first time. "The *Konzentra-tionslager*, dummy!" Ella said. "The one on the Heuberg," she went on, with a wave of her hand implying other such "concentration camps" throughout the country.

Her father's old friend Herr Gerber was among those sent to the camp on the Heuberg, because he belonged "to the wrong party," the Social Democrats, Uschi said in a hushed voice behind the back of her hand, as if mere mention of the party's name, even within the four walls of Grandfather's house, were enough to bring disaster over their own heads as well.

"Like Günther's father—he is a *Sozi*, too," she whispered, her freckles standing out sharply against her blanched skin, her wide green eyes welling up.

"Günther? The boy on your Maccabi *Völkerball* team, Uschi?"

Uschi nodded. "Yes, Günther Rehfeld. His father used to write for the *Thalstadt Guardian*." She bit her lip, but suddenly burst into racking sobs.

"They *stomped* him, Günther said. When they broke into the *Guardian* the day after they came out on top in the election and smashed the printing presses and beat up the printers and journalists. When Günther's mother was allowed to go to the Heuberg to bring him fresh clothes, there was blood all over his shirt, Günther said, so much blood . . ."

■

A few weeks later, Herr Gerber himself showed up unexpectedly but punctually for his Thursday evening chess game with Eva's father, his face haggard, his clothes hanging loosely from his shoulders, as if his body had shrunk underneath them. He waved away their anxious questions.

"Bad enough for us *Sozis* and others of the democratic coalition," he said, his jaw set defiantly. "Worse for the *Kommunisten*. And Jews, of course—whatever their politics," he added grimly, after a moment's pause.

He glanced across the small inlaid table where Eva's father was setting up their game with uncertain hands, in a futile attempt at normalcy.

"We've been through a lot together, Bentheim," Herr Gerber said in his brusque Swabian speech. Eva knew he meant the war, when he and her father had served together in the trenches—a place that had none of the glory ascribed to it in the poems and songs taught at school, her father had made plain.

Herr Gerber's hand came to rest on one of the chessmen without making its move. "I'd never thought I'd hear myself say it, Bentheim, but I am scared—scared for you and your family, now that Hitler is tearing up the Constitution and dissolving the democratic parties. We're dealing with criminals here, with beasts—they'll stop at nothing!"

"Herr Gerber, Herr Gerber, don't make our hearts so heavy!" cried Eva's mother, dropping her embroidery on her lap. A tiny trickle of blood formed on her finger where she had pricked it with the needle in her haste to look up. "This cannot last—the German people are too civilized for this. Putting a decent man like you in one of those places!"

Herr Gerber shook his head. "If you had seen them where *I* did, Frau Bentheim, you'd change your mind about who's civilized."

He dabbed his flushed face with his large handkerchief.

"You belong here as much as anyone I know, Bentheim. I'd never thought I'd hear myself say it," he repeated, the chess game pushed aside for good, "but write to those relatives of yours, in America. You're not a well man, Bentheim," he added urgently. "Nazi Germany is no place for you!"

"Is it for anyone?" her father said softly. He glanced across the room to where Grandfather sat in his armchair, the *Thalstadt Mittagsblatt* on his knees. The paper had been *"gleichgeschaltet,"* as the Nazis put it, "brought into line," like all the newspapers in Germany. No wonder Grandfather was dozing over the unread pages.

"I share your fears, Gerber," Eva's father said. "They are as valid as your concern for us is genuine, and I am thankful for it. But what about an old man who has put his roots down in this town, like one of the old chestnut trees on the Schlossplatz? Can I transplant him in the twilight of his life? Or leave him to his fate?"

He shook his head.

"My brother feels we mustn't act in haste, and for my father's sake, I cannot bring myself to dissuade him. Perhaps, sometime in the future, if things don't improve . . ."

He picked up the paper that had slid from Grandfather's hands and put it facedown on the table next to his chair.

"Come down to the bookstore for a few minutes, Gerber," he said, as his friend reached for his coat. "I've got a new shipment, from Hamburg: books by the Manns, Upton Sinclair, Stefan Zweig . . ." He smiled his rare, flashing smile. "Eva has already picked her latest Kästner—I'm sure there are some of *your* favorites, too!"

Herr Gerber studied his animated face. "It isn't only those trees on the Schlossplatz, Bentheim—or even your father, is it?" he said huskily. "It's you, too—and this house, and your books . . ."

He shrugged into his loosely fitting coat. "I hope to God you won't regret your decision. We're heading into rough times, your people and all of us who won't be 'brought into line . . .' "

He tipped his hat to Eva's mother, gave Eva's shoulder a quick, gruff pat, and followed her father down the steps to the bookstore on the floor below.

When Eva was younger, one of her favorite books had been *A Happy Family*, a title that perfectly described the large and lively household of the Müllers. Sometimes she even daydreamed herself into the midst of that bevy of sisters and brothers, with its sibling camaraderie and rivalries, its fun and adventure, watched over with amused detachment by Herr and Frau Professor Müller. Still, she would not have relinquished her single status in her own family to join the one in her book. She had the best of two worlds: Ella and Uschi upstairs, near enough to be *almost* her sisters; but also that special closeness with her parents—if, at times, their overprotectiveness, too—that came with being an only child. She had Grandfather, teasing her from his saggy armchair by the window; visits with her mother's parents, the Weils, in Ettingen, where Eva slept on the sofa in the little white room belonging to Sabine, her mother's youngest sister. Beautiful Sabine, who "adored" Hollywood movie stars and was going to study drama under Max Reinhardt in Berlin and become a famous actress herself, and who sometimes let Eva come along on one of her rendezvous with one of her many admirers, each of them in turn admired in silence by Eva. On other days in Ettingen, Eva would visit her mother's older brother, Uncle Lutz, who lived on Lindenplatz with Aunt Tilla and their small son, Eli. Then Eva could help give Eli his bath, shampoo his hair—blond like Aunt Tilla's—and hold him on her lap in his fluffy blue bathrobe, inhaling his subtle, sweet baby scent as she read him a story.

In Thalstadt, after Eva's return, her mother's sister Cora would drop by with her gentle, craggy-faced husband, Alfred, to find out "how things were going" in Ettingen. Aunt Cora, with the knot of black hair at the nape of her white neck and the ready, self-confident laugh, suffered a permanent case of homesickness for her mother. She took the train to Ettingen on every possible occasion, taking along her daughter, Karoline, years younger than Eva but, lanky like Alfred, already catching up to Eva in height.

Sometimes with Uschi, sometimes alone, Eva would roller-skate down Hauptstrasse to look in on her father's widowed sister, Aunt Hanni, and sit on the green plush sofa, with Hexle, the calico cat, purring next to her as she petted her silken fur. Aunt Hanni did French translations at the polished old mahogany desk in the corner of her living room, "to keep her independence" while Stefan, her son, studied law at Heidelberg University. But she was always glad to see Eva and let her leaf through the pearl-gray, satin-bound album to look at old family pictures, among them faded sepia photos of Eva's father as a shy-faced boy and keen-eyed young man. "That was before he got so sick, in the military, during the war," Aunt Hanni said, dabbing her eyes with her lacy handkerchief. "Before that botched appendectomy in the field, from which he never really recovered." It helped explain to Eva something about her father's frail health, the racking abdominal pains that seemed to assail him more and more often these days, sapping his strength; the visits and consultations with doctors and specialists, which never seemed to produce results or even answers. But she said nothing, sensing her father's wish to preserve his privacy, even though Aunt Hanni had spoken out of love and concern for him: a love for her younger brother second only, Eva felt, to her love for Stefan.

It was photos of Stefan at Heidelberg that filled the last pages in his mother's album—Stefan looking rakishly handsome with his ribboned student's cap askew over his forehead; Stefan on his trusty old motorcycle, kept shipshape "for study trips," as he had told her with a self-mocking grin that hinted otherwise; Stefan with a fellow student—his "mentor," she had heard him tell her father—a young man with an aristocratic "von" before his name who befriended Stefan and had somehow succeeded in getting him admitted into his fraternity, which had always excluded Jews. Looking at Stefan's jaunty smile in the photo, at the fresh fencing scar sported on his cheek like a badge of admission, she remembered how appalled her father had been at Stefan's joining one of the elitist student associations known to be "ultranationalistic and antidemocratic." And when Stefan, seduced by the flashy glamour and prestige of the fraternities and by his need to belong, flared up at him, her father had said quietly—and it was the note of sadness in his quiet voice that made Eva remember his words—"If the Republic falls, Stefan, your scars and ribbons won't buy you entry into the Valhalla of the new Reich."

■

Now the Republic had fallen. The Nazis had outlawed all other parties; Hitler was in full control of the government, issuing laws and decrees no longer under the Weimar Constitution but by force of dictatorship. Compared to what had happened—the jailing of thousands of opposition leaders and trade union activists; the prohibition on publishing or broadcasting dissident views; a "Boycott Day" of "non-Aryan" businesses, with storm troopers pasting hateful slogans on shop windows and ordering customers away—Stefan's sudden expulsion from the fraternity was a small matter.

Except to Stefan himself. Unwilling to swallow his pride, he left Heidelberg in mid-semester—and was promptly notified not to return. With Jewish law graduates no longer permitted in any case to take the state exam and open a practice, Grandfather offered to help Stefan finish his studies in France. He was the first of Eva's relatives to leave, rending the closely woven fabric of what had always seemed to her a "happy family" of her own.

She thought of this, seeing him off on a windy April morning with Aunt Hanni, looking up at Stefan's glum face at the open window of the train—Stefan without his student cap and usual dash, his gray eyes squinting "from the smoke," he said with a shrug. "I'll visit your mother, Stefan!" Eva called up to him, and he nodded distractedly: "You do that, Eva," blowing a haphazard kiss in their direction. Then the voice of the stationmaster boomed over the bustling platform: "Train to Strasbourg—Nancy—Paris. All aboard . . ." Aunt Hanni, standing on tiptoe in her high heels, barely managed to touch her fingers to Stefan's lowered hand; then the conductors banged the compartment doors shut and Eva put her arm around Aunt Hanni, who was waving her lacy handkerchief forlornly in the sooty wake of the departing train.

■

She couldn't fall asleep that night, with the whistle of the locomotive still in her ears and the rumble of Stefan's train shaking her bed. Why should her family, and other families like hers, be singled out for separation, for persecution—as so many had been many times in the past; even for death. Why should their store have been defaced on Boycott Day and barred to customers who had always shopped there by shouting, menacing storm troopers? Her father, looking down on Wielandplatz through the sheer curtains at their living room windows in shocked disbelief, had quickly drawn the drapes so Grandfather should not "see his honorable old firm dragged through the mud."

"It's the beginning of the end, Ludwig," he had said to his brother. "The road back to the Middle Ages, when Jews were without civil and human rights."

And Uncle Ludwig, trying to wring a drop of hope from the deluge bursting in on them, had shrugged. "It will blow over, Jonas. Hitler will go, as Brüning, Papen, and Schleicher did before him. The Nazis will lose the next election—in spite of the violence and intimidation, they didn't even win an absolute majority in the *last* two."

"Hitler seized power *without* it! He's announced the removal of the 'cancer of democracy.' No power on earth, he says, will ever again get him out of the Chancellery alive . . ."

Suddenly aware of Eva listening from the piano bench, her

father managed a wan nod in her direction and told her to see if she could be of some help to Anna.

In the kitchen, Anna was slamming pans and pot lids in anger at the slap of boots and shouting voices reverberating through the window. She tried to take Eva's mind off it by whipping up cookie dough for her to bake. But Eva's thoughts could not be so neatly and easily shaped by her cookie cutter, any more than she could stop up her ears against the hate-filled clamor on the square. Why were Jews resented, even hated, for running a store, for practicing medicine or law, or doing any of a hundred things others did, too? She thought of the people in her family and wondered why anyone should dislike and defame them. True, Ella could be bossy; Sabine flaunted her beauty; Uncle Lutz, who could make people laugh, could also hurt them with the sharp point of his wit. But she had heard girls in her class complain of such faults when talking about *their* uncles, sisters, or aunts. It seemed to go with being family, being human.

No, it wasn't what Jews did or said or how they earned their livelihood that caused their suffering, the hatred called anti-Semitism. Was it, as she had heard her father wonder in that troubled voice of his, "a short-circuiting of society in time of crisis—a breakdown of reason succumbing to historically in-stilled prejudice and stereotyping?" His friend Herr Gerber had shaken his head. "Anti-Semitism is the socialism of fools," he said, quoting one of his labor heroes of the last century. "What Bebel meant, Bentheim, was that anti-Semitism is used to turn the anger of the unemployed and underpaid against the Jews instead of the system that exploits and discards them." Her father had shrugged. "Perhaps, Gerber. But what if *your* system needs its scapegoats, too?"

Uncle Lutz, in Thalstadt on a visit to the British Consulate to look into the possibilities of a *Zertifikat* for Palestine for his family, joined in the conversation. The failure of the democratic parties to stem Fascism and anti-Semitism, he told Herr Gerber, had rekindled his long-standing interest in Zionism. "Tilla and I are, in fact, among the recent founders of the first Ettingen branch! Jews need a homeland of their own, like every other nation. In the Diaspora, they're demonized for whatever goes wrong anywhere—like witches burned when the crops failed or the milk went sour."

Then, turning to Eva with a straight face but with the telltale glint of humor in his eyes, he asked if she knew that all the troubles in Germany—inflation, joblessness, losing the war— had been caused by the bicycle riders and the Jews.

"Why the bicycle riders?" Eva blurted out in confusion.

"Why the Jews?" Uncle Lutz shot back, clinching his point. And everyone burst out laughing a little too loudly, relieved that there was still a shred of sanity in the world.

Herr Gerber's laughter ended in a coughing fit. "Careful to whom you tell a joke like this, Lutz Weil; it might get back to the wrong ears. These gentlemen have no sense of humor. Where I spent my winter vacation, some of my bunk-mates were made to take the cure with me for nothing more than a joke."

He got up heavily, waved to Eva's father not to trouble himself, tipped his hat to Eva's mother from the door, and was gone.

■

Once, when Eva had asked her father why people said "such things," believed such things about Jews, he had replied that there were many learned theories, but that only history would tell the full story. "A long time off, I'm afraid," he had added softly. It had made her think about the time of the Messiah—"Moshiach," Rabbi Gideon pronounced it in Hebrew from the pulpit. A time when human beings would be "redeemed"—would live together in peace and loving-kindness—"and none shall make them afraid," as the Prophet Micah had envisioned. A time when humankind in all its manifoldness would be a happy family, she thought—not only families like the Müllers in her book but like her own as well.

It seemed a far-off time indeed, these stormy April nights of 1933. Sleepless in her bed, Eva thought of Stefan's bleak leave-taking, of Uncle Lutz already planning to leave as well, taking Eli from her, too. At the thought her heart suddenly started to thump wildly, gathering speed like Stefan's train rushing from the station. The way it sometimes did when she hadn't studied for an exam or had put off her geography assignment. But now she couldn't simply switch on the bedside lamp and try to catch up on her homework without waking her parents. The very place where they were living—Grandfather's house, where her father had been born, which had always appeared so solid and permanent to her—now seemed to have lost its moorings, tossed on the waves of change like the little boats on the Neckar River that she had once been afraid to board. Her father's hand had steadied her then, lending her courage and strength. But now her father, too, was rendered helpless, powerless—*rechtlos*, she had heard him characterize the status of Jews in Germany: outside the protection of law.

On nights like these, when she slipped fitfully in and out of sleep over the bumping and flipping of her runaway heart, her mother, sensing that something was wrong, soundlessly opened the door and glided into the room on a wisp of light from the hall. In her soft robe she sat down on the edge of the bed, smoothing Eva's hair with her rough-gentle hand, until the tightness in Eva's chest lessened and lifted and she felt herself drift off to sleep.

One sunlit afternoon in May, as Eva was on her way home from school, the boy selling newspapers from the kiosk near the Old Castle cried out a high-pitched *"Extra! Extraaa!"*

Curious, yet already filled with the sense of foreboding aroused by anything "extra" these days, she dared no more than dart a quick, half-averted glance at the papers. But the red headline on the *Mittagsblatt* leaped up at her like a slap in the face: BURNING OF DECADENT BOOKS A BEACON OF NEW ERA! In the photo below it, students wearing ribboned caps and swastika armbands were stoking a roaring bonfire of books by tossing more volumes into the flames, as their professors in academic gowns and caps looked on with evident approval. *German Students Against Un-German Spirit!* proclaimed a poster held up to the cheering crowd.

"Extra! Banned books burn in Frankfurt, Berlin, cities throughout the Reich!" the newsboy called, handing out papers for coins pressed into his palm by hurried passersby. Two girls a few years older than Eva, perhaps even university students themselves, exchanged a stunned look and rushed on, talking in subdued voices. An old man stopped to buy a paper, shaking his head. A bunch of HJ boys in their Hitler Youth uniforms swaggered past, craning their necks for a look at the screaming slo-

gans on the *N.S. Banner*. "*Ja, der* Goebbels is giving those Jews and 'intellects' a taste of the New Order!" one of them said, to the jeering laughter of the others.

"Hey, are you *buying* the *Mittagsblatt?*" the newsboy asked impatiently, as Eva stood staring at it, rooted to the ground. He picked up a copy and urged it into her hand, but she recoiled from the picture of Goebbels with the soft fedora shading his fanatical eyes and the wide sycophant's smile spread over his pinched face. Hitler's choice for guardian of German Culture, presiding over the burning of books outside the University of Berlin and the great library! She thought of her father, whose very touch on the cover of a book was a gesture of tenderness, almost of reverence, and pushed back the paper, turning on her heels to run home.

■

J. BENTHEIM & SONS—STATIONERY AND BOOKS read the reassuring sign above the family store on Wielandplatz. Inside, Eva felt herself enveloped by the familiar late afternoon calm: the soothing shadows and soft lights after the sun-flooded streets, the scent of leather from the gleaming rows of briefcases and school satchels, the cool whiteness reflecting from the neat stacks of stationery and typing paper.

Uncle Ludwig, leaning against a counter and frowning at the *Mittagsblatt* spread out on it, shrugged his head toward the little curving staircase leading to the second floor. "Your father is in his office, Eva."

With a wave of her hand to Viktor, the dark-haired young salesman who was unpacking a set of marble inkwells and blotters, she hurried upstairs.

"There you are, Eva!" her father said, drawing up another

chair at his desk in the unpretentious space he had managed to set aside for himself to select and order books. His "office" and the bookstore that surrounded it, with its thoughtfully arranged shelves and tables displaying their finely bound or brightly covered treasures, were his favorite places to be, she knew. Uneasily, she scanned his face for signs that he had already seen the *Mittagsblatt* on the counter downstairs, but she could not tell.

"I heard it over the radio, Eva, hours ago," her father said after a while, as if he had read her face better than she had his. "Did the teachers bring it up at school?"

She shook her head. "Maybe they were waiting for someone to tell them *how*." She tried for a lame quip. "Maybe we'll be taken to the local bonfire site for a study trip tomorrow."

"There *is* no site," her father said. "It would be in the *Mittagsblatt* if there had been a fire here, but there was no mention of it."

"Then nothing will *happen* in Thalstadt? People can go on reading and buying the books they want?"

"I'm afraid not, Eva," her father said. He gave her a fleeting smile. "You see, Swabians aren't very demonstrative; they're embarrassed by theatricality, grandiose gestures. They're also frugal folk, brought up not to be wasteful. So the idea of a public burning of books just doesn't go over in Thalstadt, I suspect. But as for reading and selling those books, it won't be any different in Thalstadt than anywhere else in the Reich. And that, unfortunately, is what counts."

He took a pad out of his desk drawer, lined with notations in his fine handwriting.

"They're going after everybody who is anybody—popular writers, literary figures, world-renowned scientists. Einstein. Freud. Heinrich Mann, whose novels called on Germans to be free citizens of a democratic state, rather than obedient subjects of Authority. Stefan Zweig, who with Romain Rolland sought to save French and Germans from killing each other in war. Zola, whose *J'Accuse* helped to free Dreyfus. Jack London and Upton Sinclair, two American writers and critics of social conditions. Franz Werfel, whose outcry against the mass murder of the Armenians appealed to the conscience of the world . . ."

He stared into the space above the calendar on the wall. "And many more. Even Heine. Germany's greatest poet next to Goethe. But a Jew."

"What will you *do*?" Eva asked in a small voice.

"I will have to give up the bookstore, Eva," her father said, taking off his glasses to polish the lenses with the soft cloth he kept in the desk drawer. "I cannot tell you how sad this makes me feel. I know how much you've enjoyed spending time with me here, browsing through the children's books, discovering your own favorite authors as you were growing up, lending a hand with the shelving and sorting . . ."

He put his glasses back on and gazed at her intently. "You see, Eva, booksellers must be free to make their own selections. I don't always agree with a particular book I buy, but the point is to make different views available for readers to form their own opinions. As long as a book doesn't incite hatred and contempt, I want to be free to decide whether it belongs in my store or not. That choice is being taken from me now. Instead, booksellers will be forced to carry the books the *Nazis* want people to read."

"Can't you at least keep the *children's* department?" Eva asked with a catch in her throat. "Those authors on the verboten list don't even write for children!"

Her father fumbled among the books piled on his desk. "This picture-book sample just came in from one of those publishing houses, new as well as established, who're trying to get in on a good thing in a hurry!"

He flipped the pages open. Eva caught a glimpse of a green meadow strewn with flowers—except that each blossom was a tiny red swastika! There was also a fox drawn in imitation folktale style with a sly, wily grin, walking arm in arm with one of those vicious caricatures of Jews on the front page of the *Stürmer* on the kiosks. Below the picture was a two-line poem, printed in the wide-looped script of a child's copybook. "Don't trust a fox upon the heath" the first line went, but before she could read on, her father slammed the book shut.

"I'll spare you the 'poetry' that goes with the 'art,' Eva. You get the drift. Even if I were not Jewish, I wouldn't help push vile anti-Semitic trash on children's minds."

"Can't you *do* something about it? This is *your* store!"

"If the large bookstores and their organizations were doing something, and the publishers, the universities, the press—those institutions that claim to stand for 'German culture'—I could and I would, certainly. The sad truth is, Eva, that they have capitulated or are already verboten. The only protest left to me is a very private protest: closing the store."

"But what would you do instead?" Eva asked again, sensing

how much the store had meant in her father's life, not only because he had been supporting his family from it but because its bookshelves had been a bulwark of sorts for him against the changing, threatening world beyond.

"I'll have more time to help Uncle Ludwig elsewhere in the business. Adding the book department was really *my* idea after the war, when my illness and what I suppose could be called the illness of the times would not allow me to teach literature at a university, as I had hoped . . . And you know, Eva," he added after a moment, "it's time not only to *think* about leaving here but to do something about it."

He got up to pull down the shades for the night and dim the lights. Downstairs, Uncle Ludwig and Viktor had already left, plunging the store into darkness.

Her father walked to the door behind his office that led into the main stairway of the house, turning for a final glance over the shelves and tables before switching off the last light.

"By the way, Eva, there is at least *one* children's book author on that honor roll of burned writers—your own favorite, Erich Kästner! The Nazis can't swallow the biting social satire of his adult works, so who knows how long his *Emil* and other children's books will be allowed. Make sure you have your copy of *The Thirty-fifth of May* and the rest."

He locked the door behind them and, with his arm around her, started up the stairs toward their apartment.

"What will you be doing with all those banned books when you give up the store?" Eva asked, hardly aware that she was dropping her voice like the grownups when speaking about "certain matters."

Her father, about to reply, visibly checked himself. "Some things are better left unasked these days, Eva. For your own sake as well as mine and—anyone else's," he finished quickly, opening the door to the apartment to let her walk inside.

FOUR DECEMBER 1933

Sometimes things seemed to be the way they had always been.

Winter mornings were best. Night still clung to the rooftops when Eva left for school, and it was lovely to walk in the uncertain dark between the streetlamps, with the cottony feel of freshly fallen snow under one's feet. From the trolley stop, she watched the gleaming lights of the streetcar as it emerged through the haze and came to a halt under a burst of sparks overhead. Inside, sleepy-faced passengers dozed on the wooden benches while the car wound its way uphill toward The Heights surrounding the town.

Renate's streetcar, coming from the opposite direction, always reached their stop at exactly the same moment. Eva ran across the tracks as Renate waved to her from the sidewalk. They walked on together, no longer carrying their school satchels on their backs as they had in the lower grades, but as easily in step as they had always been.

One cold winter morning, as Renate and Eva were walking more quickly than usual, their bright scarves, knitted in Fräulein Kugler's class, fluttering in the wind, two tall, dark shapes suddenly appeared before them out of the dawn. Approaching swiftly, they turned out to be two upper-grade teachers at Buchberg School: Dr. Seyboldt, a square-shouldered man with a square-cut chin who taught physics and chemistry, and Herr Klaeger, soft-spoken and lean-faced, who had been Ella's history teacher. Eva and Renate had encountered the two teachers on other mornings, walking briskly in animated conversation punctuated by an occasional burst of laughter. They shared a daily train ride from Karlsdorf: neighbors and friends, though they must be living very different kinds of lives, because Herr Klaeger was a married man with many children and Dr. Seyboldt was a bachelor. This morning, though, to the girls' stunned amazement, the two men were walking not *toward* the school but *away* from it, coming down the street in grim silence so hurriedly that they were directly in front of them before Eva and Renate had recovered from their surprise. They managed a startled smile and mumbled greeting. But Dr. Seyboldt, hatless and with his massive chin thrust forward from the thick folds of his muffler, seemed utterly oblivious of them, and Herr Klaeger offered a mere nod with barely a hint of recognition. When they had stormed past, Eva and Renate wheeled and stared at their backs, watching their retreat with the same uncomprehending fascination with which they might have watched the sun rise in the west.

"Perhaps someone is sick," Renate ventured at last, walking backward into the stinging wind so as not to lose even a moment of the amazing spectacle. "Come to think of it, Herr Klaeger did look ill, didn't he, Eva? Pale and shaky, somehow— as if he could hardly keep up with Dr. Seyboldt."

Eva wasn't so sure. "If Herr Klaeger were sick, Dr. Seyboldt wouldn't make him walk so fast, Renate. It must be something else."

The two men, already blurred shadows in the thin winter light, passed by the streetcar stop and disappeared down the steep flight of stone steps that led from The Heights. For an instant, Herr Klaeger's hat wavered above the top step, a last vestige of his professional dignity. Then they were gone from sight.

Renate turned around. "If he were sick," she said, slowly putting one foot before the other, "they would have waited for the streetcar."

They walked on in silence. Something had happened to the predictable order of their schooldays: something perplexing which they could only puzzle over, but which they perhaps already knew to be bound up with other changes, all of them disquieting—unbidden interlopers in their schoolgirl lives.

■

In the schoolyard, groups of students stood together in tight little knots, voices ringing in the frosty air. Diete Goetz, surrounded by a circle of wind-reddened faces, was stamping her feet on the ground to keep warm.

"It's happening in *all* the schools," she was saying as Eva and Renate walked up. "I heard my father speak of it the moment the Führer became Chancellor. It's simply a matter of cleaning house."

"And to think he was *teaching* here, having been in *jail!*" Inge Beisswanger whispered, shuddering deliciously.

Diete looked at her sternly. "Jail means nothing," she said with an airy wave of her hand. "The Führer himself sat in Landsberg Fortress for nine months after his Munich Putsch: remember, he wrote *Mein Kampf* behind prison walls. The Führer was in jail to save Germany from the *Juden-Republik—*

an honorable thing! But Dr. Seyboldt was a coward and a traitor!"

"A traitor?" Renate asked, horrified.

"Anyone who refused to fight for Germany in the war is a coward and a traitor," Diete said flatly. "Dr. Seyboldt prefers to call it pacifism, no doubt—but the name didn't save his job for him. There is no place for people like him in German classrooms."

"And Herr Klaeger? Is he a . . . pacifist, too?" Dorle Hohnegger asked in a faltering voice.

Horst Reuter tossed a forbidden snowball across the yard.

"Klaeger is a horse of a different color," he said, brushing the snow off his hands. "And the color happens to be *black*—like a monk's cowl!" He wheeled, glaring at Anton Huber.

Anton flushed to the roots of his sandy hair. "Just because he's a Catholic . . ." he began defiantly.

Horst laughed contemptuously. "Let your Herr Klaeger save his soul any way he sees fit," he said, hulking over the smaller boy. "But when he plays the intellectual and puts out a forbidden magazine . . . *Der Katholische Humanist*," he quoted sarcastically. "Sound familiar, Anton? You probably get it at home!"

Anton stared back at Horst. "We read all kinds of things at our house," he said in a shaky voice, thrusting his fists into the frayed pockets of his coat.

With his lazy smile, Horst raised his hand and tightened it around Anton's thin arm. "Do you?" he said softly, blowing his breath into Anton's face. "How interesting—how very interesting! Things from Rome? Or from Moscow, maybe? An interesting combination—but then, you've always been an interesting little fellow, with an interesting Herr Papa—a Catholic-Bolshevik Herr Papa!"

"Leave him alone, Horst!" Monika von Ahlem said in disgust, shrugging her long, pale hair back over her shoulder.

With a grimace of pain, Anton jerked his arm free. "My father is no Bolshevik," he said through his clenched teeth. "His union wasn't Communist, and you know it!"

Horst shrugged. "Whatever they were—Free Trade Unions, Christian ones—it's down the drain! They're all verboten—unions, sports clubs—it's all going to be handled by the *Party*!" He rubbed his fingers quickly up and down the swastika pin on his lapel, as if to make it shine.

Renate drew a circle in the snow with the tip of her boot. "And how is Herr Klaeger going to feed his children this Christmas?" she wondered aloud, trying to keep her voice quite neutral, as if her question were one of mere curiosity.

"Herr Klaeger wasn't a bad teacher," little Helga Boehm said in her singsong Saxon speech. "My brother says he always made you feel you were right *there*—like when Columbus found America by chance, or when Napoleon's soldiers froze to death in Russia. And that he's always . . . objective!" she added, looking around for the effect of the upper-grade word on her classmates.

"That's exactly the trouble with intellectuals—why the Führer doesn't trust them!" Diete scoffed. "There is no place for 'objectivity' in the Third Reich, Helga—that's why the Führer says: 'Who is not for us is against us!' "

She turned back to Renate. "And that's why those who're not

with us have to be taught a lesson. Even if they have *seven* children!" she finished coolly, following the school bell into the lobby.

■

It was warm and inviting inside. Renate and Eva stepped gingerly over puddles of melted snow on the stone floor and drew in the chocolate scent that drifted through the closed door of the custodian's ground-floor apartment: Frau Munze, the custodian's wife, was preparing the cocoa she would sell to the students during recess at ten. From the gym below came the rhythmic thud of a medicine ball; two floors above them, in the music room, someone struck a tentative chord on the piano, first in one key, then in another. They were the sounds and smells of every school morning that had ever been. And the sights, too, Eva thought uneasily, watching the children on the stairs beside her doing the same things they had always been doing: jostling one another, pulling pigtails and making faces, worrying about unfinished homework, unannounced tests. It was as if the two dismissed teachers were already forgotten—as if, indeed, they had never been part of their school lives at all. And, coming up the stairwell behind Inge Beisswanger's broad back, Eva almost wanted to forget them, too, as if by doing so she could bring back the old, already quite unreal days when nothing had ever "happened"—when she had never been afraid. "Let Herr Klaeger save his soul any way he sees fit," Horst had said. In retrospect, it was almost possible to draw a treacherous kind of reassurance from the facetiously spoken words. Perhaps Horst had really meant it; perhaps if one's father *had* fought for Germany in the war, had never put out a forbidden magazine . . .

"Look, Eva!" Renate cried suddenly, pulling Eva's sleeve.

A small, plump woman was coming down the stairs, fumbling in her pocketbook as she hurried past them.

"It's Fräulein Metzger, the math teacher," Renate whispered. "And she is leaving, too!"

Indeed, Fräulein Metzger was crossing the lobby toward the door with rapid steps, making her way through the receding crowd of staring children unseeingly, as if walking in her sleep. She had nearly reached the door before Renate saw the glove on the landing: a white woolen glove, or one which, at any rate, had been white before the indifferent shoes of boys and girls had trampled it into the schoolhouse dust. The math teacher, a plain, aging woman given to subdued colors, always carried white gloves.

"Fräulein Metzger!" Renate's voice rang out clearly over the heads of the children. She waved the glove overhead like a tiny, battered white flag.

Below them, the teacher stopped hesitantly and looked back. She had evidently found what she had been searching for in her pocketbook, for she was pressing a damp handkerchief to her red-rimmed eyes.

"Your glove, Fräulein Metzger!" Renate cried, elbowing her way down the stairs.

Diete Goetz caught her arm.

"She won't need her glove, sitting in her room for the rest of the winter. Non-Aryans are no longer permitted to teach!"

But Renate slipped from her grasp and ran across the lobby, unmindful of the sudden silence around her, the curious eyes.

"Your glove, Fräulein Metzger," she repeated unnecessarily, urging her soiled offering into the teacher's uncertain hand.

For a moment they faced one another speechlessly, the pig-tailed girl and the elderly woman with the tear-smudged face. Then, with a visible effort, Fräulein Metzger managed a melancholy smile.

"Thank you, my child," she said, in a voice so small it could be heard only because of the unnatural quiet about her. She held the glove up to her nearsighted eyes, gazing at it wonderingly, as if the familiar object were now a relic from the past. And lowering her voice to a mere whisper, which in the dead silence carried farther than would have seemed possible, she added slowly, "What good is one glove without the other, after all? No more, I'm afraid, than a teacher without her pupils."

"Off to the Wailing Wall!" Horst Reuter cried, making a snorting noise into his grimy handkerchief.

But no one laughed.

FIVE FEBRUARY 1934

She was dreaming of rain. Round, luminous summer raindrops falling against the windowpane in a persistent, drowsy pattern of sound. A faraway sound, growing nearer as she struggled to free herself from sleep.

She sat up with a start. It was dark; the frilly edge of the curtain made a dim silhouette against the dusky pane. A shred of fog hung over the streetlight; it was winter and there was no rain.

But after a moment, the sound of something beating against glass came back. The same instant, the light in her parents' room clicked on, seeping through the crack beneath the connecting door. Along with the light, her parents' whispered voices rose from the darkness, her mother's slippers swished across the floor. The front door of the apartment opened softly; her mother must be in the hallway, huddled into her warm robe, peering with sleepy eyes down the dimly lit stairwell.

Eva dug her fingernails into her blanket, holding on to a childhood safety no longer part of the familiar objects of her room. "They came for our neighbor last night, but he got away," Anton Huber had whispered during recess the week before. "Out the back window and into the woods behind the house . . ." But *their* house had no back window on the ground floor, no dense and sheltering woods beyond. If they were coming for her father, where could he run to, he who was barely able to stir from his bed these days, too sick and weak even to go downstairs to find out, as her mother was doing . . .

Eva threw back the covers and tiptoed into the hall, afraid that her father might hear and call her back. The soft knocking had ceased, but in the hushed stairwell she could hear the beating of her own heart.

She leaned over the banister. Downstairs, her mother's hand was on the doorknob, her head thrust forward.

"*Wer ist denn da?*" she called in a small, muted voice, her ear pressed against the door to the street. "Who *is* it, please?"

Suddenly she turned the lock and threw the door open.

A gust of wind ruffled the folds of her robe. She drew back, shivering, and covered her mouth with her arm to stifle a cry. Fog drifted into the entrance and with it a strange and terrifying sound: a low, stricken moan of unendurable pain. Slowly, heavily, as if in the grip of an evil dream, her mother reached out her hands to someone crouched on the doorstep. Tugging and lifting, she finally raised him to his knees, but he could get no farther. On knees and elbows, his hands dangling limply, grotesquely from upraised wrists, he crept up the steps, her mother's arm in futile support about his shoulders.

It seemed hours for them to reach their door, hours during which Eva stood rooted to the cold tiles, staring numbly. When at last her feet had regained the power of flight, it was too late to run, even to look away. The twisted, spattered being on the stairs raised his head and for an infinite, shattering moment their eyes locked: it was tall, gentle, immaculate Uncle Alfred. Midway between his bloodied chin and his smeared, tattered shirt was the ubiquitous polka-dot bow tie, perfectly straight and in place, as if someone had played a final, obscene joke on him.

"Eva! What are you doing here?" Her mother's face flushed painfully.

"No, Martha, let her see!" Uncle Alfred shook off her restraining arm and thrust out his bruised and broken hands. "*They* did this to me, Eva—ten, twelve of them, with their boots and sticks! What *are* we doing here, among men turned into wolves? We have to leave, Martha, all of us—wherever there is a crack in the wall!"

Eva held the door open for them, forcing her trembling legs to keep still so her mother wouldn't notice. She switched on the foyer lamp over the scroll-backed chairs that had flanked the hall mirror since the grandmother she had never known had placed them there long ago. From Grandfather's room came the rumbling sound of his snoring. *"Ein ruhiges Gewissen ist ein sanftes Ruhekissen,"* he would quote, only half-jokingly, when someone teased him about his deep old-man's sleep. "A clear conscience is a soft pillow." In the world of yesterday, her grandfather's world, it had always made perfect sense.

"Your father is calling, Eva," her mother was saying. "Tell him it's Uncle Alfred, that he's been . . . in a slight accident, that he's all right." Her voice was toneless, perfunctory, as if she knew that the well-meant deception would not be believed.

Her father was sitting up in bed, his face as white as the pillow propped against his back, a half-smoked cigarette crushed in the ashtray on his night table.

Eva stood at the door, dreading his question. Of all her childish sins, it was an untruth her father could least forgive.

"Come over and sit by me, Eva," her father said quietly.

She did, and drew a deep breath.

"Uncle Alfred has been in a slight accident," she heard herself say. It was easier than she had imagined. "But he's all right now."

The lamp etched a bright circle on the sheets, and on her father's fragile hand on her arm. She thought of Alfred's hands, the broken fingers dangling grotesquely from his wrists, and threw her face against her father's nightshirt, with its familiar scents of linen and tobacco.

Her father's arm tightened about her.

"Accident, Eva? The accident of having been born a Jew? Of being a Jew in Germany, in the year 1934 of the one they call the Prince of Peace?"

He lifted her chin and gazed at her intently. "Much has changed, Eva, in a few short months. And will keep on changing. But let nothing change between us in this house, or within us. That must be *our* victory, not theirs."

He seized her shoulders and gently held her at arm's length. "I know Mother and you want to shield me from pain, Eva. But I have no right to be spared at least the truth."

He picked up the empty glass on his night table. "Bring me a little fresh water, Eva, please. And do get into some warm things. Then ask your mother if there is anything you can do to help."

Something rustled under her foot as she stood up—yesterday's *Mittagsblatt*. The bold red headline caught her eye, but it took another instant for the meaning to sink in:

IRATE GERMANS BATTLE RACIAL ENEMY!

It meant Uncle Alfred, though the leering caricature on the front page was utterly unlike the suffering human face she had seen in the stairwell.

■

From the sofa in the living room, Alfred pushed back the cup of tea and cognac her mother held to his lips. His face moved, but the words would not come.

"Don't talk, Alfred," her mother pleaded. "I've phoned Dr. Neuburger—he'll be here any moment now."

". . . crashed down the door to my hotel room, Martha—dragged me out. Beat me in the room, down the stairs, in the courtyard. Must've been four or five of us, at the King David in Friedlingen—traveling salesmen away from home, screaming, asking what we had *done!* I told them I'd been a front-line soldier, earned the Iron Cross Second Class at Verdun. 'So you're a brave *Jud*'?' one of them said. 'Let's see how brave you are *now!*'"

"Please, Alfred, you mustn't think about it anymore! Try to take a little of this."

"I wouldn't have come here, Martha, if I could've made it back to Reinberg. Jonas is a sick man, you have your own tsores, but where else could I have gone?"

"You did the right thing, Alfred."

The doorbell rang: three firm staccato sounds.

"It's Dr. Neuburger, Eva!" her mother said. "Quickly—the door!"

Dr. Neuburger always rang the bell like that, apologizing afterward that he was a busy man; but tonight the familiar sounds were a reassuring signal that it was *his* hand pressing the button, not the ominous one of a stranger. He brushed past Eva without his customary pat on her cheek.

"Thank God, Herr Doktor, you are *here!*" her mother said, rushing to take his hat and coat. "I've been fearful for you out there, after what happened in Friedlingen tonight!"

The doctor shook his head. "In Thalstadt, violence mainly happens behind closed doors, in 'official' places. In villages and little towns, such 'spontaneous outbursts of healthy folk instincts'—as the *N.S. Banner* puts it—can be more easily orchestrated. And without causing those 'crocodile tears in the foreign press' that Goebbels keeps fuming about."

He opened his bag on the living room table and drew up a chair next to Alfred with a matter-of-fact greeting.

"I haven't even phoned my sister yet," Eva's mother murmured, reaching a tentative hand toward the receiver.

"Well, let us have a look before we do any calling," the doctor said.

Grandfather's early morning cough, demanding attention, came from his bedroom. Dr. Neuburger's familiar ring had accomplished what the horror of the night had not: roused him from sleep.

"If I'm not needed here, Herr Doktor," Eva's mother said uncertainly, "I'd better go and speak to Father."

The doctor nodded. His square, stubby hands held those of his patient with a touch at once tender and impersonal. It must have been like this, Eva thought, when he took care of the wounded soldiers and prisoners of war in the field hospital in Belgium—like this, too, when he ministered to an injured worker at a factory. How strange that the doctor, a plain, peaceable man, with his Bavarian dialect and soggy cigar, was always caught up in a world of violence, always binding up its wounds.

"I'm very sorry," the doctor said softly, as Alfred drew in a sharp breath of pain.

"Come, child," her mother said quickly, putting her arm around Eva and drawing her from the room.

■

Before he left, Dr. Neuburger asked to see Eva's father. She led him into the bedroom; no one had told her to go back to sleep, as if the happenings of the night had suddenly earned her a place in the closed society of the grownups.

"I shall be back tomorrow to change the dressings," the doctor said through the smoke of his hastily lit cigar. "He is in great pain, but his face and body contusions will heal."

"And his hands?" Eva's mother asked anxiously.

Dr. Neuburger shrugged. "I'm making an appointment for your brother-in-law to see Dr. Detleff, the surgeon—tomorrow morning, if possible. Perhaps with proper treatment he will be able to use his hands again, but to what extent I am not prepared to say. The trauma is severe, perhaps irreversible."

Her father put his frail hand over his eyes, his voice a stifled sob. "Yes, it is as Heine wrote with his usual irony: his 'sickness' is being the persecuted Jew—'the ancient family affliction no medicine can cure.' "

"Permit me a supplementary diagnosis, my friend," the doctor said. "In recent months I have treated patients who had been given a taste of Gestapo hospitality in its notorious cellars on Theodorastrasse. A *Wandervogel* leader who would not lead his hiking troop into the Hitler Youth. An auto worker unlucky enough to be elected shop steward just as the regime outlawed the labor unions. An elderly seamstress and Jehovah's Witness who could not be persuaded to place Hitler's *Mein Kampf* above the Word of the Bible."

He picked up his bag and turned to leave.

"The patients' symptoms vary: an eye to be saved, bones to be set . . . But the cause is always the same: call it conviction, conscience—or simply an inability to let oneself be processed by the regime, a stubborn propensity for sticking in its craw . . ."

Eva's father reached for the glass of water on his night table. "We Jews, too, have been among those indigestible ones, throughout our history. By our very presence we affirm liberty of thought—beginning with the right to stand by that elusive God of ours, though we may sometimes rebel against Him, even despair of Him. We won't surrender our spiritual birthright—that is why we have suffered so much."

"That is why we have endured," the doctor said, shutting the door behind him.

SIX SEPTEMBER 1934

With so many things changing all around them, it was Grandfather who seemed to remain the firm, fixed center of their lives. It was as if he had willed himself to remain untouched; by refusing to acknowledge change, he had put himself above it. In his armchair after dinner, he scarcely wasted a glance at the *Mittagsblatt*, and when the radio program was interrupted by the glib voice of the news announcer, he turned the set off abruptly, with a contemptuous flick of his hand. Otherwise, his day followed the same pattern in which it had long ago become fixed: he rose early to breakfast with Eva and visit the store, went for his midmorning jug of wine at the Rathskeller, and in the evening, for his game of cards at the coffeehouse. If anything, he held his head even higher than before, and his conversation became even more caustic and curt. Under his smooth white brows, his eyes shone with an icy disdain, asking no pity and allowing none for others less sturdily fashioned to withstand the storm.

When friends and relatives came to say *Auf Wiedersehen* on their way to Hamburg or Bremen and the foreign ports for which their ships were bound, his handshake was frosty and formal.

"You'll be back, you'll be back," he said, shrugging aside their well-wishings and warnings. And pulling his neat mustaches over his faintly curled upper lip, he added in his deceptively gentle Rhenish drawl, "That's the trouble with us—we're always too quick to throw up our hands and run! Jakob Bentheim goes where he wants to go and stays where he wants to stay: he never takes orders from inferiors!"

Those whom he ridiculed laughed weakly out of deference to his years, but when they spoke again, their voices sounded strained. Eva wondered uncomfortably why Grandfather persisted in taunting the refugees; their burden seemed heavy enough. Was he really hoping he could shame them into remaining—or was it perhaps himself he was trying to convince, his own doubts he wanted to still?

Among those who came for a last visit were her mother's sister Cora and her family. They were the only ones who were spared a taste of Grandfather's bitter humor. The memory of that terrible night when Alfred had fled to their house lay unspoken between them all. His wounds had healed, as Dr. Neuburger had promised, and his hands at long last had mended—but mended into a gnarled and twisted shape, like the hands in medieval paintings of the Crucifixion that Fräulein Waegele, the visiting art history teacher, projected on the screen. Eva kept her eyes from straying to those poor hands, tried not to notice the tremor that seized them spasmodically, as if they were still feebly knocking at bolted doors, begging soundlessly to be let in . . .

Karoline, tall and gawky, told Eva she was scared of being seasick. Aunt Cora's hair had been cut short, and instead of the classic knot at the nape of her neck she wore a pert new style with saucy waves at the temples. It made her look even younger and more beautiful, but at the same time she had already become a stranger. Gone, too, was her husky laughter; the smile that had taken its place, though bright enough, seemed a thing she had bought along with her good new suit and pert little hat.

"When we arrive in La Paz, Alfred's cousins will put us up for a few days—then it's on to the farm settlement that has promised us work and a place to stay."

Aunt Cora's voice was as brave as her smile, and no more convincing.

"La Paz!" Eva's mother said, shaking her head. "It sounds so very far away. If it were only Zurich, or Paris—or even London . . ."

"Martha, you're being terribly provincial," Aunt Cora chided. "Bolivia is a beautiful country—we've seen pictures at the travel agency: mountains higher than the Bavarian Alps, and marvelous flowers. And Alfred has the promise of work he is able to do—we're so much luckier than most."

"Just the same," her sister persisted, "if it were only Paris or London—or even New York . . ."

"We must go where a door is opened to us," Aunt Cora said quietly. "And a possibility to build a new life. What else can I say, Martha?"

But later, in the kitchen, Aunt Cora suddenly laid her head against her sister's shoulder. "Ach, Martha, how hard it was to part from Mother in Ettingen—how hard it is to leave you all! Last night, when our train came into Thalstadt and the lights gleamed below us in the valley, I couldn't bear looking, knowing it was for the last time."

Eva watched her mother smooth Aunt Cora's hair, as she had done, perhaps, in days when they were both small girls in Ettingen, with childish sorrows so different from those that had come to them now.

"Then why not wait, Cora—wait a while longer before deciding on this final step! Perhaps things will quiet down after all."

But Aunt Cora shook her head and resolutely blew her nose into her perfumed handkerchief.

"I don't know, Martha—I only know I can no longer stay. Sometimes I feel as if the very ground were burning beneath my feet."

She shivered, unaccountably, in the mild breeze that lifted the kitchen curtains.

"Do you remember the Schiller ballad we learned in school, Martha—about the tyrant Polycrates, so favored by fortune that the gods became jealous and willed his destruction? I often think of it these days. I see the flags and the uniforms and the triumphant faces—but it is a triumph born of evil, feeding on evil, like the evil perpetrated on Alfred. There is a Judgment that will not be mocked, sister. It is well to leave in time, before that Judgment is visited on Germany."

Strange words, it seemed to Eva, to come from Aunt Cora's lips—but then these were strange times, bewildering times, that seemed to leave few unchanged, on either side of the dividing line the Nazis had drawn. Eva wondered if *she* had changed, too, and if others could read the changes on her own face. And perhaps it was because she *had* seen that Aunt Cora suddenly put her arm about Eva and drew her head against her ruffled white blouse.

■

Soon after, Cora, Alfred, and Karoline sailed from Bremerhaven. It was September, the week of the Nuremberg Party Rally; in Thalstadt, too, the houses were hung with flags; bands blared and men in uniform goose-stepped in wide ranks down the Hafenstrasse, with cheering crowds lining the sidewalks.

In school, the loudspeaker crackled, and Eva's schoolmates listened entranced as the announcer described the Führer's triumphal progression through the ancient streets of Nuremberg. "And now the people's ecstasy is breaking all bounds! 'The Führer leads, we follow! The Führer commands, we obey!' They are beside themselves, filled with gratitude and adulation for this singular man, humble at his most exalted moment! They reach out their hands to him to feel his touch— they lift up their little children to see for themselves this man who is their savior, this man who into their tiny hands bequeaths a new and glorious Germany destined to last a thousand years!"

"*Sieg Heil! Sieg Heil! Sieg Heil! . . .*"

In the assembly hall, students and teachers sprang to their feet, their voices merging with the airborne voices at the rally. Their hands were raised in salute, as were the hands of the shouting multitude at Nuremberg, and millions of hands in schools and factories and public squares. They were saluting the new Germany, Hitler's Third Reich destined to last a thousand years. But Eva, standing alone in that forest of upraised arms, thought of a ship leaving the pier at Bremerhaven, and of Alfred raising his crippled hand in a last gesture of parting from the lost Germany, the land of his birth.

■

Summer took its time leaving that year. It hung on into late September, reluctant to give way. One almost came to take for granted those warm days and glowing afternoons, last constants in a time of uncertainties.

One such unseasonable afternoon, as Eva and Uschi were crossing the Marktplatz on their way home from the park, the sun-tinged clouds overhead broke suddenly under their burden. A torrent of rain lashed the cobblestones and within seconds Eva and Uschi were drenched to the skin. Giggling they ran toward the City Hall and sought refuge under the striped awning of the Rathskeller, where Grandfather's eightieth birthday had been celebrated more than two years before. Catching their breath, they leaned against the wall and peered across the rainswept square. It was as if they had found a small safe island all their own in the midst of a vast, treacherous sea.

Suddenly Uschi's eyes widened and her face went white under her freckles. There, at the Rathskeller door, fastened to the oaken beams dark with age and venerability, was a sign. A sign discreetly printed in Gothic lettering, in keeping with the patrician aura of the tavern. Eva suddenly remembered Herr Engelberth, the white-haired proprietor, taking leave of the family at this door after Grandfather's birthday dinner. "May I make reservations for your Herr Father's *next* big anniversary, five years from now?" he'd proposed genially.

There was something preposterous about the sign at the familiar door. Eva stared at it in disbelief, waiting for the words to fade away as if written on the wind. She had heard about such signs appearing in other places—in Nuremberg and Munich, even in sleepy old towns along the Neckar. But they had seemed scarcely more real than strikes in America and floods along the Nile, their impact blunted by other stories. Compared with the sound of doors crashing under a hail of fists and boots, the silent closing of doors had made a faint noise.

Now the place was Thalstadt, and it was Grandfather for whom the door had closed, a door that had stood open to him for a lifetime. The sign said that Jakob Bentheim could no longer enter—that Jews were Not Welcome.

Anger, which could make one cry, could also stop one from crying. Turning her back, Eva walked out into the rain, pulling Uschi along.

"Uschi, Grandfather mustn't be told about this—not yet! Perhaps Herr Engelberth was *forced* to put up the sign, and when Grandfather's Rathskeller companions find out . . ."

Uschi said nothing. Her shoes, swollen with rain, spurted little cascades of water with each step, but she trudged on sullenly, her small face set. By the time they reached the corner of Marktstrasse and the great clock of the Roeblin watch store across from their house, the cloudburst had dwindled into a soft rain. Behind the storm-splashed windows of the Roeblin store, the carved figures of a Black Forest clock made their quaint turns, and the bracelets and golden watches shone on their velvet cushions. It reminded Eva of the gift Herr Roeblin had presented to Grandfather on his eightieth birthday in the name of his Rathskeller friends the spring before the Nazis had come to power. Grandfather, touched but trying to hide it, had handed the gift around the table of the assembled guests. A watch chain in a white box with the inscription ROEBLIN'S HOUSE OF CLOCKS embossed in glossy gold, and under it, in finer, fainter print: *Where Time Never Stands Still.*

A sudden thought came to her.

"Uschi, let's go in and speak to Herr Roeblin. Remember the speech he gave at Grandfather's birthday dinner? They've been neighbors for a very long time, Uschi—I think he ought to know."

Uschi glanced down at her dripping skirt.

"It's no use, Eva. It doesn't *matter* whether he knows or not, don't you see? He won't *do* anything about it—*none* of them will."

She started across the street, but when she saw that Eva was not coming, she turned back slowly and followed her into the watchmaker's store.

■

It was quiet inside; the rain had kept the customers away. There was only the sober ticking of the clocks, like the heartbeat of time. Their faces gazed down on them remotely, beyond good and evil.

"*Ja, Kinder?*" A voice spoke out from the dim interior of the store. The watchmaker's wife sat behind a counter, manicuring her fingernails.

Eva fumbled for words. She had always been a little shy of Frau Roeblin, with her marble features and improbably dark hair. She was as unapproachable as her paunchy husband was jovial; even toward close neighbors she maintained an air of studied reserve. In the store, she never tried to persuade a wavering shopper, but merely shrugged her shoulders and slipped the tray from the counter into its vacant niche under the glass. Sometimes she would pick a necklace or brooch from its box and hold it aloft with a deft motion of her hand, letting the lamplight strike the stones and sparkle seductively. Her hands, pale and slender, were like an afterthought to her somber plainness.

"Yes, children?" she repeated, as they stood dumbly, feeling the chill of the stone tiles creep into their wet clothes.

"We'd like to speak to Herr Roeblin, please," Eva began, her courage slipping away under the storekeeper's indifferent gaze.

"My husband has gone out. If it's a necklace you want restrung, you can give it to me. I'll see to it myself."

She held out her hand across the counter, a hint of a smile in her dark eyes.

Eva shook her head, not knowing what to say. It was such a simple thing that had occurred to Frau Roeblin: a girl's broken string of beads, to be mended in secret, perhaps, before the mother might find out. What could this cool, self-contained woman know about the troubled lives in the house across the street?

"It's about our grandfather," Eva said at last, wishing she had not come. "Something important. I think Herr Roeblin would want to know."

Frau Roeblin looked up sharply. For an instant her eyes held Eva's shrewdly, as if she was trying to guess her thoughts, indeed had already done so.

She shrugged, as if she had slipped the message under the counter.

"Well, he's gone home for the day. If you care to come back tomorrow . . ."

Uschi tugged at Eva's sleeve. "Thank you, Frau Roeblin. I hope we haven't disturbed you."

"Good, then," said the watchmaker's wife, bent over her hands. She was rubbing her oval nails with a polishing cloth, intent on her task. After a moment, her voice spoke up behind them, absently: "I'll tell my husband you were here."

■

Her mother and Anna were in the kitchen, canning peaches and plums.

"Not enough sense to come in out of the rain," Anna said, scowling at the wet footprints on her freshly waxed floor.

"Well, just in time to help set the table!" her mother said, smiling through a plum-scented cloud of steam. "And to get to the piano for a while before dinner."

For once, Eva did not stop to think up excuses. It was good to force one's mind on other things; good to be in the quiet room, playing a Haydn adagio, with Grandfather sitting in his armchair as he had done yesterday and the day before, an undemanding and unappreciative listener. After supper, as soon as she could find a moment to be alone with her father, she would have to speak to him. Meanwhile, one could pretend that everything was as it had always been—as if beyond the drawn curtains the world were not changing piece by piece, incomprehensibly and perhaps forever.

Was something different about Grandfather, too? In some odd way, his face seemed larger this evening, his features dif-

fuse. In the light of the reading lamp over his chair, his droop-
ing eyelids had a bluish cast.

"Grandfather!" she called out in sudden apprehension.

He looked up with a start, his eyelids fluttering. With a gesture so leadenly at odds with his usual briskness it seemed like
the slow-motion dream scene that had frightened her in the
movie about *Emil and the Detectives,* he tugged at his watch
chain and puzzled over his watch.

"The days are growing shorter," he said petulantly, shrugging
his jacket about his shoulders as if to seek warmth. He got up
stiffly, groping along his armrest for support, as she had never
seen him do before.

"Are you all right, Grandfather?" she cried in alarm, pushing
back the piano bench to rush to his side.

He waved her away with an uncertain motion of his arm.
"Tell your mother I'm going to lie down for a while."

But when her mother, alerted by Eva, hurried into Grandfather's room, she called out in a stricken voice, "Jonas, quickly,
get Dr. Neuburger—Father is *ill!*"

Eva was given a hurried meal in the kitchen and hustled upstairs to sleep at her cousins' for the night. "Grandfather must
have rest, Eva," her mother said firmly. "It's best to have everything very quiet."

At any other time the prospect of sleeping on the couch in
her cousins' room would have sent Eva flying up the stairs. Now
she gathered her things bleakly and crept wretchedly down the
hall, past the closed door to Grandfather's room. It was incon-
ceivable that behind it Grandfather should be lying sick in his
bed; he had never been ill before, and his illness now seemed
yet another baffling token of a world gone awry.

Upstairs, as in a kaleidoscope, the world reassembled itself; she fitted herself into it snugly, feeling whole. Ella, perhaps put in a mellow mood by the happenings of the day, consented to play Aggravation with them till bedtime. None of them spoke of the sign on the Rathskeller door; nor did anyone mention that Grandfather, by falling ill, had himself found at least a temporary solution. Uncle Ludwig came upstairs from a talk with Dr. Neuburger and stood at the window, hands folded behind his narrow back, looking owlishly inscrutable. Aunt Gustl came to treat them to a bedtime sweet.

"Grandfather is resting," she said soothingly, easing their scruples at the sight of the raisin buns she set before them.

The lamp with the purple beads shed its comforting light over the little round table. Ella, picking the raisins from her bun to save for the last, cast a wary sidelong glance at darting fingers with designs on her hoarded treasure. It was an old game of theirs, and they clung to it now, guarding the pattern of their childhood against the shadows beyond the lamp.

Catching her unawares, Ella tapped Eva's fingers. "I'll tell Mother never to let you have *Schneckennudeln* again!" But when it was time for bed, she suddenly relented and let Eva have her own moss-green quilt for the night.

Afterward, Eva lay in the dark, listening to the faucet dripping in Aunt Gustl's kitchen. Through the curtains, the electric sign above Herr Roeblin's store blinked its blue light into the room, flitting along the ceiling and across the frilled coverlet on Uschi's bed. Eva counted the seconds it took to traverse the darkness, flaring up brightly and ebbing away, but always coming back. She lay very still, fighting to hold off sleep. For some odd reason it seemed important to stay awake, watching the light come back.

She woke to Aunt Gustl's parting the curtains. Daylight streamed into the room and with it, sharply, remembrance of yesterday.

She scrambled up from her pillow. The air from the opened window felt raw on her face; overnight the wind had turned, auguring fall.

"How is Grandfather, Aunt Gustl?" she asked, pulling Ella's quilt over her shivering arms.

Aunt Gustl sat down heavily on Ella's bed. She blew into a soggy handkerchief and quickly wiped her eyes. "I'm sorry, children . . ."

Before Eva had fully comprehended, Uschi had thrown back her covers and run from the room. The sound of her bitter weeping filled Eva with vague surprise. She had always thought nobody loved Grandfather as much as *she* did.

■

At the same early hour, as Eva later learned, her father received an unannounced visitor. Red-faced from having puffed up the stairs, Herr Roeblin was led into the drawing room and eased his paunch over the edge of her father's desk, declining a seat.

"You can imagine how difficult this is for me, Herr Bentheim—for all of us—but our hands are tied. Engelberth says he has to swim with the stream. If it were up to *us*—but we have our families to consider. My youngest, Berndt, expects to be called into the army any day—I can't involve myself with anything that could bring harm to him."

Her father rose and walked his visitor to the door.

"I am sorry you inconvenienced yourself, neighbor Roeblin. My father is beyond bringing harm to anyone—beyond hurt and humiliation, too. He died early this morning."

■

Grandfather was laid to rest in the consecrated Jewish part of the Thalstadt cemetery, under the headstone that bore the name of his long-departed wife, the grandmother Esther for whom Eva had been named. Eva had cried herself into being allowed to come to the burial—by custom, children were not. None of Grandfather's old neighbors or Rathskeller friends accompanied him on his last journey, nor did his tenants who for decades had made their homes in his house. Only her father's staunch friend Herr Gerber stood quietly among his Jewish townspeople.

Rabbi Gideon, Grandfather's *Landsmann* from the Palatinate, spoke to the assembled mourners. Standing at the graveside in his black suit, his dark beard accentuating the pallor of his scholar's face, he towered over his top-hatted congregants and their primly clad wives. He spoke sonorously, eloquently, of Grandfather's simple virtues and quiet, generous acts of *tzedakah*, and commended his prickly spirit into God's sheltering care. Eva, huddled into her mother's arm and holding on tightly to her father's sorrowing hand, listened almost rebelliously.

"Jakob Bentheim, a good man, a proud man, led a long and good life. His life spanned the Golden Age of German Jewry. He was born in the wake of the Emancipation, when Jews were granted their rights in the ranks of their fellow citizens. He died, in God's wisdom and mercy, just as these rights are wrested from us again."

To Eva, God's mercy seeming a long way off on that autumnal day of 1934, it was almost as if Grandfather's indomitable will had triumphed to the last.

One late afternoon the following March, as he was preparing to close the store, Viktor, the dashing salesman who had worked for J. Bentheim & Sons for as long as Eva could remember, hung back over the array of gift-packed fountain pens he was putting under glass for the night and asked "for a word with Herr Bentheim."

"I could tell at once it would be something disagreeable," Uncle Ludwig told Eva's father later that evening; since Grandfather's death, the Upstairs no longer showed up for an almost nightly chat over coffee and cake, but Uncle Ludwig dropped in on his own once or twice a week to talk things over with his brother—business matters or the news of the day, which he usually summed up with the same all-inclusive word: *disagreeable*. What had happened earlier in the store, Eva found out quickly enough, was not merely disagreeable but almost unthinkable: Viktor had "given notice"—he was leaving J. Bentheim & Sons.

"He hemmed and hawed, of course, but it was in his *eyes*, Jonas—I knew at once what he was about to come out with," Uncle Ludwig went on. "It wasn't his *own* idea, he wanted the family to know, and I haven't had cause to doubt his word since I took him on as an apprentice straight out of school a dozen years or so ago. And it wasn't his fiancée either, he was eager to assure us . . ." Eva remembered Viktor's red-haired fiancée, who rode in the sidecar of his motorcycle on Sunday afternoons, a perfect counterpart to Viktor's fetching dark looks.

"It's her *brother*," Uncle Ludwig went on, shrugging his narrow shoulders. "A Nazi, a little bureaucrat hoping for a promotion, who tells his sister he won't have anyone in the family who's working for Jews. Susi and Viktor want to get married the week of Pentecost, you see, and so . . ." He spread his hands in a gesture of resignation. "I'll miss having him at the store— and not only because he has learned the business inside out. He had become almost like . . ." His voice trailed off.

". . . a son to me?" Eva completed the sentence in her mind. Was that what Uncle Ludwig had meant to say, before he stopped himself just in time, afraid to sound sentimental? She had heard grownups use the phrase now and then, and perhaps Uncle Ludwig, who had two daughters . . .

"Try not to take it so much to heart," his brother was saying softly. "Try not to take it personally at all. Would you take scarlet fever personally, Ludwig? What happened is a *symptom*— the symptom of a raging virus that very few people are immune to or sound enough to fight."

"*I'm* taking it personally," Eva heard herself blurt out. "I *like* Viktor, he's nice. Why should anyone tell him where he can work or not? Why should he *do* what someone is telling him? And it isn't as if he'd just found *out* we're Jewish; he knew it all along."

She stopped, expecting Uncle Ludwig to look at her with his

usual skeptical gaze and wonder aloud since when was it permissible to interrupt adults' conversation. But he was pacing the floor, his shoulders hunched, his hands folded behind his back.

"Everything you say is true, Eva," her father said into the sudden stillness. "That's what makes it all so incomprehensible, so painful . . . I wish I had answers for you, to make it easier to understand. But I don't."

In Ettingen, that spring, the Passover Seder around her grandparents' dining room table was observed with mixed emotions. Uncle Lutz and Aunt Tilla had obtained their *Zertifikat* for Palestine; and when Grandfather Weil, looming over the Seder table with his wide frame and gloomy patriarch's face, came to the part in the Haggadah that read: "This year we celebrate here, next year in the Land of Israel!" his voice faltered for a moment before he raised his glass with the holiday wine in his son's direction and gravely wished him and his family safe passage and God's blessings. Eva, sitting close to Eli to guide him in turning the pages in the children's Haggadah with the bright illustrations, thought of Karoline and her parents, whose places were empty now—and ahead to the *next* Passover, when Eli's chair next to hers would be empty as well. The Seder, commemorating the Exodus from bondage to deliverance, was a time of celebration; and in the festive mood of its customs, readings, and songs, Eva and Sabine used to exchange whispered banter and suppressed giggles behind Grandfather's back, their eyes sparkling from the wine that even Eva was allowed to sip on this night so "different from all other nights." Now, though she tried to rejoice with those about to leave, her well-wishings were tinged with a bitter taste, like that of the maror root on the Seder plate that symbolized the bitterness of slavery in Egypt. Deliverance, too, could have its bitterness, when it meant leave-taking and separation, Eva discovered. Even the scents of Grandmother's fragrant soup simmering on the stove, with its fluffy dumplings and bits of chopped parsley floating on the clear broth, had lost their magic to soothe the ache in Eva's heart. All the more when she saw the pain in Grandmother's eyes, despite her efforts at holiday cheerfulness.

Still, they went on with the celebration bravely, breaking the matzoh and partaking of the unleavened "bread of affliction": first with the maror to remind them that they had been "slaves in Egypt," commanded to cherish freedom not only for their own sakes but for all who suffered oppression; then with the sweet haroses—chopped apples and nuts flavored with cinnamon and wine, symbolic of the mortar and brick used for doing Pharaoh's labors. "Before we were brought forth out of Egypt to the land of milk and honey promised to Moses," Uncle Lutz added, smiling at Eli, who, with Eva's help, had asked the Four Questions assigned to the youngest at the Seder table.

Later, the ancient story of redemption having been told, the festive meal savored, and grace said, Uncle Lutz intoned the "Had Gadya"—the song of the One Kid, the baby goat bought for two coins, that was a favorite of children everywhere around the Seder table; Eli's, too. A song with many dire happenings, except that at the end the Angel of Death is destroyed by God. And they all joined in: Eli and Eva, her small voice dimmed with the hurt of losing him; her mother's warm mezzo and

Sabine's light coloratura; Grandfather's rumbling baritone to his son's stronger, steadier one; and Aunt Tilla's fine, trained soprano befitting the soloist of the Ettingen synagogue choir that Uncle Lutz had always conducted. They were a singing family still, the Weils: had not their great-grandmother Vögele—the Little Bird—been sister to the "Swabian Caruso," the celebrated tenor at the Royal Opera in Thalstadt? Eva's eyes strayed to the singer's portrait over the piano: a mustached gentleman of the last century, with the white silk shawl worn to safeguard his voice against the changeable Swabian seasons. Now the seasons had turned and another family among his descendants was about to join the latter-day Exodus across the Neckar River and beyond.

Only her father's voice had not joined in the singing, or in the songs of praise and thanksgiving that followed. The Bentheims were *not* a singing family. But beyond that, Eva sensed that her father felt too burdened to make even his usual self-conscious attempt at singing along.

"And what of your own efforts to emigrate, Jonas? And your brother's?" Uncle Lutz asked during a pause in the ceremonies.

"*Ach*, Lutz—this isn't the time or place . . ." Eva's mother said quickly, protectively.

But the question, no longer to be retrieved, was already being answered.

"My brother allows himself to be lulled from what lies ahead by the fact that we are still earning a modest living from the store," Eva's father said. "And our American *mishpocheh*—the cousins who visited here just before Hitler took over—aren't very encouraging either. Richard now lives in London, where refugees aren't admitted except on temporary visitors' visas, and not permitted to work unless they are lucky enough to find a coveted spot as butler or maid. Arthur, in New York, writes ruefully that he is supporting his daughter through medical school, and reminds us that 'there is a depression' and refugees are perceived as competing for much-needed jobs with Americans. All of which, he and many American Jews fear, is likely to ignite the anti-Semitism smoldering everywhere beneath the surface."

He shook his head. "Arguments all too similar to those voiced not so long ago in our own communities, Lutz, when Jews coming here from Warsaw or Lodz needed *our* support. A case of Jewish history coming full circle—with all of us the losers, of course.

"If only I had my health," he went on after a moment, barely above a whisper, "nothing could deter me from taking my wife and child to safety, from making a new start *some*where, with no more than the ten marks allowed to be taken abroad. But the thought of lying helpless and penniless in a hospital ward in New York, while Martha is forced to scrub floors to support us—"

"Jonas, dear, dear Jonas!" Eva's mother said softly, touching her hand to his wan cheek. "You'll make yourself ill worrying! We can work it all out, we two, here or there, as long as we have each other!"

Eva, struck to the core by her father's ashen face and her mother's pained eyes, quickly turned to help Eli pull the tab on the Haggadah page that made the basket with the baby Moses glide across the painted blue waves of the Nile, where Pharaoh's

daughter waited in the reeds with outstretched hands to re
ceive him.

Eli's clear, unknowing child's laughter pealed over the awkward adult silence in the room. Sabine rose from the table and
returned carrying Grandmother's sugar-dusted Passover hazel-
nut cake.

"Oh, it tastes better than ever, Mother!" Aunt Tilla called
out, ladling a dab of Sabine's foamy white wine sauce over the
slice on her plate. "May I have your recipe to take along for
next year?"

"Next year in Jerusalem!" Grandfather said firmly, solemnly,
the wineglass raised in his hand, and they all chimed in, holding their glasses aloft and gazing fondly, wonderingly at one another, between sorrow and hope.

"But he didn't come *in*!" Eli suddenly burst out, the corners
of his mouth turned down in consternation. "Opa told me to
leave the door ajar so the Prophet Elijah could come into the
room, but he never did!"

"If Grandpa said he would, it must be so, Eli," Sabine said,
with a smile in her lovely eyes both teasing and consoling.
"Maybe you weren't *looking* at the right moment."

"I did look, but he never came!" Eli persisted with a throb in
his voice. "And he never drank his *wine*—see, Sabine!" He
pointed toward the ornamented silver cup set aside for the
Prophet Elijah and still filled to the brim, and burst into sobs.

Grandmother, who had been so quiet all evening with her
tasks and her thoughts, quickly put her arm around Eli and laid
her hand over his small, heaving chest. "He is *here*, Eli—in our
hearts. And when Moshiach is about to come, Elijah will reap-
pear and let us know."

Eli's face brightened. "Next year, Oma? Will Moshiach come next year?"

Grandmother smoothed the soft blond tendrils at the nape of his neck. "We don't know when, Eli. Not until people are ready for him, you see. When that time comes, I think children may be the first to know."

And she gently picked him up and held him close for a moment before she laid his suddenly sleep-heavy body in his father's arms to be carried home.

Frau Ackermann, though no longer their class teacher, still came to their room each day to teach her special subject, German. The events of the past two years, which had changed so many others, seemed to have passed her by. She taught with the same blend of enthusiasm and subtle irony; and she continued to reward a probing question with the same flashing smile with which she received a correct answer. "Questions are the birthright of the young," she said. "The only thing silly about a question is not to *have* one." Sometimes she stood at the classroom window with her head expectantly cocked to one side, as if she were waiting for the questions to come—big questions, deserving of big answers that she might set forth in her just and reasonable way: questions not about the umlaut or declensions or the meter of a poem but about right and wrong, truth and sham. But none were raised. The time for questions was already past. Eva knew it and the others knew it, and when Frau Ackermann turned tiredly from the window and wrote the date on the blackboard in a fine spray of chalk, Eva knew that *she* knew it, too . . .

■

At the end of the last day before summer vacation, Frau Ackermann asked Eva to help her carry some books upstairs to the

Teachers' Room before leaving. The halls were emptying, and the students running down the steps had already cast off the restraints of the schoolhouse before they burst through the door into the summer promise of endless free time.

When Eva and the teacher reached the third floor, they seemed to be the only ones left in the building. "Come in for a moment, Eva," Frau Ackermann said at the door, after an instant's hesitation. "I have something to tell you."

Embarrassed at this invitation to enter the teachers' retreat, as well as by Frau Ackermann's air of confidentiality, Eva awkwardly stepped inside. She set down the books on the round table where, through a door left ajar, she had sometimes glimpsed the teachers drinking coffee during recess. Frau Ackermann gave her a fleeting smile. "I'm glad we have this chance to say *Auf Wiedersehen* to each other, Eva," she said. "I won't be coming back."

"You *won't?*" Eva asked incredulously. "You'll be teaching at *another* school?" Frau Ackermann seemed to have been at Buchberg School forever and ever, and Eva could not conceive of a reason why she would no longer be.

Frau Ackermann was stacking her books on the shelves of the metal cabinet along the wall.

"I won't be teaching anymore at all, Eva," she said with her back turned, and clicked the lock shut.

She sat down at the table and shook her head, as if she were as surprised to find herself saying it as Eva was to hear it.

"You see, I am a *Doppelverdiener,*" she said, pronouncing the unwieldy new word with the kind of disdain barely tinged with amusement she reserved for what she called Bad Poetry.

Eva tried to break the long word into its component parts, the way Frau Ackermann had taught them. "A double earner? You mean you are earning—" she stopped herself in time from asking if the teacher was earning two salaries, but it seemed the only possible interpretation.

Frau Ackermann, following Eva's thoughts, flashed her bright smile and laughed, but the laughter had an unaccustomed edge.

"No, Eva, nothing of the kind. But I'm considered to be earning a double *income* in our household—there is my husband's and there is mine. And that has become verboten, it seems."

"But why?" Eva asked, puzzled. "You studied to be a teacher. It's what you've always *done*." And what you're so good at, she would have liked to add, but did not dare for fear it might sound at once ingratiating and condescending.

Frau Ackermann shrugged. "It's one of many new things that are not to everyone's liking. It's supposed to do away with unemployment—though if you *make* work for some by putting others *out* of work, it doesn't seem to make sense. Except perhaps on some skewed statistical charts that ignore unemployed married women."

She pushed back her chair, picked up her big pocketbook, and waved Eva through the door, pulling it shut behind them.

"Anyway, Eva, I won't be back. Strange, I hadn't ever thought it would happen to me. When they got Fräulein Metzger and Dr. Seyboldt and Ulrich Klaeger, I felt bad for them. But I did no more about it than any of my colleagues did."

They were walking down the stairs, over the steps on which, that chilly morning two winters past, Fräulein Metzger had dropped her woolen glove.

"I wasn't 'political,' you see. And I wasn't Jewish. I was just a teacher of German who loved what she was doing and did it reasonably well, I was told. For a while back there, when things looked so bleak for our country, I even thought—and I'm not proud of it now—that a *new* government, a *strong* government, might do some good—though never the *Nazis!*"

They crossed the silent lobby. Their footsteps must have alerted the custodian's wife, for the door to her apartment opened slightly and the faint meow of one of her cats came plaintively through the crack. Frau Ackermann doubled her steps and drew Eva into the schoolyard.

It was a blindingly blue afternoon with all the brilliance and fragrance of midsummer. Frau Ackermann cast a parting glance at the flower beds in bright bloom that always competed for Eva's attention at her desk near the windows.

"It used to be a fine place to work, Buchberg School," the teacher murmured. "I'll miss being here." She turned resolutely and, taking a deep breath, walked through the gate.

"Maybe you'll be here again," Eva said, as much to console herself as to cheer up the teacher. "Maybe *Doppelverdiener* will be allowed back."

Frau Ackermann, walking on briskly, shook her head. "No, Eva, it's over. And in a way, I'm glad. I would have stayed on, holding on to my post, making compromises in *what* I teach, *how* I teach—not Heine, he's a Jew; not Thomas Mann, he's an outspoken critic of the regime. Watching my step with colleagues and school directors, and with some of the students I needn't mention by name . . ."

She slowed her step. "It wasn't only my own post I had to worry about, you see. My husband works for the radio station, and he's holding his breath wondering if they'll let him go on reporting the weather, or put one of their old party members in his place. What I did or didn't do at school could have been held against him at any time."

"Dr. Laemmle wouldn't have told anyone," Eva said, thinking of the elderly director, as gentle as his name implied, who with his white-haired wife presided over the school. Though in truth she had seen them only infrequently and fleetingly in recent months.

"The Laemmles are leaving, too!" Frau Ackermann said, walking on. She rested a hand lightly on Eva's arm. "They haven't had a full say in running the school for years now—all these dismissals have been forced on them. And by the time you come back from vacation, the regime will have taken over officially and put in its own director, as everywhere else."

They had reached the streetcar stop, where Buchbergstrasse merged with the winding avenue that dropped down toward the city. Frau Ackermann, suddenly overcome by the heat and perhaps by the reality of it all, sat down on the waiting bench and gazed toward the rooftops in the valley below. Glancing at her sideways, Eva noticed a few white strands amid the teacher's gleaming chestnut-brown hair, the fine lines around her eyes and mouth.

Frau Ackermann looked up with a start. "There is your Number Seven, Eva!" She pointed toward the car coming down the gleaming rails.

Eva shook her head. "I'll be *walking* home, taking the shortcut." She scanned the teacher's flushed face. "Will you be all right, Frau Ackermann?"

"Oh, I'll have time for a lot of reading, things I haven't been able to get to for a long time," the teacher replied, interpreting Eva's question in her own way. "We're lucky—Rolf and I can do without my salary, at least for a while, at least for as long as he can hold on to his post. But what about those other *Doppelverdiener,* the women in poor families who need that second wage? Or the young professional women told to stay home and make soldiers for the Führer?

"And what about *you,* Eva?" she added softly. "You have a hard road ahead of you—will you be able to keep your pride intact, the way you always have? Even when certain students made things very tough for you. Even when I wasn't always the kind of support I should have been."

Frau Ackermann's streetcar came clanging around the bend and she got up to meet it at the curb.

"*Auf Wiedersehen,* Eva." She quickly pressed Eva's fingers in her firm, suntanned hand and turned to board the car. "And thanks—you always *were* a good listener!"

"I'm glad you were at Buchberg School," Eva said, blushing over the compliment. "I learned a lot!" she added, barely loud enough for the teacher to hear.

Frau Ackermann, one foot on the step of the streetcar, looked back over her shoulder. "So did I, Eva," she said. "God knows, so did I."

■

The new teacher, Herr Froenlich, arrived at the end of September—late but highly recommended.

"He's spent the summer at a National Socialist Teacher Camp," Diete Goetz let it be known. "At last we're going to have a truly German teacher, without a vestige of outmoded liberal tendencies, my father says."

"And good-looking!" Inge Beisswanger giggled. "I just caught a glimpse of him in Dr. Lang's office. Wavy blond hair—and he wears *knickers!*"

"I hear he hates *fat* girls!" Horst Reuter shouted across the classroom, his eyes impudently on Inge's chubby shoulders. Her new peasant blouse, richly embroidered, showed her full figure to painful disadvantage, but the true German girl dressed *völkisch* these days—copying the old folk costumes of the countryside.

Renate put her freshly sharpened pencils on her desk. She passed one to Eva, a red one with silver stripes. "Keep it, Eva. It's got a fine stroke, great for shading!"

Renate still had hopes of making an artist of Eva. But in all the years of sitting next to Eva on the school bench, her talent hadn't rubbed off.

"I'm afraid even your pencil won't do it, Renate!" They both laughed, but stopped abruptly.

The new teacher strode into the classroom, snapping his hand upward as if it were jerked by an unseen puppet master.

"Heil Hitler!"

All around Eva, her classmates jumped to their feet.

"Heil Hitler!"

Hers was the only hand not raised in the new German salute. "Non-Aryans," fortunately, were exempt.

She felt his eyes on her at once, bland, watery-blue eyes in a face that seemed oddly spent despite its youthfulness, lacking in strength despite the tanned veneer.

"Sit down, class." He put his briefcase on his desk and picked up a piece of chalk. Hitching up his knickers and cinching his belt, he strode toward the blackboard.

"Karl-August Froenlich," he wrote, underscoring the family name with a thick line of chalk.

He turned to face them.

"*Jungens und Mädels,*" he said, clipping his consonants smartly, "I come to you directly from our beloved Führer."

A gasp rose from the classroom. Diete shook her forelock into place and sat up straight as the ruler in Herr Froenlich's hand. Inge Beisswanger barely suppressed a sigh.

Herr Froenlich waited for a brief moment to let the effect of his pronouncement sink in.

"Directly from the Führer and his Youth Deputy, Baldur von Schirach, who reigned in spirit over our summer community in our magnificent Bavarian Alps. I come to you imbued with the message of our National Socialist destiny, cleansed in body and mind of all traces of alien ideologies and decadent un-German thought and sentiments . . ."

Next to Eva, Renate shifted uneasily on her bench.

"Education!" Herr Froenlich was saying, with another cinch of his belt. "In the Third Reich it serves but one purpose: the unquestioned, unquestioning, unquestionable subservience to the aim and purpose of our Führer and his hallowed Vision."

He paced slowly back and forth between the rows of benches, scanning the upturned faces on either side.

"Those of you," he began in a tone whose mildness matched the bland look of his eyes, "who will follow me in this glorious venture of becoming German *Jungens* and *Mädels* worthy of the lofty task the Führer sets for us—those of you shall find in me an elder comrade faithful to, and full of faith in, the Youth of the Third Reich."

He drew a comb from his pants pocket and surreptitiously fluffed the waves at his temple. From the corner of her eye, Eva watched Monika von Ahlem bite her lip.

"But *those* of you," Herr Froenlich's voice suddenly thundered at her elbow, "those of you who hide their cynicism behind futile dialectical probings, who stick their noses into books like ostriches and find a sterile intellectualism more exhilarating than the healthy cultivation of strong Nordic bodies and spirits—those will get to know me as an implacable adversary!"

Satisfied with the hush of awe that had descended over the classroom, Herr Froenlich sat down at his desk.

"If there is a single form through which the German folk soul finds its ideal expression, it is poetry. From time immemorial, beginning with the myth-shrouded Edda, through the heroic *Nibelungenlied* and the minnesingers, to our own day when Horst Wessel forged for us his immortal song . . ."

If Herr Froenlich had skipped seven centuries in his haste to get to his own heroes, Eva thought, so much the better. Goethe and Uhland would scarcely have wished to be mentioned in the same breath with the writer of the Nazi anthem.

"*Blut und Eisen*—Iron and Blood—the Life Force of the German spirit, make up the main theme of our poetry," Herr Froenlich went on. "*Lebensraum*—living space conquered on the tips of spears or bayonets—this is the age-old yearning of our invincible nation. Not the beauties of nature, not the favor of woman, but a victorious death on the battlefield—that is the highest aspiration, the most sublime theme for a German poem!"

Herr Froenlich, with a sidelong glance at his reflection in the window, rose from his chair. It had been a strange speech, in a classroom in which, not so very long before, Frau Ackermann had read the lyrics of Heine and Mörike. But those were not the poems Herr Froenlich had in mind.

He was standing on the far side of Renate's bench, a book open in one hand, his free arm swinging from his shoulder as if he were marching toward invisible battlefields. But he was only reciting a poem.

> "A *student, eager to enlist,*
> *Stood waiting at the gate,*
> *'Your chest is much too narrow, boy!'*
> *The doctor told him straight.*
>
> " *'Sir, for a bullet broad enough!'*
> *Smartly the boy replied.*
> *'And if it pleases God on high,*
> *An Iron Cross beside!' "*

Herr Froenlich waved his hand toward the boys' rows and had them repeat the second stanza along with him. They shouted in unison, rhythmically, raucously—and shot bravado glances across to the girls basking in their attention.

Herr Froenlich snapped his book shut and waved it toward his students. "Of course, the next to last line of the second stanza is not to be taken literally. The author clearly does not have a Semitic, Old Testament God in mind but rather a kind of Cosmic Force . . ."

He smiled his big-comradely smile. "You've all heard the Führer invoke the *Vorsehung*—Providence, the Almighty . . . The Führer is a marvelous orator, who knows how to personify the will of the people through the use of such symbolisms. Our best nationalist poets have often had similar gifts."

Herr Froenlich, with a quick glance at the clock in the back of the room, leafed through the black notebook on his desk that contained the class list of names.

"Bentheim?" he called out suddenly, with a cursory look along the rows of benches, turning his watery-blue gaze on the dark-haired, dark-eyed student before Eva had recovered enough to raise her hand.

"You will be excused from first period Monday, Wednesday, and Friday, starting next week," he told her curtly.

"That will be our time for an exciting new adventure, class," he went on in a voice husky with fervor. "The Reich Education Ministry has instituted a course in *Rassenkunde*. Folk and Race Science is mandatory for all Aryan students, and I promise to make it as interesting as I can, with slide shows supplementing my lectures and assignments."

The bell rang, and the unseen puppet strings jerked Herr Froenlich's right arm forward. "Heil Hitler! Class dis*missed!*"

They jumped to their feet. "Heil Hitler, Herr Froenlich!"

■

It had been the last of the morning sessions—time to go home.

"An*other* subject," Klaus Herzog grumbled under his breath on the way to the door. "You're lucky," he told Eva in passing, in a voice none too friendly. "You're always getting out of things!"

"Luckier than he thinks," Monika von Ahlem muttered behind his receding back. " '*Rassenkunde!*' It's unscientific rubbish! Well, things have been going downhill ever since they kicked out the Kaiser!"

She slipped her books into her elegant leather case, shrugged her pale hair back over her shoulder, and followed the others out the door.

Renate collected her pencils and put them away in their long flat case. "The way he talked about God, Eva," she whispered, although they were the only ones left in the room. "That's *blasphemy!*" She shook her head. "My parents say we will be punished for the sins we're committing—the ones against God and the ones against human beings."

"Maybe they're one and the same, Renate," Eva said softly. She waited to hear Renate say something more, something that concerned *them*, that was happening to them here in this classroom. But she sensed the tears gathering in Renate's eyes and the fear that had trembled in her voice, and looked away.

"Thanks for the pencil, Renate," she said, closing her fingers around its silver-striped ridges. It had a nice, wooden, solid feel, something to hold on to. At least for now.

■

There was little enough to hold on to these days, even at home. Her parents walked around with a perpetually dejected look. Her mother no longer played the piano for them to sing to, "in harmony," as they did Before—before the Nazis came to power and everything changed. Her father worked in his little office on the second floor of the family store when he felt well enough to do so, but he did so joylessly, she could tell, now that he dealt with stationery and children's school supplies instead of the books he loved. And the campaign against Jewish businesses, the continuing barrage against them in the papers "kept customers away," she had heard Uncle Ludwig say to her father with a shrug—though many "stayed loyal," as her father replied with a catch in his voice. "But for how much longer?"

Next to the grownup worries oppressing her parents, her own schoolgirl hurts seemed to Eva petty concerns. She began to keep them to herself and, when asked in the absentminded way her parents spoke these days what was happening in school of late, she shrugged off their questions with a quick and noncommittal Not *much*.

It was to Anna she found herself turning more and more for someone to confide in, to hear her make short shrift of "that *Quatsch* they're teaching nowadays," or of a snide remark flung at Eva by someone in class. "What that one needs is a good whack on the bottom of his brown uniform!" Anna said, furiously scrubbing away at the spotless white sink. "Swaggering around playing the hero and picking on a girl half his size!" She straightened up from the sink, the scouring brush raised in her hand like a weapon brandished in Eva's defense. It made Eva laugh, which was just as well, or she might have thrown her arms around Anna and asked if she knew how fond Eva was of her. And that would have startled Anna's unsentimental Swabian heart almost as much as Eva's teachers and classmates shocked and angered her.

■

Her parents were not at home when Eva came back from school the day Herr Froenlich had begun his reign at Buchberg School.

"They've gone to some foreign consulate or other, your mother told me, Eva," Anna called out from the kitchen. "Come in and help me slice up these plums for a *Zwetschgen-kuchen*, would you?"

Visiting consulates for "orientation" was something many people busied themselves doing these days, to find out what their prospects were of finding refuge and earning a livelihood in countries ranging from Australia to Zanzibar. The results tended to be discouraging, hinging on occupation (doctors and farmers were more welcome in South America, for instance, than shopkeepers and attorneys), age, finances, and health. Some countries were willing to let a limited number of people immigrate, but would not let them work for a living; others made no secret of the fact that while their doors were open to some, they remained closed to Jews. In Palestine, the British used their "mandatory power" under the League of Nations to restrict entry, favoring those with agricultural and similar skills; for those waiting for their *Zertifikat*, the Zionist youth groups ran hachsharahs—training farms in Holland and Germany to prepare young Jews for the communal settlements in Eretz Yisrael, the Jewish homeland. To get into the United States, whose Statue of Liberty proclaimed it a place of refuge, required a coveted visa from the American Consulate, which in turn required an "affidavit" from relatives in the United States, to guarantee that the new immigrants would not "become a burden on the State." The unfamiliar vocabulary of flight confused and bewildered Eva, and she was glad to sit down at the old kitchen table with Anna to help her bake the tartly sweet plum cake and talk about less worrisome things than how to leave a country that wanted them *out,* for some other country that didn't want them *in.*

Anna had already rolled out the yeast dough and spread it on a flat baking pan. Its fresh, homey fragrance teased Eva's nostrils. "Remember when I was little and you'd take a bit of dough and bake a small loaf just for me, Anna?" she said, picking up one of the plums for slicing.

Anna looked at her curiously. "Funny that you should ask, Eva!" She pointed to the windowsill, where a raisin-studded little yeast loaf was rising in its own pan. "I know you've outgrown those special treats I used to make for you. But somehow I thought of them today and decided to make one once more, for old times' sake."

Something in her voice made Eva uneasy. She cut into a plum, feeling the sweet juice drip down her fingers. "You make it sound so final, Anna," she said, trying to keep her voice level, seemingly amused.

"I have something to tell you, Eva," Anna said, the words coming very quickly, almost stumbling over one another. "Remember Karl, my mother's cousin from the Remstal? Who comes to visit now and then and once brought a kite he had made for you, and the three of us walked up to the top of the Buchberg to let it fly?"

Eva nodded. Of course she remembered Karl. A nice man many years older than Anna—a quiet man who spoke even less, Eva sensed, when Anna brought *her* along, though she could not imagine why her presence should have that effect on anyone.

"Well, you see, Eva," Anna went on, speaking a little more slowly now, in her usual voice, "Karl has asked me to marry him, and—"

"*Marry* him?" Eva wondered if she had heard right, or if Anna had suddenly lost her senses. "Why should you want to marry Karl, Anna? You hardly ever *see* him! Do you *love* him?" Not like the childhood sweetheart her father wouldn't let her have, because he was poor and out of work!

Anna ventured a smile. "I'm very fond of Karl, Eva. I've known him all my life—he is a good man, a decent sort—and he's been waiting for a long time for me to decide. I think now is the time for me to tell him yes. He's got a little house in the fields outside the village. It will be good to come home again."

"But this is *your* home, too, Anna!" Eva burst out in a choked voice. "You've lived here as long as I can remember, you be*long* here!" She knew, of course, that she sounded entirely unreasonable, knew that she had no claim on Anna, that Anna was free to live her own life anywhere and with anyone she pleased. But her fear of losing Anna was greater than anything "reasonable" she was trying to tell herself.

Anna reached for Eva's plum-stained hand.

"Didn't your parents explain those new laws to you, Eva—the Nuremberg Racial Laws, the Nazis call them. Stupid, horrid 'laws,' no better than those leering cartoons in the *Stürmer* that tell the worst kind of lies about Jews. Well, under those new 'laws,' marriage and any close bonds between Jews and 'Aryans' are verboten. And young women like me can no longer work in Jewish households, didn't you know that, Eva?"

Eva shook her head, though a small voice inside told her she *did* know, hadn't *wanted* to know, had done everything she could to blot it out. But how *could* she? The same "racial laws" had stripped Jews of their citizenship and made it "legal" to take away their legal rights.

"I'll have to leave here, Eva, don't you see?" Anna was saying. "So I decided to do it for my own reasons, not the Nazis'. I've thought about Karl's proposal for a long time, Eva. I've told your parents that we'll be getting married next month and that I'll be leaving in two weeks. That way your parents don't have to give me notice, won't need to let that 'racial law' touch them at all!"

She set the pan with the risen dough into the warm oven. "Your parents don't really need me anymore, Eva. Grandfather is gone, the store is less busy, and your mother, who used to help out in the office now and then, has more time for the household. And *you*'re growing up, Eva; you'll lend a hand when you can—right?"

Eva nodded, a bit dubiously.

"You'll come visit us in the Remstal, Eva," Anna went on. "And did I tell you that Karl is saving up to open a little store here in Thalstadt in a few years? A place where we can sell fresh country butter and eggs from the village, vegetables and fruit. Then you can come and shop and see us, huh, Eva?"

Eva nodded miserably, watching Anna's practiced hand sprinkle brown sugar over the *Zwetschgenkuchen* that no one could make as well as she.

"Aren't you going to wish me luck, Eva?" Anna asked softly, sliding the plum cake into the oven.

And so she did.

NINE APRIL 1936

Sometimes even still, perhaps by willing oneself to believe it, things seemed to be almost the way they once had been. There was school, there was homework to be done. There were piano lessons one afternoon a week, and afterward Eva would read in Fräulein Lehmann's living room until Thea Rubin, her best and oldest friend, had finished *her* lesson, too. Together they would walk down Verastrasse, talking, laughing, racing each other to the rambling city garden in back of the Rubins' apartment building, where they would sit on the creaky swings and talk some more, while Thea kept an eye on her younger sister, Miriam, and the baby. Sometimes Eva could stay for supper, and later Thea would walk her toward Wielandplatz before she had to turn back at the corner. Then, every time Eva looked over her shoulder, Thea was doing the same, and they would double up laughing and wave to each other through the descending dusk.

On other afternoons, Thea and Eva shared the same bench at Hebrew school in the Community House next to the synagogue, listening to the cantor tell the Bible stories Eva loved and teach the Hebrew lessons that Thea absorbed with such enviable ease. Then it was Thea who would stop by Eva's house on their way home, sometimes to play four-handed pieces on the piano together, other times simply to talk—and not only "girl talk," as Martin, Thea's scholarly younger brother, teased them with mild condescension. They were studies in contrast in many ways, beginning with appearance: Thea's crisp blond hair and shining blue eyes to Eva's dark. Thea's parents had come to Thalstadt as children with their families from Poland and met and married here. They were observant Jews, whereas Eva's family was "liberal," and Thea could stay for supper at the Bentheims' only when there was no meat on the table that evening.

But the most fascinating thing about Thea was that, like all of her family, she was a Zionist. With her youth group she would dance the hora and sing the songs of the kibbutzim, the collective farms in Palestine where Thea, too, would live and work, as soon as she was able to "make Aliyah" with the others—to obtain a *Zertifikat* from the British permitting them to immigrate. There were many people, mostly young, waiting to enter, and not nearly enough places under the British Mandate Quota. But Thea knew that it was only "a matter of time." Hadn't Herzl, the founder of modern Zionism, written: "If you will it, it is no dream!"

And she proudly showed Eva a new photo of her cousin Michael, who was "in charge of milk production on his kibbutz," and sent her frequent letters urging her to join him soon.

"Do you think you *will*, Thea?" Eva asked, looking from the sturdy young man with the tanned, open face in the picture to Thea's sparkling blue eyes.

"Oh yes, Eva—as soon as I can! You know that Michael and

I are old friends, not just cousins—well, really *second* cousins, anyway!"

She slid the photo back into the envelope along with Michael's latest letter and put an arm around Eva.

"You'll meet someone, too, you'll feel this way about, Eva! Then you'll understand . . ."

It was then that Eva told her about Arno, for the first time, though she would have liked to do so long ago but never quite could. About her father's old schoolfriend Herr Valtary, an art dealer who used to sell books about painters and their work to Eva's father when he still had the bookstore. About the time he had brought his nephew along, the son of an artist. A boy who played the violin and didn't do much talking, but who had walked her to her piano lesson and carried her sheet music, and looked at her sideways with a certain smile. And how he had promised to come to see her again, the next time he was in Thalstadt. And never had.

"Then you must *wish* for it, Eva!" Thea said. "Or get his address from his uncle and write—did you think of that?"

She shrugged. She hadn't seen Herr Valtary in a long time: not since her father had closed his bookstore. But she didn't want to tell Thea about this. There could be many reasons why he no longer came to see her father—none of them good.

■

Thea walked her to the corner, where she said "Shalom!" and turned back. Hurrying across the square with her thoughts still on their conversation, Eva almost slipped on the cobblestones made slick by a sputter of April rain, but suddenly found herself steadied by someone's hand on her arm. She looked up, embarrassed by her clumsiness, and stared into a pair of amused dark eyes. "I told you I would come to see you when I was back in Thalstadt, Eva," Arno said. He glanced at his watch. "I must run now—violin lesson in twenty minutes! I'll try to come next week and walk you to Fräulein Lehmann's house—all right?"

She nodded, speechless, and he shifted his violin case to give her a quick, awkward hug and hurried off.

■

But he did not come for her the following week, nor the one after. The third week it rained, and Eva made a dash for the streetcar, hugging her music books to her chest under her small red umbrella. Of course he hadn't come again and it was just as well, because the April rain sweeping across the empty square in windblown sheets dampened her hair and made her cotton skirt cling to her legs.

It was still windy when she left Fräulein Lehmann's house, but the rain had let up a bit and the sun flitted intermittently between the swift, scattering clouds. As she turned the corner, there was Arno leaning against the wall of a building, petting a wet and shivering dog. When he saw her, he straightened with an embarrassed grin. A man's umbrella over his arm clattered to the ground and he stooped to pick it up and held it out sheepishly in Eva's direction.

"I thought you might be without one, and since it was pouring, I thought . . ."

Whatever she did, she mustn't laugh. "Thanks, Arno," she said, folding her own small umbrella and opening his over both of them. "But you should have used it yourself! You're as drenched as . . ."

"A wet dog?" Arno finished for her with a laugh, taking leave of his bedraggled companion with a last ruffle of the slick fur.

"You know, Eva, it never occurred to me to open that umbrella—I don't even own one. This one's my father's—I brought it along from Munich for him. For when he gets back."

He put his hand over hers to steady the umbrella against the wind, and his free arm around her waist, matching his step to hers. The rain beat a swift staccato overhead. "I think I'm beginning to like this," he said with that remembered smile.

They walked down Uhlandstrasse, following the streetcar tracks. Arno tipped back his head and scanned the sky. "A bit more sunshine and we might have a rainbow," he said, reaching across her to take her music books, the way he had that other time. She realized suddenly how much she had missed him, and perhaps he knew what she was thinking because he gave her a quick, quizzical look and drew his eyebrows together in a half-frown of concentration.

"I wanted to come those other times, Eva, as I told you . . ." he began uncertainly, as if even now he hadn't quite decided on a plausible excuse.

"Oh, did you? I don't remember you saying anything," Eva parried coolly, the way Sabine, her sophisticated aunt, might have done. Though her voice didn't seem quite arch enough to be convincing, at least not to her own ears.

Arno bit his lip. "Well, I did," he repeated stubbornly, his dark hair falling over his forehead. "And I meant it, too. But for the last two weeks my father's visiting hours were changed, so you see . . ."

Eva abruptly folded the black umbrella, hoping he wouldn't

notice that her hands were fumbling. It wasn't always so wise, after all, to be like Sabine.

"I'm sorry, Arno—you hadn't told me your father was ill. Is that why you live in Thalstadt now? To be near him?"

"I'm here to study music with Professor Zeller," Arno said. And added, after a moment, "My father isn't in town, Eva. He's more than an hour's ride from here by train. I used to visit him from Munich, too, from boarding school—it wasn't that much longer."

She wanted to say: My father is also sick, Arno. It might have helped him, knowing she knew what it was like. But somehow she didn't dare say it, for Arno's face seemed closed to her, like a shut door.

They were passing the stone fountain on the Uhlandplatz. Behind it, a flight of tree-shadowed steps led steeply down toward the Old City. "Let's turn in here, Arno," Eva said, out of a vague sense that she should let him change the conversation. "It's a shortcut—and there's a good view from the top of the steps."

But the lingering mist had cast a gray shroud over the valley and the town was barely visible beneath, as if it were hiding its face from them. Only the copper cupola of the Art Museum shone under a patch of blue.

"I'm staying right near there," Arno said, pointing past the museum building, his other hand gently turning her head in the same direction, brushing her cheek.

"Oh, I know where your uncle lives," she said quickly, flustered by his touch. "We've visited there, my father and I. Not for a while, though," she added, remembering ruefully how long it had been since Herr Valtary had invited them, since he had been to see her father. Had he found new friends for himself?

"I'm not living with my uncle; I'm staying at the music school," Arno said. "Professor Zeller takes in a few out-of-town students as boarders. Swiss, mostly, like himself. But others, too," he added, giving the phrase some weighty meaning that escaped her.

A wave of resentment rose inside her. Why did he speak and act in riddles, making her feel ill at ease, wary of every word she was about to say? Following him down the rain-washed stones, with no sound between them except the hollow ring their footsteps made in the stillness, she almost wished he had not come back.

Suddenly Arno stopped and caught her arm. "Look, Eva—a rainbow! Didn't I tell you we'd have one?"

He was pointing not toward the sky but toward a patch of rain-furrowed earth to the side of the steps. A pool of sunshine had painted a thin film of red and indigo over the stagnant water.

She shook her head, confused by his even glance. She had expected him to laugh at his own silly joke.

"But this doesn't count, Arno. It isn't a *real* rainbow!"

His gaze swept the cheerless sky. "No, Eva, it's only an ersatz rainbow. But we found it and it's ours, yours and mine." He put his arm around her. "Until the sun shines for us again."

It sounded like a promise, a promise she desperately wanted to believe. Something began to change in her, to grow at once sweeter and keener, that moment on the stone steps, with Arno's grave eyes upon her, safe within his arm. She felt she could never be angry at him again, for anything he might say or do, no matter how vexing it might be, no matter how foolish it might make her look.

■

That evening, when her mother came into her room to turn off the reading lamp, Eva drew her down to sit on the edge of her bed. There was something she had to ask, though she felt vaguely treacherous for doing so. But was she not doing it to help Arno, to stay away from things that were troubling him, from careless questions?

"I saw Arno today, Mother," she began, hesitantly, for she realized only then how strange it must seem to her mother that she had not mentioned it before.

"Arno?" Her mother did not remember at first. Then she smiled a serious kind of smile and smoothed Eva's hair from her forehead. "You mean Herr Valtary's nephew, don't you? I didn't know he was in Thalstadt."

"Oh yes, he lives here now. He's studying music with Professor Zeller. He called for me today, after piano lessons."

Her mother shook her head. "Yes, of course—and to think it was I who suggested he walk you to Fräulein Lehmann's that afternoon his uncle brought him here . . ."

"What has happened to him, Mother—to him or his family? Something is wrong. Is his father very sick?"

There seemed to be something secretive about his father, beyond the fact of illness.

"I don't know very much about it, Eva," her mother said, still in that curious, cautious voice. "And I don't think it would be right for me to pass on the little I do know without Arno's permission. It's up to Arno to tell you as much as he wants you to know."

But she was not to be put off by her mother's clever appeal to her fair-mindedness.

"You don't seem to be happy about my seeing him, Mother. Has he done anything wrong? Is his father . . ." A terrible thought struck her, as she suddenly remembered Herr Valtary's hostile remarks against the democratic government in the last days of the Republic.

"Is his father a Nazi?"

(This, too, could be seen as sickness, in the eyes of someone like Arno.)

"No, no, Eva—nothing like that! Arno's parents were good people, both of them. But I'm afraid they've left him a troubled heritage in these cruel times."

She took Eva's hand between her own and leaned closer. "Have you never wondered why Herr Valtary felt inclined to bring Arno to our house that time? And why I can let you walk down the street together now, when such a friendship between a boy and girl could be very dangerous for both?"

Slowly, things began to fall in place. Why had it not occurred to her that, as Herr Valtary's nephew, Arno would be assumed to be "Aryan," and forbidden to be with her? None of the boys in her class, not even Anton, dared any longer to be seen with her outside the classroom.

"Then Arno's mother is Jewish?"

"She *was* Jewish, Eva, yes. I never knew her, but your father met Arno's parents in Florence many years ago. His mother was a beautiful young actress, a Hungarian. She died in an automobile accident. I wonder if Arno was old enough at the time to remember her at all."

Her mother got up quickly, as if she wanted to get away before Eva might draw more of Arno's secrets from her.

Her eyes lingered on Eva's face.

"It's hard growing up in Nazi Germany, Eva, and perhaps harder still for parents to watch hurt come to their children without being able to help them. But at least we have each other, we know where we belong. Sometimes I think it is saddest of all for young people like Arno, who are no longer at home anywhere, who grow up in a no-man's-world."

She knew that what her mother said was a quiet warning, as if she had been present when the troubled look had come into Arno's eyes, involving Eva in his own hurts, his own unsolved riddles. But when her mother glanced back at her from the door, she shut her eyes quickly, making her face grow blank, promising nothing.

TEN SUMMER 1936

That summer, something close to a holiday feeling enveloped the city. There were no arrests, no further decrees, no humiliating incidents. In school, even Herr Froenlich had shifted his daily opening remarks from "the Führer's lightning-speed reoccupation of the Rhineland" and Mussolini's "gallant conquest" of Abyssinia to a lighter topic: the Summer Olympics to be held in Berlin in August.

There was a seductive normalcy to this talk of games and records and meets and scores. And while Herr Froenlich insisted that it would be "the Nordic athletes, of solid Aryan stock" who would be excelling, he conceded that "other nations," too, might give their German hosts some competition. The names of runners, swimmers, women jumpers, and vaulters from Hungary, Italy, Finland, and Japan whizzed about Eva's astonished ears; though when Klaus Herzog brought up Jesse Owens, Herr Froenlich, flush-faced, curtly turned their attention to the achievements of another American runner instead.

Still, Eva puzzled over the changed ambience in the classroom, freer and more spontaneous than it had been since Frau Ackermann's days. Had Herr Froenlich received a new set of instructions from Berlin, substituting the triumphs of the sports arena for the glories of death on the battlefield? Could this mean that there would be no war—that Hitler really had "no further territorial demands," as he had told the French after his troops had marched into the demilitarized Rhineland? "He's got all he wants now!" Renate had whispered that day on their way back from the assembly hall, where the school had listened to a broadcast of Hitler's "victory" speech to the roaring Reichstag—the rubber-stamp Nazi "parliament" in Berlin. "Things will get back to normal, Eva, you'll see!" Renate's fingers had closed about Eva's furtively—a stolen gesture of reassurance behind Herr Froenlich's back.

And though it seemed an impossible idea in this year following the Nuremberg Racial Laws, something inside Eva could not keep from wanting to believe Renate. Lately, she caught herself counting the brown uniforms in the streets—there seemed to be fewer—and noting the gradual disappearance of signs forbidding Jews to enter a restaurant or sit on a bench in the park. Could Thalstadt, by some miraculous turn of events, become Thalstadt again? Would the regime "change," as a very few visitors around her parents' coffee table still clung to hoping? Or was this the kind of wishful thinking that her father, with a shake of his head, dubbed the "striped leopard theory of history"?

Arno, too, meeting Eva halfway on her walk home from school on the last of these perfect afternoons in July, shrugged off such notions with a toss of his lank dark hair.

"It's the Olympics, Eva. They don't want the foreign press and visitors to see what Germany has really become under the

Nazis. So they cover the dark underside with a show of hospitality and sportsmanship. Did you hear Goebbels on the radio spouting 'peaceful competition among the youth of the nations' instead of his usual Tomorrow-the-World stuff? Followed by a chorus blaring Schiller's 'Be embraced, you millions, / This kiss to the whole world!' in place of the 'Horst Wessel Song.' "

And he began to whistle the Beethoven choral theme set to Schiller's "Ode to Joy." Whistling it with an impudent, jazzy beat that mocked the Reichsminister for Folk Enlightenment and Propaganda for using Schiller's poem in praise of joy and humanity as a smoke screen. "The fox luring the chickens into his den," Arno scoffed, breaking off the Ninth Symphony theme and snapping his fingers in disgust. "They'll make it work, too, the pageantry and propaganda—'filmed by Leni Riefenstahl.' Whether it's at the Party Rally in Nuremberg or at the Olympic Stadium in Berlin!"

They turned toward the flight of steps behind the stone fountain on the Uhlandplatz. It had become *their* way down into the center of town, away from the broad sunlit streets where the streetcars ran and the swastika flags fluttered from too many houses. Here in the leaf-shaded world on the descending steps it was silent and cool, with only the slap and splash of the fountain above them and the hollow ring of their footfalls on the dank stones. They were passing a newly painted bench on a landing, free of the usual JUDEN VERBOTEN sign, and Arno suddenly grabbed Eva's arm and pulled her down beside him. "Courtesy of the Olympics, Eva!" He stretched his legs out, put his arm around her shoulder, and leaned his head back against the wooden slats, squinting into the dappled sunlight falling through the leaves. "Nice to sit here like *people* before the signs go up again," he murmured. "Before the 'youth of the world' go home with their medals and the Nazis go back to making bombs and bullets with their names on them!"

Eva, longing to hold on to the moment—the filtered light on her skin, their cheeks nearly touching, his arm urging her close—turned Arno's face toward her own and laid a silencing finger on his lips.

But the voices in her own heart would not be stilled so easily. She knew as well as Arno that the jubilant façade of the "Olympic host country" masked the dark realm of the concentration camps. She thought of Alfred raising his broken hands in the hushed stairwell: *"They* did this to me, Eva!" She saw herself, newly banished to the last bench of the classroom, a barely acknowledged presence rather than the fellow student she once had been—or had imagined herself to be. Even the Olympics, debated endlessly and enthusiastically by the others, were not for her. Germany's Jewish athletes were not allowed to compete, among them Gretel Bergmann, Swabia's high-jump champion, whom Eva had once seen training on the Maccabi ball field in the Crow's Nest woods. And across the border, in Switzerland, the Emperor of Abyssinia had pulled his slight frame to its fullest height, imploring the League of Nations delegates in Geneva to stop Mussolini's tanks and planes from slaughtering his spear-carrying soldiers. To the jeers and laughter of Italy's Fascist delegates, echoed by their Nazi allies in Hitler's Reichstag. Her schoolmates, brought into the assembly hall for their weekly government broadcast from Berlin, had joined in the laughter, unmoved by the drama of the bearded dark monarch and his abandoned people; she sat among them blank-faced, herself one of the scorned and abandoned . . .

"What is it, Eva?" Arno said softly, scanning her face. "What are you thinking?" She drew a deep breath, wishing it could be the "green thought in a green shade" that Dr. Brachmann had cited from a poem in English class that morning. But she could not shut out the world from the borrowed bench Arno had claimed for them, from this moment between them, with the leaves swaying over their heads and the white stems of birches shimmering in the shade.

Arno, sensing the drift of her unspoken thoughts, got up and gently pulled her to her feet, to the tips of her clumsy schoolgirl's walking shoes, meeting her flustered, upturned gaze. "I've spoiled the afternoon for us, Eva; I'm sorry. No talk about politics next time, I promise. We'll find another Olympic bench and be just *people*—just *us!*"

She laughed, willing herself out of her conflicted mood without much success. "Just *us*, Arno, next time!" Just you and me and the summer, she wanted to add, but was afraid that it would tell him too much about herself and the way she felt about being with him.

But perhaps he already knew, she thought with a sudden rush of blood to her face, catching his sideways glance and letting him reach for her hand and hold it all the way down to the last flight of steps to Verastrasse.

At the corner of the Bahnhofsplatz, in the late afternoon jumble of traffic and hurrying pedestrians in the shadow of the station tower, Arno let go of her hand and glanced at his watch.

"There's a train leaving for Weissendorf in twenty minutes,

Eva. I'm going to visit my father, tell him that I'll be staying with him at the sanatorium for a while, when school vacation starts next week. Professor Zeller will be going home to Switzerland, and most of the other students won't be around either. So this is a good time for me to be with my father." He gave her a searching look and added softly, "Where I belong, Eva."

She nodded, a sudden lump in her throat stifling her voice. "But where will you be staying in Weissendorf?" she finally managed to get out.

Arno shrugged. "On the floor in my father's room, Eva. In my old sleeping bag. We used to wander about the woods a lot, my father and I, during summer vacations. So now I'll be camping out in his room instead."

Her heart flip-flopped in her chest. She would miss him, and worry about him, and wonder if he would forget her. Perhaps even meet someone else in Weissendorf. Someone prettier, taller, smarter than she.

"And I'll be helping out in the kitchen to earn my keep," Arno added, luckily misinterpreting her silence. "The cook can use an extra pair of hands."

He kissed her lightly on the cheek. "I'll be back the end of the month, Eva. With all of August still left to be together. Just *us!*"

She walked him across the square, their arms about each other, and up the flat steps leading to the station. "I hope your father is feeling well," she heard herself say—the kind of thing grownups said, expected one to say, not always quite sincerely. Now she had said it on her own, because of the way Arno felt about his father. And she about *him.*

He gave her arm a little squeeze. "Would you want to meet

my father, Eva? I think you'd like each other. I could ask him if I can bring you along sometime."

She nodded. She would go anywhere with Arno. She wasn't sure how her parents would feel about such a visit—or even how she herself would, awkward as she always was with strangers. But she nodded yes, anyway.

"Your ticket, Arno," she reminded him. "You'll miss your train."

"I'll write," he promised. "It won't be long."

She smiled, putting up a brave front. The end of July was a very long time to wait.

Arno got in line at the ticket window, behind three young Wehrmacht recruits not much older than he. They were teasing each other about going home on leave rather than off to war, as they would have been doing if the French hadn't given in on the Rhineland remilitarization without firing a shot. Even Herr Froenlich had acknowledged how very close to the brink of war the "Führer's lightning stroke" had brought the countries of Europe. Listening to the soldiers' adolescent voices, relief mingled with bravado, Eva suddenly remembered her father saying that France had not bought peace by its inaction but only war at a later date, at a far more terrible cost. "Oh yes, especially for *us*," Dr. Neuburger had added calmly, but shaking his head as he did when inspecting an inflamed throat or listening to a hacking cough. "Unless we are blessed with a stray cousin in Indianapolis who might be persuaded to get us out in time." She had been setting the table, the two men so deep in conversation they seemed hardly aware of her, and she remembered the sudden jolt of fear tightening her chest like a band of steel. Remembered it now so vividly she could almost see the doctor's cigar, smoke curling toward her mother's white curtains.

Arno was slipping his ticket into his shirt pocket. "I'll call as soon as I get back, Eva." He gave her a quick last-minute hug too hurried for him to catch the look in her eyes and bounded up the shallow steps two at a time. At the top, where the acrid cinder fumes of the trains hung heavy in the close air, Arno turned and waved. "See you soon!" he said soundlessly over the heads of the milling travelers, and her lips formed the words back from where she was standing below: "See you soon!"

But before they met again, flames seared the sunny European skies. Civil war had broken out in Spain.

■

Herr Gerber, on one of his visits for a game of chess with Eva's father, spoke grimly about General Franco's revolt against his Spanish Republican government.

"Of course, he knew that Hitler and Mussolini would send him weapons and planes! Troops, too, Bentheim! Spain is their testing ground for another world war." Herr Gerber dabbed a gloomy brow with the same gesture of foreboding that had accompanied other pessimistic pronouncements over the years. All of which, Eva realized with the now familiar pang that tightened her chest, had one by one come true.

If he were younger, Herr Gerber went on to say, he'd find a way to get to Spain himself, just for the satisfaction of fighting the Fascists—"theirs and ours!"—as a free man, with a gun in his hand. But as things were, he was too old, and too closely watched by his block warden, if not the Gestapo itself, to make it to the border, let alone across it.

"Take care you don't get yourself in trouble over a game of chess, Gerber," Eva's father said warily, his fingers poised over one of the carved figures.

Herr Gerber shrugged. "Let 'em, Bentheim! If I can't visit a sick war comrade anymore, if *that* has become verboten, then they can—" He stopped himself in the nick of time, with an embarrassed glance in Eva's direction, from finishing an earthy Swabian saying that a beleaguered knight of yore had flung at his imperial foes. Her father, with a hint of a smile, came to his visitor's rescue. "It's all right, Gerber. If Goethe could put that immortal line into his play . . ." And they both chuckled, looking down on their game—two old friends whose world had come to an end as swiftly and finally as if a curtain had dropped on a stage.

But Spain was far away, across the brown mountain range of the Pyrenees that seemed to seal off the Iberian Peninsula from the map of Europe in Eva's old geography textbook. On the streets of Thalstadt, wearing its best "host country" face that summer of the Olympics, it was difficult to imagine the scenes of bombarded cities and homeless children in a distant land one did not know. And Eva, thankful for a Thalstadt summer in which "nothing happened," tried not to think about Spain, and to live only for this brief season of tenuous serenity, one she had scarcely remembered could exist. When Arno came back from Weissendorf at last and they spent long hours walking together on The Heights, along the crest of forests encircling the town, they seemed to have a tacit conspiracy of silence about Franco's war and the shattered lives it meant for young people much like themselves. They played a game of pretending that they were living in an ordinary world, with time enough to be young, to grow and unfold like the flowers and leaves in the summer landscape about them. A world that would let them bring to fruition that strange, elusive, and disturbing thing happening within and between them. But of this, too, they never spoke.

■

The last week of summer vacation, Arno suddenly asked Eva if she would come to Weissendorf with him on Sunday to visit his father.

It was a rainy Friday afternoon when Arno had unexpectedly "happened by" after a violin practice session. They settled down for a game of Aggravation on Eva's tattered old board, giggling over their errors between bites of the buttered Thalstadt pretzels that Eva's mother had brought in for them, as if to assure herself that they were still children in need of an afternoon snack. Through the door left ajar—perhaps for the same reason?—came the fragrance of freshly baked *berches*, the braided white Sabbath bread sprinkled with poppy seeds already set out on its special platter, to be served with the evening meal. Sheltered in her parents' living room, with Arno across from her frowning down at the board and tossing his lank dark hair back from his forehead, Eva could almost have shut her eyes to the swastika flag whipping from the tower of the City Hall, and to the headline of the *Mittagsblatt* lying unopened on the corner table: FRANCO FORCES MASSING FOR MADRID!

Arno, the game finished, was putting away the blue and green tokens. With the rain still pelting the windowpanes, he wondered if Eva would go over a Handel sonata with him. It was a piece she had heard him play with Dora Silber, a piano student at the music school who was expecting her American visa any day.

Eva, conscious of her own amateur musician's standing, agreed reluctantly, tackling her part diffidently in a flush of effort and concentration. At the end of the stately adagio movement, just as she was beginning to feel her way through the music and learning to weave her instrument's voice into the web of sound Arno spun on his violin strings, he looked up with a nod and asked if she would come to Weissendorf with him.

It was the first time he had brought up the visit since the day he mentioned it on the Bahnhofsplatz. She had almost forgotten about it in the intervening weeks; more truthfully, perhaps, had shrugged it off. There was a secrecy—a mystery, almost—about Arno's father, about his stay at Weissendorf, that both intrigued and troubled her, as if the hidden complications she sensed might entangle her own life, her parents' safety, her friendship with Arno. Nor had she ever asked Arno to explain. In Nazi Germany it was wiser and safer not to ask questions, better not to know anything that might somehow be used against those one loved and hoped to protect.

Sprung at her now so suddenly—almost as if the visit were a prize that had to be earned by passing the test of the Handel sonata, she thought with a twinge of anger—the idea so unsettled her that she nearly dropped the heavy music book on the piano keys.

Arno quickly reached to steady it before it came crashing down on her fingers.

"What are you afraid of, Eva? It's not much farther to Weissendorf than going to Ettingen to see your grandparents.

And my father is looking forward to meeting you. He asked me to tell you."

"Are you quite sure it's all right?" she asked uncertainly. "For him to have visitors, I mean."

Arno bit his lip.

"Because he is in a sanatorium, Eva? Don't let that fool you. Some of our sanest people are behind bars of one kind or another. The most insane are outside, holding the keys."

He fitted his violin into the faded plush lining of its case and snapped shut the locks. "I wouldn't let you endanger yourself, Eva," he said, taking her hands from the piano keys and pulling down the lid. "If your parents object, I'll understand, of course. But if you decide to come, let's catch the nine-fifteen train on Sunday morning. I'll be on platform five, looking for you."

■

Just before Ettingen, the tranquil landscape swaying past the train windows in a fine spray of mist became suffused with light. Eva, standing beside Arno in the corridor outside their compartment, blinked into the sudden shaft of sunshine flooding the rain-spotted glass. "When angels travel, heaven smiles," she told him teasingly, quoting one of Aunt Gustl's Bavarian sayings. He lowered the blind enough to keep the glare from hitting her eyes. "And do you *feel* like an angel traveling?" he teased her back.

No, she did not. For perhaps the first time, she had not told her parents the truth about her plans. Not that she had lied. She was going to spend the day with Arno, she had said offhandedly, letting her mother assume that it would be another day spent walking on The Heights, perhaps taking a bus ride to the castle in the woods, and afterward sitting in while Arno practiced with Dora or one of the other music students. Her mother, knowing that she could "trust Eva," had inquired no further.

Now Eva had violated that trust. Not that she was doing anything "wrong." Visiting the sick, as she had heard her parents say, was a mitzvah—an act pleasing to God and incumbent on Jews, even on those who did not consider themselves to be "religious." But she felt instinctively that her parents would not have let her go with Arno on this particular visit, out of the same troubling, half-formed fears for her safety that had kept her from asking him any questions.

And so she had not told them. Had simply packed their usual sandwich lunch, put on her pleated skirt and walking shoes— hadn't Arno warned her that the sanatorium was a good half hour's walk from the Weissendorf train station?—and stomped deliberately out the door while her mother was fixing breakfast. "Be back for supper!" she had called over her shoulder, hating herself for her deception yet hurrying off to be with Arno, her stomach tied in knots.

Rounding a bend in the tracks, the train slowed toward the familiar Ettingen station. Through the late summer haze, the sober streets and structures of the town swam into view, and beyond it the wooded hills with the faded medieval glories of their crumbled castles. They passed beneath the footbridge on which Eva had often stood with Sabine and watched her lean over the railing toward the passing trains, letting the smoke-laden wind blow through her long dark hair and filling her lungs with the acrid air. In those days, Sabine had always longed to leave "this philistine little town" and go to Berlin to study acting under Max Reinhardt, the famous director. Now Max Reinhardt had fled Germany, along with hundreds of others of the artists and intellectuals Sabine had so admired. And she was "stuck in Ettingen," unable to continue her education or to find work—coming to Thalstadt whenever she could to "catch a breath of air" at some of the events still taking place at the Jewish Community House.

"Shall we get off for an hour and visit, Eva?" Arno asked, sensing her thoughts. She shook her head; she did not want to take time from Arno's day with his father. Or was it, she wondered with a pang of surprise, that she was unwilling to share Arno with anyone today? Least of all with Sabine?

Just as the train lumbered to a halt at the Ettingen platform, one on the adjoining track pulled out in the opposite direction. Looking across with that faint sense of vertigo caused by the jumbled sensations of motion, Eva caught a glimpse of a striking profile behind the window of the other train. Even with the hat pulled stylishly over the young woman's forehead and the averted gaze at once furtive and determined—not unlike, Eva suspected guiltily, her own look this morning as she had stalked past her mother to the door—she recognized the face in the split second before the cars pulled away from each other.

She wheeled to face Arno. "Why, it's *Sabine!*" Where was Sabine going in the Thalstadt-bound train? She had told Eva's mother not to expect her this weekend.

"Sabine?" Arno asked. "There? On the platform?" He was turning in the direction of a kerchiefed young woman, pretty enough, with the prim, provincial look of, well, a young woman from Ettingen, but with none of Sabine's dark wild beauty.

"No, on the *train*, Arno! She looked wonderful, too bad you missed her!" Her heart lurched as if it were stumbling over her own words. If only *she* were beautiful, too, she thought wistfully, regarding her faint reflection in the glass with the old sense of sorrow and self-pity. It was hard growing up in Sabine's shadow, loving her, wanting to be like her, yet always left to wonder how *any*one seeing Sabine could keep from falling in love with her.

"There's my grandparents' house, Arno!" she said quickly, pointing across the tracks as the train rumbled toward the outskirts of town. "And Grandmother's little garden with the pear tree!"

A troop of Hitler Youth boys, wind-reddened thighs strutting beneath their shorts, elbowed their way down the crowded corridor toward the front of the car. Arno propped his arms against the window frame as they pushed past, his body forming a protective wall about Eva. And for the rest of the journey they looked out on the passing rural scene to the rhythm of the wheels, aware of each other's closeness and the elusive sense of comfort they drew from it.

"Weissendorf!" the conductor called out at the next stop.

"Weissendorf—that's where they keep the *crazy* people— useless mouths to feed!" the HJ leader said loudly, sizing up their city visitors' clothes as they passed his troop near the door. Arno turned back sharply, his fist clenched for a punch at the boy's spiteful face—but suddenly found himself seized from behind by three of the others and heaved off the train, clattering down the iron steps to the station platform. Eva, her heart pounding giddily, jumped after him with her eyes squeezed shut just as the train began to pull away.

Arno stooped to pick up the bag of fruit for his father he had dropped in his fall. Behind them, where they stood shakily on the empty platform, the train rumbled off, HJ boys hanging from lowered windows, gesturing, jeering. Eva, aching for Arno's pain and outraged pride, reached for his hand and drew him toward the gate. "You don't have to *listen* to them!" she said fiercely. For the first time, she felt older and wiser than Arno. Not listening was something she knew all about; she had already served a long apprenticeship in it.

They walked out into the bright sunlight of a small-town square—old houses, eyes shuttered against the glare—closed in on itself with the languor of a summer Sunday, as if time held its breath. Arno squinted over his shoulder at the clock on the wooden station building, beneath the ubiquitous Nazi flag, even here. "They send a car to pick people up if you call ahead," he said, frowning down the country road baking drowsily in the unexpected heat. "But I never call them, myself." He caught her puzzled glance. "I guess I don't want to chance being turned down. Or draw more attention to my father's being there than can be helped."

He turned the corner into the country road, matching his pace to hers. "It isn't true, you know. About my father, I mean. Not in the way he said it, on the train."

You don't have to defend your father to me, Arno, she wanted to say, but sensed that he needed to talk, needed her to listen. "He isn't sick, then," she said, as evenly as she could manage.

"People can be sick in many ways, Eva. Some can be so heartsick at what they see around them they can't take it anymore. My father hates bullying, lies. Official decrees on anything from what is art to who is human. And when they took away his right to teach, to sell or exhibit his work, even to sit quietly in his studio and paint . . ."

". . . he couldn't take it anymore?" Eva said softly.

"He thought he'd be freer in There than out Here. That's what he told me, anyway." He shrugged. "It really was my uncle's idea, you see. When you're Hans Valtary, in charge of 'Cultural Affairs' in Thalstadt, it's safer to have a brother buried in the sanatorium than openly on the Nazi blacklist of 'Degenerate Artists,' perhaps even in the KZ. And so he told my father that it was the only way he could 'protect' him—and me."

His hand tightened about Eva's. " 'Protect your half-Jewish son against the consequences of your youthful folly' was the precise way my uncle put it."

He tossed his hair back from his damp forehead.

"That's when I instantly decided where I belonged. Not with my uncle's crowd. Even if I could have toadied my way into it by letting him 'Aryanize' my mother posthumously, as he in all seriousness offered to try. 'What sort of birth certificates do you think were kept in those little Balkan villages behind the moon in your grandparents' day, Arno? We'll come up with a new set of progenitors for you, boy, with unassailable Magyar bloodlines all the way back to Attila the Hun!' He laughed at his own 'joke' and added that if Göring, in Berlin, could boast, '*Wer Jude ist, bestimme ich!*'—why shouldn't *he*, Hans Valtary, decide who is a Jew in Thalstadt!"

They stopped by a stone well at the side of the road, and

Arno pulled up the iron cup by its chain and dipped it into the bracingly cold water. They passed it thirstily between them, drinking in great, splashing gulps, wetting their flushed faces with the overflow and flicking cool droplets at each other from the tips of their fingers, pretending a lightheartedness they could not quite bring off.

"And then . . . ?" Eva asked in a small voice, as they walked on.

"I packed my bag and walked out of his house, what else? Which didn't require any great heroics—Zeller had already offered to take me in."

"And your uncle? Did he try to stop you?"

"He didn't put down the brandy in his hand! Just wondered aloud, in a stage mutter, what kind of gratitude this was for his willingness to save me from my Jewish *Mischling* status, at great risk to himself!"

"And *then*, Arno?"

He shrugged.

"I told him to spare himself the trouble. That I considered myself Jewish on *both* sides, since my father's courage and decency had put him in the ranks of the persecuted. That I wouldn't be made into 'an Honorary Aryan.' 'Convenient as it would have been for your career,' I managed to get out with all the sarcasm I could come up with, before he threw my violin case into the hallway and told me, dramatically, 'never to darken his door again.' 'Except under the most extreme circumstances, and only after a warning phone call,' he added, red-faced, covering all his bets."

So this is how you came to us, she wanted to say. How we came to be walking down this road together to visit your father.

Who may be sick or not, I don't think you really know, perhaps he himself doesn't know. So this is the mystery you kept to yourself all this time . . .

"Do you remember your mother at all?" she said instead, putting her arm around him as they walked on. "I know she died in a car accident; my mother told me. She said you were very little at the time."

"I was almost four when it happened. Old enough to remember her. Dark eyes and hair. Beautiful—her voice, too. She would sing me to sleep; I can still hum the melodies. Melancholy, minor keys. Hungarian songs, maybe Yiddish—the words are gone . . ."

"But you remember *her*," Eva said. "That she loved you. And you *her*."

"My father loved her so much," Arno said softly. "Losing her nearly killed him, too. He's never really recovered."

He looked at her intently. "All that remained to him was his painting, you see. That's why he let his brother talk him into the sanatorium. The Director allows him to paint. The Nazis have branded his work Degenerate Art and placed him under *Malverbot*. The Director pretends it's simply the creation of one of his patients."

He put his hand on Eva's arm and pointed across a wooden bridge toward a sprawling country house surrounded by lawns and a stone wall.

"Yes, it's the sanatorium, Eva—are you surprised? My father calls it his golden cage. But it's a cage nonetheless, even if it's not Dachau. A prison of the mind. Like all of Germany."

■

It was a small room, spartanly furnished, almost cell-like in its unforgiving spareness. A narrow rectangle with a small window set high opposite the door. A bed made up with the precision of a soldier's cot along one side of the bare, institutionally gray walls, a metal table laden with paints and canvases, flanked by two straight-backed pine chairs. The only touch of color flared from the easel in the corner between table and window, where a half-finished painting at once caught her eye. The painter, intercepting her gaze, shook Eva's hand and pulled out a chair for her, then turned to draw Arno into a brief, hungry embrace.

"Things haven't been too bad," he said in response to Arno's inquiry, but with a shrug and a quick, surreptitious gesture toward the door. "Remember, walls have ears, Eva," Arno had warned her on the way. No wonder he and his father were talking in carefully even voices about carefully chosen things: the heat, a new sonata Arno was working on, an errand his father needed him to take care of. She kept out of their conversation, her self-consciousness heightened by fear of what she might unknowingly disclose to the listening ear behind the wall. The room was cool but oppressively airless; even the strip of curtain at the window barely stirred. The torpor of the room and the drone of the two low-pitched male voices put her into an almost somnolent state, until her eyes were drawn back to the painting: the vivid slashes of greens and angry reds, punctuated by daubs of black, of purples and yellows. A puzzling and intriguing riot of colors and shapes that seemed to exist for their own sakes and for the coiled energy they emanated. Yet suddenly—as though she were looking at one of those vexing, almost inexplicable images called optical illusions—the tangled lines and planes seemed to reassemble, to hint at hidden meanings: concentric waves whirling into a narrowing abyss, sweeping along the gabled roof of a house, a charred and shattered building, the face of a bearded old man, an infant's screaming mouth, a soldier's blood-spattered uniform, its empty sleeves and legs flapping wildly, a young woman pulled by her long yellow hair into the swirling vortex . . .

"I call it *Maelstrom,* Eva," the painter said, looking up at her from his conversation with Arno, as if he had caught her wondering aloud.

He tore open the paper bag filled with fruit that Arno had brought for him and flattened it on the tabletop, letting the red and golden globes spill out, feasting his eyes on the supple round velvet of the peaches, the contoured sheen of the apples. "Cézanne was lucky to paint his still lifes," he said softly. "Who was it that said, 'May God protect us from interesting times'?"

■

When their time was up, Arno's father walked them back across the well-tended lawn—"We push the mower ourselves: exercise, therapy, and economy combined, the Director tells us!" He gave Eva a wry smile—a sandy-haired man, barely taller than Arno and without Arno's striking dark looks. "My father is an *artist,*" Arno had told her long ago, saying it as if he meant: My father is a *king.* But the painter's spare, compact body and pleasant, unremarkable face might have been those of a workingman or artisan, Eva thought: a face curiously boyish, yet etched with wariness and care. At the wall at the edge of the grounds he leaned his shirtsleeved shoulders against the cool stones in the shade of a willow trailing its listless branches over the wooden bridge.

"Someone has to say no, don't you see?" he said simply, as if it was the most reasonable thing to agree on. "A painter must paint what he *sees*, what he *feels*. Not what someone *tells* him to see and feel—least of all the government, least of all one whose ideal work of art is a *boot* ground into a human face!"

His hand tested the rough texture of the stones. "The Nazi culture police say it's Degenerate Art to see the rot beneath the green meadow and paint it brown—or soaked in blood from the concentration camps. But art isn't about painting pretty pictures; art doesn't fawn or lie or glorify. Art looks *beneath* the uniform to expose the emperor's nakedness. It tears the blinders off people's eyes—sounds the alarm."

"Alex," Arno said under his breath, his eyes on two figures in white smocks coming toward them across the expanse of lawn. His father glanced over his shoulder and scrambled to his feet.

"Time for you two to hurry for your train!" He held Eva's hand lightly in his own, his free arm around Arno. "Thank you both for coming. For listening." He turned to her. "One day, when I have my studio back, when this madness has ended"— his wave took in the world beyond the wall—"I'd like to paint you, Eva. Will you let me?" His eyes scanned her features frankly, impersonally. "Your face is so—"

"Interesting?" she broke in, trying to make a joke of it, to ward off pain. It was what Sabine called her face: interesting, a consolation prize for not being pretty.

He shook his head. "All faces are interesting. It's what makes them human, beautiful. Blond girls of Friesland, dark women of

Kenya, Polish peasants and Hasidic rabbis—I painted them all"—his gaze flickered back to the house, perhaps to the bare walls of his room—"when I still had an artist's free choice of subject, of theme."

He looked at her intently. "Each face has its own aura, its innate essence. Yours is a transparent face—your skin, your eyes. It tells more about you—what you think, what you feel—than you mean to let on."

She felt herself blush, but he had already turned to Arno.

"The Director has taken some of my paintings home, to hold for me 'for the time being,' as he delicately puts it. The Director's face is *not* transparent—is he sticking his neck out for *my* benefit, or for his own?" He shrugged. "Not that I'm sure about my own brother, either! He tells me the same thing when he drives over at night for one of his rare visits and makes off with a couple of paintings he finds in the back of my closet."

"Alex," Arno said in a choked voice, drawing his father into a tight embrace. "Keep well and be careful. Till next time."

"Is there anything I can get for you in Thalstadt?" Eva asked shyly. "For Arno to bring along?" She knew she wouldn't be back to visit. Arno and his father needed time together; they had so little of it. And her parents needed *her*.

He nodded. "Write something for me, Eva. Arno tells me you like to write—and we need poems and paintings more than ever now. Even if we can only write and paint them for the drawer. They bear witness for us, if not for now, then for later. As art always has done."

They left him at the gate, where the two figures in white—

orderlies? guards?—were already waiting for Alex Valtary, their faces impassive, impenetrable. He turned and walked between them toward his "golden cage" without looking back, flinging his arm high for an instant against the dark entrance in a mute gesture of parting and defiance before the door closed behind him.

ELEVEN SUMMER 1937

Her father's health had worsened again.

Almost daily now, instead of going home after school, Eva went to Königin Luise Hospital for a visit with him. It was a long streetcar ride through the midsummer city, with a transfer at Steinachplatz from one stuffy car to another. But Eva, always on the lookout for new and solitary walks through Thalstadt, had soon discovered another of her shortcuts: a narrow lane running beside a low stone wall lined with pink hedge roses and raspberry bushes that wound its way downward in back of the school toward Luisenstrasse far below.

Summer lay warm and heavy over the gardens and fields, and apples ripened in the sun-shot air. Dry twigs snapped under her steps, and sometimes a stone would roll beneath her on the steep incline, carrying her a little space along with it. A sense of satiated peacefulness spread over the landscape and the green hills beyond, as if nature, self-contained and self-concerned, had shut out all not in harmony with its own cycle of growth and fruition. Even the rain fell only at night, and the next day there were once more the cloudless skies and the verdant fragrance of blossoms and berries and grass. And as the days passed and her father's strength seemed to ebb from him almost visibly from visit to visit, so the apples seemed to grow larger and rounder and the green of the leaves deeper; and there was something about this glowing summer that was at once healing and heartless, she scarcely knew which.

One afternoon, as Eva was walking in the secluded lane, there was a sudden sound of footfalls behind her, and when she looked back, she saw Diete Goetz coming quickly down the path. She carried her BDM uniform jacket slung over one shoulder; perhaps she was going straight from school to one of her Bund deutscher Mädchen meetings. In the instant before Eva turned away, Diete raised her head and their eyes met.

It was a strange meeting, the two of them alone in the summer calm, for in school Diete and Eva no longer spoke to each other. Diete's father, the economist Dr. Goetz, was a prominent Thalstadt Nazi, and Diete had been the first in Eva's class to join the League of German Girls. On the school grounds, they were enemies—unequal enemies, Eva knew, with all the power on Diete's side and nothing on her own, except the will to resist that power as long and as well as she could. And yet, now and then, almost in spite of themselves, under their cloak of silence and mutual contempt, it seemed to her that they were hiding from each other, and from themselves, a glimmer of truth: that in another time, another place, things might have been different between them.

Now Eva turned her back on Diete and hurried on, determined to put distance between them. But Diete, easily catching up with Eva, abruptly slowed down and matched her pace to Eva's, her jacket swinging jauntily from an outstretched finger.

Eva, without acknowledging Diete's presence, glanced at her from the corner of her eye, scanning the blank face with its tightly pressed lips. The sun put a glint of copper on Diete's short brown hair; she might have been almost pretty, except for the usual tenseness about her mouth and eyes, the graven immobility of her features.

Suddenly Diete turned her head and looked at Eva with narrowed eyes. "What are you doing here? You don't live anywhere near here!"

"Visiting my father in the hospital," Eva said, keeping her voice flat and her eyes straight ahead.

"At Königin Luise? Since when has he been sick?"

"For a long time," Eva said in the same noncommittal tone as before. "Since the war, Diete," she almost caught herself adding, recalling, in a sudden flash of memory, Aunt Hanni saying, bitterly, "My brother hasn't had a well moment since he came home from the war." But she stopped herself, unwilling to grant Diete a glimpse into the private realm of her family or let herself be suspected of playing for Diete's sympathy. It was not sympathy she would have wished for but justice; and justice, even less than sympathy, was what Diete was neither able nor willing to grant her.

Diete's voice broke in on her thoughts. "Aren't you surprised that I'm walking with you, Eva?"

Eva shrugged. "I guess there's no one here to see, one way or the other."

Diete gave a short laugh. "Not a bad guess! It's because of the others that I keep away from you in school. I have nothing against you personally, but there is a principle involved."

"A principle, Diete?"

She snapped her fingers impatiently. "You know perfectly well what I mean! Because your father was a soldier in 1914, you are still permitted to attend our school. But as far as our German class community is concerned, you must be *ausgeschaltet*—totally segregated. Some of the others are slow to learn."

A stone had come loose under their feet; it bounced on the rocky path before them, downward, downward. Eva kept her eyes on it, listening to the diminishing thud until it had merged with the throbbing insect hum of the summer stillness. No longer there to drown out Diete's voice.

". . . back in the lower grades, when the girls loved brushing your hair, saying it was as silken as a Chinese doll's. It always disturbed me, even then, that they could be so taken with the very things that set you apart from us—that black hair, that look as if the wind could blow you over, those foreign, almond-shaped eyes!"

"Disturbed you, Diete?" It was too late now to run from those stinging words, downhill into the shelter of the summer day that Diete had invaded and destroyed. "There used to be a saying that opposites attract. But I guess that is verboten now."

It was also verboten to allude to the many things that were verboten, Eva realized with a belated pang of fear; remarks like this could land a grownup, or a girl's parents, in jail or worse.

But Diete had other things on her mind. ". . . to think that now, years since the New Order was established, there are still some who compromise Dr. Brachmann by calling out *your* name when he asks whose essay should be read aloud, or who should recite a poem. You will have noticed that I am never among those who do."

"I don't care whether you do or not, Diete. If you don't like what I say—"

"But that's beside the point! I've already told you there is nothing personal about any of this. I'll even admit: you do have a peculiar affinity for our German tongue. Peculiar, because you are, after all, *artfremd*—alien in your very being! This language you use so cleverly, the poems you recite with such a facile show of feeling—they are not yours, any more than these trees and skies are yours, simply because you happen to walk under them!"

Shadow and light shifted in the treetops over their heads. "A tree is neutral, Diete: it belongs to those who look at it with love. Language is like water, like air: it takes on the shape into which it is poured. I've heard it spoken only in kindness in my parents' house; never in hate."

"You don't belong here anymore," Diete said stonily. "You never did."

Eva turned away from that relentless face. Below, the Neckar glittered in the distance, and somewhere in the blueness beyond the terraced vineyards and green hills was her grandfather's childhood home, the small village where his family had lived for generations before she was born. She had a sudden recall of another blue and golden day, when he had let her peer past an iron fence at crumbling rows of headstones white as bone, their faded Hebrew inscriptions whittled smooth by the winds and rains of countless years.

She drew a deep breath. "You can drive us out, Diete, but you can't take back the past, can't undo the traces of our lives—"

"We can do more than drive you out!" Diete said in an icy voice, her set face more scary than open rage. A rush of fear seized Eva; she had an almost physical sensation of being pushed back over the low stone wall to hurtle headlong down the steep drop into the valley below. But she held fast, steadying herself on trembling legs against the trunk of a tree, keeping Diete at bay with her own guarded, unswerving gaze.

"Yes, you can take our lives, as Cain took Abel's," she heard herself say. "But do you remember, Diete, when we read Schiller's *Maria Stuart* in Frau Ackermann's class? 'It is not the living Stuart you need fear, it is the dead one!' Lord Shrewsbury warns Queen Elizabeth, to keep her from signing Mary's warrant of execution. We were no threat to you in life, Diete—our scientists who won Nobel Prizes for Germany; our writers, artists, and musicians who enriched its culture; the tailors and booksellers and shopkeepers on the Marktstrasse. Our lives brought honor to Germany—our deaths will stain its name for centuries to come."

Diete, her knuckles white on her clenched fists, grabbed Eva's arms and shook her. "You little—Hebrew prophet!" she spat out. "Shut up—shut up—shut *up*!" She shook Eva so hard that the back of her head struck the tree. A momentary look of fear, perhaps even a hint of something more, stole over Diete's face. She stopped herself abruptly.

"You've made me late for my meeting! If you tell anyone about any of this, you'll be visiting your father in the KZ next time!"

She turned on her heels and stormed down the path, and Eva, her head reeling, followed her with her eyes until Diete had reached the bend in the lane and disappeared from view. Then she let herself slide down into the soft grass with her back to the tree and leaned her cheek against the rough grooves of its bark. She sat for a long time, watching the ants teem across the knobby roots while the sun sank lower over the hills. A leaf, perhaps starved for sunlight in the green cupola overhead, floated down and sailed into the blue void beneath the wall, turning in the light breeze until it drifted out of sight.

TWELVE   FALL 1937

In the fall, the Jewish Kulturbund—the Cultural League formed to bring theater and music to the ostracized communities to raise their spirits and affirm their heritage—decided to give a concert. The repertoire would be somewhat limited: it was verboten for "non-Aryan" musicians to perform "German music," unless the composer happened to be "racially Jewish." "Thank God for the Nuremberg Laws—they're leaving Mendelssohn to the Jews!" Arno said sarcastically. "Felix Mendelssohn, whose music is the essence of German Romanticism, who dusted off Bach from a century of German neglect!"

It was poems by Heine set to music by Mendelssohn that Sabine had been invited to sing. Coming to Thalstadt for rehearsals once a week that fall, she would go home with Eva to spend the night on the sofa in Eva's room.

Even now, in these days of upheaval and leave-takings, Sabine did not lack for admirers. During rehearsals, with the old mixture of pride and pain, Eva noticed the appreciative male glances lingering on her lithe body and animated face. But though she flirted outrageously, Sabine rarely accepted an invitation for a Saturday night dance at the Community House or a Sunday afternoon outing. "My father is very strict, you see," she would say demurely, with a toss of her head at once regretful and final. Her firmness surprised Eva; she had never known Sabine to be so mindful of Grandfather's wishes before, always lamenting her fate as the late-born daughter of aging parents with "outmoded ideas."

Once, when a young man with earnest eyes and the beginnings of a small paunch had brought them to their door after rehearsal, carrying Sabine's little overnight case in one hand and his formidable cello in the other, Eva had asked her about it as Sabine sat brushing her hair before the mirror.

"But he is so *dull!*" Sabine said, stretching her arms over her head and lifting her hair away from her neck. "Decent and dull—a typical Thalstadt burgher!"

"He plays the *cello*," Eva said reproachfully from her bed, recalling the look in the young man's eyes as Sabine coolly retrieved her belongings and closed the door behind them.

Sabine laughed, letting her hair fall loose so that the dark waves cascaded over the white ruffles of her gown.

"Ah, if it were the *violin* now!" she shot back teasingly, cupping Eva's chin in her hand. But Eva shook off her touch and turned her face to the wall. She did not like to be teased about Arno.

The light clicked off, and when Eva cautiously turned her head on the pillow, she saw Sabine standing at the window, gazing out on the lamplit street, her lovely face silhouetted against the white curve of the curtain. It was the same angle, Eva knew with a sudden flash of remembrance, from which she had seen Sabine through the windows of the moving trains that Sunday afternoon in the Ettingen station. "Where were you going,

Sabine?" she had asked her the following week, trying to make her voice sound casual enough to hide her curiosity.

She half expected Sabine to turn on her, with a reminder that she was Eva's *aunt*—closing the door to the world of grownups as firmly in Eva's face as she shut out an unwelcome suitor. Instead, after a mere instant, Sabine had smiled one of her dazzling smiles and given Eva's shoulder a little shake. "What were *you* doing on that train with Arno—playing Emil and the Detectives?" she joked good-naturedly, even paying Eva the compliment of remembering her favorite childhood book.

"Well, I was visiting Manya Mankovsky, in Düningen, if you must know," Sabine had added with an amused chuckle. "As simple as that, Eva—but thanks for your concern!"

And Eva, who had never met Sabine's friend with the alliterative Polish name, had laughed along with Sabine, feeling foolish and, indeed, like a clumsy intruder in Sabine's world.

Was it one of the mysterious young men of that world she was thinking of now, Eva wondered, watching Sabine stand by the window enveloped by the night, as by a veil drawn over her secret other life.

▪

Professor Zeller had come up with an unusual piece for Arno to play at the concert: a Vivaldi violin sonata, as rarely performed as it was beautiful. But the week before, Dora Silber, who was to accompany him, suddenly received her long-awaited visa and found herself in a tangle of last-minute paperwork and emigration regulations. Arno, unable to find a fellow student to take Dora's place on such short notice, tried to hide his disappointment beneath his shared joy for Dora's good fortune. But Eva, aware of the many afternoons he had spent practicing and re-hearsing, knew how much it would have meant to him to play the sonata at the recital. For there was this about Arno: his music made him forget his innate reticence, his reluctance to reveal himself. It was a little like the way he had once described his father, when he had said, "His paintings are him*self.*" With Arno, one had only to listen to him play to know him for who he was.

"I wish I'd been more serious about my playing, so I could do the concert with you, Arno!" she blurted out the afternoon he called for her at Fräulein Lehmann's house that week. It was a windy, gray October day; the last brittle leaves were falling from the linden trees and blew forlornly along the streets.

Arno nodded, unable when it came to music to let her off so easily. "Yes, the Vivaldi is difficult. Dora worked hard at it, even though she's been playing for quite a while longer than you."

He looked so downcast she took his hand and swung it as they walked on. "I went over the piano part of our Handel sonata today, with Fräulein Lehmann. She said it sounded fine—'just a bit less *feeling,* Eva, and more *practice!* ' "

Arno laughed, as she had intended him to. But only for a moment. Then he stood still, perfectly still, even stopping their arms from swinging in midair. "Did you mean what you said, Eva? Would you play the recital with me?"

"Of course I would, if I *could!*" she said airily. "But you know the Vivaldi is too difficult for me, Arno."

He shook his head. "We'll do the Vivaldi next year! Or the year after next. This year we'll play our Handel sonata."

She stared at him. "But Handel was German, Arno. Out of bounds for us."

He held up his hand. "No excuses, Eva, I'm sorry! Handel isn't quite pure enough for the Nazis, it seems, because he composed *Judas Maccabaeus* and all those other oratorios on biblical themes. And chose the freer air of London over the provincial German courts that never fully recognized the genius of Bach. The Nazis are leaving us Handel, for the moment. I have it on the best of authorities!"

"Herr Valtary?" she asked, avoiding his eyes. He disliked being reminded of his uncle.

He nodded. "That's what he told me on the phone. He made quite a to-do about it, as if he were making me a gift of something that already belonged to me. And I doubt he'd dare act on his own; all his 'cultural activities' in Thalstadt are cleared with Goebbels' Reich Chamber of Culture in Berlin!"

He put his hand on her shoulder in a gesture that was almost solemn. "Will you do it, Eva? I know you can."

She couldn't say no, then, to those questioning eyes. But because she was afraid to say yes, she suddenly broke free and flew ahead of him down the stone steps behind the Uhland Fountain, giggling wildly, the brittle leaves scattering before her feet, and Arno's steps echoing in pursuit until he caught up with her on the sidewalk of Verastrasse and swung her around.

"All right, Arno!" she burst out breathlessly, hammering her fists against his urging, encircling arms. "All right, then, as long as it's all right with the Reich Chamber of Culture!"

And they laughed as they had not laughed together for a very long time at the sheer lunacy of it all, until Arno suddenly fell silent, very silent, and drew her closer still into his arms, his face coming closer, too, until his lips found hers and she let herself lean back into those firm, enfolding arms as if she had always belonged there.

■

That Thursday, even though it was a rehearsal night, Sabine did not show up at her usual hour from the train station. Eva's mother held up supper in the kitchen, listening nervously for her sister's swift footsteps on the stairs, and her impetuous ringing of the bell. Eva sensed her mother's unstated fears: *any*one's unexplained absence or tardiness caused apprehension these days; and Sabine's conspicuous dark beauty and self-assured stride alone might be a provocation. In the end, it was only the telephone that rang, and Sabine's hurried voice against Eva's ear.

"I caught a cold, Eva," Sabine was saying, coughing delicately as in her imitation of Garbo's consumptive Camille. "Tell the Concert Committee that I must stay in bed with warm milk and honey, or I'll be sick for the performance!"

Over Eva's shoulder, her mother called into the receiver, "Is something wrong, Sabine? We've been waiting for you—you had me worried!"

There was another staccato of coughs. "All I need is some rest, Martha. I'll be in Thalstadt Sunday morning for the next rehearsal!"

"Have you a fever, dear?" Eva's mother persisted. "Let me speak to Father!"

But Sabine's ears must have been affected by her cold. "Father is fine, yes—I'll see you Sunday!" And the receiver clicked off.

Eva's mother shook her head. "Sabine never dresses properly. Only last week I told her it was time to wear her coat."

Eva shrugged. Sabine looked so shapely in her slim suit, no wonder she was unwilling to hide under a bulky coat!

She grabbed an apple from the fruit bowl, informing her mother that it had grown too late to have supper before rehearsal, threw her green loden coat over her shoulder, and hurried through the chilly dusk to meet Arno.

■

There was an air of excitement and anticipation at the Community House behind the synagogue. On the stage, a children's choir was running, sotto voce, through a medley of Hebrew rounds, the cantor conducting briskly, with an occasional exclamation of approval or reproof. Below them, around a few small tables hastily pushed together, a circle of men and women were reading a scene from Stefan Zweig's pacifist drama *Jeremias*, under the guidance of Dr. Tiefental, a former literature professor at the Gymnasium no longer regarded as "racially fit" to remain on the faculty. In the center of the hall, a large space had been cleared of chairs to make room for a Zionist youth group doing the hora, the traditional dance of the young pioneers in Palestine, arms linked and feet kicking in rhythm to a boy's accordion. Among the dancers in their white shirts and blue skirts or shorts Eva at once discovered Thea, her broad-cheeked face aglow with the sheer joy of movement and fellowship, her crisp blond hair a whirling flame of brightness among the darker heads around her. "Come on, Eva, join us!" she called out, slipping her arm from a young man's shoulder to draw Eva into the swirling circle.

Eva, conscious of her own less winged and nimble feet, shook her head. "I can't, Thea! I'm rehearsing with Arno."

But she stayed a while longer to watch their exhilarated faces, aware, with a feeling of loss, of their closeness and sense of purpose. The Zionists were the only ones whose world had not shattered into fragments. Sometimes Eva almost wished she, too, could have grown up in a family like Thea's, believing with a sure and joyous faith that there was a homeland for all Jews in that remote country of the Bible; it would be easier, then, to bear this time of turmoil and uprooting, easier to leave the place that once had seemed to be "homeland," but never really had been.

Once, and then again and again as if drawn by a spell, she had gone with Thea to one of her meetings and sat on the floor among the others, humming along as they sang their lovely Hebrew songs. The words, in the Sephardic "Ivrit" of Palestine, almost eluded her limited grasp of the Hebrew of the synagogue. But the fiery Slavic tunes and haunting Middle Eastern airs filled her with inexplicable longing, as if these love songs and lullabies, these songs of hope and defiance, contained all the anguish of her people and its ancient quest for release and redemption.

Afterward their leader, a slight, intense girl they called Rina, had spoken to them about the hachsharahs in Holland where young people like themselves were trained for life in the kibbutzim. "It will be a great honor for all of us, friends, to be admitted to hachsharah," Rina said, fixing their faces with her intent, gray-eyed gaze. "And it will be a joy to shake the dust of the Diaspora off our soles and tread the earth of Eretz Yisrael—

to come home to the Land of Israel and make it bloom after the long road of exile and persecution!"

Someone struck a diminished chord on his guitar and they sang softly, as the last rays of the winter sun slanted through the window and shone on their upturned faces. *"Artsa alinu, K'var charashnu v'gam saranu . . ."* "We have gone to the land, we have plowed and also sowed," the one with the guitar translated, fitting the German words to the melody, perhaps for Eva's sake; for he was looking in her direction, smiling encouragement. *"Aval od lo katsarnu . . ."* "But we have not yet reaped . . ."

"Chazak!" Rina cried, and all the others in the circle raised their left hands in a gesture of pledge, and called out, *"Chazak!"*

"It means 'power,' Eva," Thea whispered. "The power of our belief, the strength of our will!"

And she took Eva's hand and gently raised it up within her own among the others in the circle.

They walked home together that evening, Thea and she, through the dark streets of a Thalstadt winter that Thea hoped to be leaving soon for the sunny new land of her hope. "There will be hardship and danger, yes," Thea said, responding to Eva's troubled silence. "But we will work and suffer for our*selves*, for our *own* future, our *own* people. Our own *land*, Eva— to sow and to reap! No more pointing fingers, no ugly words. No concentration camps!"

She put her arm around Eva's shoulder, in their old, best-friends embrace. "How I wish you could join us, Eva, and come with us!"

How easy it would have been to say yes, with Thea's shining

blue eyes urging her on and the exuberant voices of the others still ringing in her ears. It was a siren song, drawing her into their midst with its fervent pride and affirmation.

But when she had told her mother about those afternoons with Thea's friends and about Thea's hope to "make Aliyah," as the young people in the circle called it—"going up" to the Land of Israel—her mother had drawn in her breath sharply and turned away. "I'm glad for Thea," her mother had said after a moment. "And for the Rubins, too. They'll have a chance to follow Thea—if not now, then the *next* year in Jerusalem."

What she had left unsaid, Eva could only too well complete on her own. Even if her father could manage to obtain a *Zertifikat* from the British, required for entering Palestine, he was far too ill to live in a rugged, subtropical country. A country that needed *halutzim*—pioneers with strong bodies and unshakable conviction.

Her father had no such unshakable faith. He prized his Jewish heritage, but he had never seen a contradiction between that heritage and his life as a citizen of his country. It was in the realm of mind and spirit that he saw himself defined, not in the concept of Land. The writings of Lessing and Schiller and other lofty voices of the Enlightenment had been her father's siren song: the promise of a humanist redemption for Germans and Jews alike, which now had been rendered null and void. The German humanism her father had believed in and supported had forsaken him. How could she now forsake him, too? Leave her parents for a place to which he could not hope to follow, and a new way of thinking he no longer had the strength to adopt?

She turned to Thea and tried to explain what she felt, groping for words that were difficult to form because the things she was trying to understand were complicated things—perhaps too difficult even for grownups to resolve.

"Your hope is for a new land for all Jews, Thea, but mine is for a new world for all people. A world where people can live in peace with one another, in the land of their birth or the land of their choice. A world that might be a homeland for all humankind, after its long Diaspora of suffering and pain."

"Oh, Eva, so do I, so do we!" Thea cried, pressing Eva's arm against her own. "It is your Jewish pain and longing that make you feel that way, talk that way! We *all* long for Moshiach—the time when the lion shall lie down with the lamb, when none shall make us afraid. We want that world, too, Eva—as Jews in our *own* land. There is no other way!"

Out of the dusk, a band of Hitler Youth boys came marching down the street, their steps and raised voices resounding on the chill air. At the head of the uniformed column, the HJ flag flew in the wind, and as they approached, people stopped to salute it with outstretched arms and shouts of *"Sieg Heil!"*

Thea grabbed Eva's sleeve and pulled her into a doorway. They stood close together, shivering with cold and suppressed fear, listening to the singing as it came nearer, swelled to a crescendo, and then receded down the wintry street. "Our flag flutters before us . . . Our flag is the new time . . . We march with Hitler . . . into Eternity . . . Yes, the flag is more than death itself!"

"It will be a long time coming, that new world of yours, Eva," Thea whispered in the dark shelter of the doorway. "Too long to wait. We've waited long enough."

■

"It's *our* turn, Eva!" Arno said, coming up behind her with his violin and music sheets. Rehearsal finished, to the cantor's beaming satisfaction, the children's chorus was leaving the stage—small feet in white socks and polished black patent leather shoes clattering down the steps toward the outstretched hands of admiring mothers.

They were very high steps, suddenly. And the piano seemed miles away, as Arno made her precede him across the stage. She sat down and opened her music book with unsteady hands; Arno would not take it well if she spoiled their piece. He who was so accepting when it came to her other failings—making him wait for her when she showed up late; bursting into tears over a silly quarrel; not being as pretty as she longed to be for him—was not so forgiving when she disappointed him with her playing. Not that he raised his voice or sulked; but she sensed his mood in the way he drew his dark eyebrows together and looked at her coolly, with the eyes of a stranger. For a moment she was overcome with regret at having agreed to accompany him at all; if she failed or embarrassed him—if she got angry in turn at his ill-concealed annoyance—it might be the end of their friendship.

"I'm *scared*, Arno!" she whispered. "And I'll feel even worse at the performance. Look how my hands are shaking!"

"You've got an acute case of stage fright!" Arno whispered back, pausing to tune his violin. "Luckily, at the music school we have Zeller's Cure for Footlight Fever: Don't think, I have to prove myself before this audience; think, I'll try to make them hear what Handel *meant* them to hear, what he had to say to them. You'll forget all about yourself, I promise!"

Below them, the hall had fallen expectantly silent. The actors sat back on their chairs, the dancers squatted on the floor, and a scattering of people who had just wandered in to watch or listen stood at the back of the hall, leaning against the wall.

Eva took a deep breath and waited for Arno's cue to begin. When they played, finally, it was almost as if they were quite alone, in their corner of her living room, playing for themselves . . .

There was a burst of spontaneous applause at the end of the last movement. Arno bowed, his face flushed; then he took Eva's hand and drew her downstage with him. She bowed, too, swept with an almost giddying sense of relief: Professor Zeller's Cure had *worked*!

They sauntered arm in arm off the stage. Arno gave her a close hug as they walked through the emptying hall toward the door. "Thanks, Eva—the Vivaldi's next!"

■

It had rained while they had been rehearsing and now the air was fragrant, like a night in early spring. One might have imagined that the earth was bound for a new cycle of growth and unfolding instead of a season of frost. They slowed their steps; it was good to walk together in the nocturnal calm of the streets, with even the sound of their footfalls diminished by the mist. On the deserted Schlossplatz, the Angel of Peace on top of the Marble Column glistened faintly in the lamplight, and the pavilion stood plunged in shadows. Eva thought back to the summer afternoons when she had sat with Uschi on its steps, sifting the fallen chestnut blossoms into their white-pleated skirts as the military band blared its rousing tunes. Now there was only the muffled sound of their steps; and the benches where Grandfather had sat, thumping his cane in rhythm to the music, were empty. Even the hateful signs, newly restored after the Olympic year, were swallowed up in the darkness.

Arno must have read her thoughts. "Eva—driven from her childhood Garden of Eden," he said softly. His glance strayed to the pillared cupola on top of the Arts Gallery building behind the trees. "My father's work used to be shown there," he said, looking away. "They've driven him out, too."

Beyond the covered flower beds, at the edge of the wide sweep of lawns, Arno took off his coat and spread it over a patch of damp grass. They sat down self-consciously, refraining from touch, content to feel each other's closeness in the dark. The lamplight cast their shadows across the white, pebble-strewn path, and from the turn of Arno's head she knew that he was looking at her. For some strange reason she did not trust herself to meet his eyes.

Arno reached for her hand. Her heart was drumming its sharp, quick beat, almost as it had earlier, when she walked up the steps to the stage. He leaned toward her, his face coming close, as it had on the sidewalk of Verastrasse—so close she could breathe the faint peppermint taste of his breath.

But suddenly he jumped to his feet and pulled her roughly up beside him.

"I shouldn't have brought you here," he said in a husky, unfamiliar voice, whisking his coat off the ground and slinging it over his shoulder.

"Arno . . ."

His lips brushed hers lightly. "If they catch us kissing on the

Schlossplatz, there'll be headlines in the *N.S. Banner* tomorrow: 'Two Jewish Brats Desecrate German Park!' "

Her laugh echoed the bitter humor in his voice. Bitterness was a sharp knife, severing pain and self-pity—at least for a little while.

"One and a *half* Jews, Arno—may I remind you?" she teased clumsily.

He shook his head. "No, thanks. I may be half 'Aryan' by *their* lights, Eva. I'm Jewish by *mine*."

Their steps crunched over the white pebble path. "Like your mother," Eva said softly.

He nodded. "And *you*."

It was past her usual hour when Eva said good night to Arno at her door and hurried up the steps. Not that her parents held her to an inflexible schedule on rehearsal nights. They "trusted her," as her mother had told her when she and Arno first went walking together, looking into Eva's eyes searchingly, seriously, and finally with a light smile. And though it had never been said to Arno, Eva knew that he felt himself included in this trust, and that, as the older of the two, he considered it his responsibility, more even than Eva's, to live up to it. And they *had*, mostly, she felt. Except for the train ride to Weissendorf that she had never confided to her parents—and this night's stolen moments on the edge of the lawn. Which must be plainly written on her face, she worried, as she let herself in.

But no one in the living room paid attention to her. Her mother briefly turned her head in Eva's direction and nodded, at once resuming her conversation with Eva's grandparents, who must have arrived unexpectedly with Sabine in Eva's absence. Grandmother sat on the sofa with a handkerchief twisted in her hands. Grandfather, slumped in Grandfather Bentheim's old upholstered chair, seemed suddenly crumpled and spent in a way Eva had never seen him before. Her father paced the floor by the window, his face drawn. And Sabine leaned against the green tile stove, tears streaming down her cheeks and sobbing wildly.

"But I'm not in love with him, can't you get it through your head?" she almost shouted at her father. "There is nothing between us—we just talk about music, his poetry—it's all platonic!"

"Platonic, is it?" Grandfather mimicked wrathfully. "Aunt Sophie had to call us from Düningen to come and take you home after she saw you walking down the street with him, arm in arm—a Jewish girl and an 'Aryan' man! Do you think the Nazis draw a line between 'platonic' and the ugly things *they* choose to call it?"

"The Nazis—always the Nazis, Father! That's why Manya Mankovsky and her friends in Düningen are a breath of fresh air! They meet in a small circle and talk about the arts, religion— the transformation of society after the Nazis are gone! Manya, a few students from the university, even one or two local ones, like Andreas. He loves me in a *spiritual* way, can't you understand? When I first met him at Manya's—he is her brother's oldest friend—he told me that true Christians must abhor the Nazis for persecuting and vilifying 'the people who gave us God'!

"And if I held on to him on the street, it's because he has a lame leg—from infancy!" Sabine went on angrily, cutting off her father's reply. "It's what makes him sympathize with others who are taunted, for whatever reason, as he was taunted in school. And still *is*, by the *new* bullies!"

"He may be one of the Just," Grandfather conceded with a catch in his voice. "But he is putting my daughter in danger of her life, her honor! And himself, too! Do you want them to parade you around the streets in Ettingen with a sign hanging around your neck, saying—"

"Stop it, Simon!" Grandmother cried in anguish. "No need to bring their gutter talk into this room!" She glanced from Eva to Sabine and fumbled for Sabine's hand. "Promise to stay away from that man and the others, Sabine. If someone informs on them and the Gestapo breaks in on that 'small circle,' they'll all be taken to the KZ! Will you promise, Sabine— please!"

"I *can't*, Mother," Sabine whispered, resting her head against the green tiles at her back and closing her eyes. "I'm in love with one of them and want to see him a few more times before he sails for Palestine and out of my life."

Grandfather sat bolt upright. "Palestine?" he asked, a note of relief creeping into his voice. "Who *is* this man, Sabine?"

"Ari," she said softly, savoring the Hebrew name on her lips. "Ari Mankovsky—Manya's brother. A Zionist activist. Who'll get to Palestine one way or another—legal or illegal!"

"Mankovsky . . ." Grandfather repeated, shaking his head. But only for an instant. "And does he share your feelings, Sabine?"

"He *does*, he tells me he *does*—but he can't marry me now!

He has to bring out Manya first—and his parents and young brothers in Poland, whom he worries about. And he is committed to work for the Youth Aliyah when he reaches Palestine—to rescue as many children as possible before it's too late!

"We love each other," she cried, tears gushing from her eyes again. "Like the doomed royal children in the song, who can't get together because the waters are too deep!"

So it was Ari whom Sabine had been seeing all this time, Eva knew in a flash! It was to Ari that she had been traveling, that summer day when their trains passed in the Ettingen station. Ari of whom Sabine was dreaming when she gazed out into the night from the window in Eva's room. Ari for whom she turned down the invitations of other young men, for whose sake she had feigned illness on the telephone so she could miss the rehearsal and go to Düningen instead!

"He can't marry you, Sabine?" Grandfather was saying. "Well, I know someone who can—and will, if you let him. A Jewish businessman from Holland, here to wind up the last of his affairs in Nazi Germany, who told me at the Café Einstein the other day that he had 'fallen in love with my daughter's picture' on the poster announcing the concert. A widower in settled circumstances, with a son attending the university—and contacts with Thalstadt families to vouch for his intentions, he told me with a smile."

"I'm not *listening*, Father!" Sabine cried, clapping her hands over her ears, but Grandfather was unmoved.

"Naturally, I waved him off, saying my daughter was too young to marry a man with a grown son. But all that has changed now. I want you to meet this Mijnheer Hartog,

Sabine—tomorrow, if he can. He'll be here for another two weeks—long enough for you to get to know him and for a wedding to be planned and celebrated."

Sabine let out a strangled cry. "Never! Bartering off your daughter to a stranger! The days of arranged marriages are over—how can you *think* of such a thing?"

Grandfather bit his lip. "I want you safely out of the country, child—that's how. Away from here, where a pretty girl's face can seal her fate," he said heavily. Grandfather, who never alluded to Sabine's beauty, not wishing to "turn her head," as Eva had heard him tell her mother.

"I don't *want* a middle-aged businessman from Holland!" Sabine moaned. "I want Ari! I want to go to Palestine and marry Ari!"

"You need a *Zertifikat* to get *in* there, Sabine," Eva's mother said anxiously. "You know it can take years for that."

"Listen to your father, Sabine!" Grandmother implored. "There are art museums in Amsterdam, great concert halls. Romantic canals, like those in Venice—he told us all that. You can have a good life, Sabine—and you'll be safe in a neutral country, if the Nazis make war!"

"Your words in God's ears, Mother," Eva's father said softly from the window.

Grandfather hoisted himself tiredly from the deep chair. "Let's get some sleep now, all of us. If your sister and Jonas will oblige us, Sabine, I shall invite Mijnheer Hartog to join us at dinner tomorrow evening. A traveler appreciates a good home-cooked meal on Shabbes Eve."

Two weeks later, just before the concert she would no longer be a part of, Sabine Weil's wedding to Jozeph Hartog of Amsterdam was held at the Thalstadt Synagogue. Only a sprinkling of Sabine's old friends in Thalstadt and Ettingen were able to attend, in these days of upheaval and dispersal; of the small circle in Düningen, none had been invited out of fear for her safety. Nor were there wedding guests on the groom's side willing to cross the Dutch border into Nazi Germany. Fräulein Lehmann, Eva's piano teacher, had agreed to play an organ arrangement of Lewandowski's liturgical music. To its strains, Sabine in a white silk suit and little tulle veil—bought in the last store on Königstrasse without a "sign"—walked down the aisle on Grandfather's lightly trembling arm to stand, pale and fragile, under the bridal canopy next to her solidly built groom. A beaming, bedazzled stranger, looking capable and dependable and rather nice, Eva had to admit, except for his square, dark-rimmed glasses. Rabbi Gideon, joining their hands in marriage, commended the bridal pair to cherish each other and make an exemplary Jewish home in "that small, untroubled land beyond the border that has been a place of refuge to many over the centuries"—saying it meaningfully without being explicit, in case a Gestapo *Spitzel*, an informer, might lurk somewhere between the half-empty benches of the sanctuary. Then the bridegroom eagerly crushed the ceremonial empty glass beneath his solid heel, and everyone called out "Mazel tov!" for good luck and watched them kiss.

Eva's parents gave a family dinner in the pair's honor at the Café Einstein, where Grandfather had so recently met the groom; and Sabine, sitting at the head of the table next to her attentive husband, looked thin and vulnerable but beautiful as ever, holding a red rose about to burst into full bloom. Arno played the Mendelssohn love songs Sabine would have been singing at the concert; and Eva accompanied him on the slightly out-of-tune piano in the corner on which, on Sunday afternoons in better days, *Tanzmusik* had been played for dancing couples between servings of cakes and whipped cream.

Later, when Sabine and Jozeph in their traveling clothes were about to get into Mijnheer Hartog's car with the Dutch license plates outside the Café Einstein, a trim young woman with close-cropped brown hair suddenly hurried out of the dusk. "*Bon voyage*, dear Sabine!" Eva heard her murmur. "From my brother, too! He sent word that he would be leaving for Haifa tomorrow, from 'somewhere in the Balkans,' and wants to wish you the best."

And Sabine, her lovely eyes welling over, turned toward her friend with the romantic Polish name and thanked her for coming. Then she took off the red rose she had pinned to her coat, and breathed in its fading fragrance.

"Take it, Manya! Press it inside one of your books and take it to Eretz Yisrael when the time comes. Tell Ari that love and friendship are more perishable than flowers these days, though we both *tried . . .*"

And she hugged Manya quickly, brushed Eva's tearstained cheek with her lips, and slipped through the car door already held open for her with a trace of impatience by her husband.

Afterward, Eva always remembered the English proverb that Dr. Brachmann wrote on the blackboard one morning at the end of March: "March comes in like a lion and goes out like a lamb." March had come in like a lion, all right—no, like a ferocious wolf that would never change into a lamb. Earlier in the month, German troops had poured across the border into Austria; and with the cry *Heim ins Reich!* Austrians had welcomed the Nazi invaders sent to enforce the Annexation and bring their country "home into the Reich." Those who opposed the Anschluss were brutalized and jailed by the tens of thousands, or thrown into the already notorious new Austrian concentration camp, Mauthausen, near Linz. Events that belied the sunny official version of "Austria's union with the Reich," shown on newsreels in cinemas and school assemblies: cheering men, girls tossing flowers at beaming German soldiers driving their tanks across the border. Women holding up babies to the Viennese drifter become Germany's Führer—and now theirs—on his triumphant journey into Vienna.

Among the Jews hunted down in the streets of Vienna, Eva had heard people say in anxious voices, were Jewish refugees from Germany now caught in the Nazi net a second time. Fear-ing for them, she tried to block out her classmates' exuberant talk about skiing vacations in the Austrian Alps already planned by their parents—about "Strength Through Joy" trips to the Tyrol and across the Brenner Pass into Italy.

Shaken anew by the events in Austria and by Hitler's threats to wrest the Sudetenland, with its ethnic Germans, from Czechoslovakia or make war, those in the Jewish community in Thalstadt and elsewhere redoubled their efforts to emigrate. One after the other, the girls Eva had grown up with left with their families: for places on any of the five continents, no matter how distant and unfamiliar—anywhere that refuge, however late and grudgingly, was granted. In July, Lilo Levi—who had sat next to Eva in the children's rows at the synagogue, casting glances at the boys across the aisle from behind her prayer book—was leaving for England. "On the *Kindertransport*," she told Eva. "But my parents will come later, on a visitors' visa—as soon as they get our papers so we can all go on to Ecuador from there." "But where will you be staying in England meantime?" Eva asked, wondering if *she* could bear to leave her parents and go alone to a strange country where nobody knew her name.

"Oh, it's all being arranged by the Committee in London," Lilo said. "Some of us will stay with Jewish foster parents. Some with Quaker or Church of England families. Some will even be put in boarding schools," she added, anticipation mingling with apprehension in her voice. "Anyway, my mother told me it won't be long!"

Eva's parents were among the few who were in no position to pursue plans for emigration. Her father was too ill.

A *personal* tragedy within the universal one, Dr. Neuburger called it, with a regretful shake of his head, as Eva's mother walked him to the door after one of his visits.

"The only thing left for me to suggest, Frau Bentheim, is an exploratory operation. I can arrange a consultation for you with Dr. Heilinger, the surgeon. But it is a serious procedure with great risk. And with no guarantee of success . . ."

His words made Eva's heart contract in fear, fear she saw mirrored in her mother's eyes as she closed the door behind the doctor.

"What shall we do, Eva?" she whispered. "There seems so little we can hope for—and we might *lose* him, if anything goes wrong!"

It was the last thing Eva wanted to hear from her mother. She didn't *know* what to do, didn't want to be asked, and so, scared and resentful, shrugged and said nothing. Aunt Hanni, too, was alarmed by the gloomy prognosis and counseled her younger brother against a hasty decision. And Uncle Ludwig, bowed by business and emigration worries, sat gray-faced and silent. Only Eva's father seemed strangely calm, willing to take any risk for a chance to regain his health. The following week her parents went to the surgeon's office for consultation. When they came home hours later in the early evening of a sultry August day, her father lay down on his bed, too exhausted to eat or even undress, and fell into a deep, night-long sleep. The next morning Eva heard him tell her mother that he had decided to have the surgery. "This is no life, Martha," he was saying quietly, reaching for her hand. "Not for me, not for you and Eva—and at a time like this!" He paused for a moment. "If all goes well, we'll find a way to leave and struggle through, like everyone else. If not, if something happens to me"—he shrugged—"it will set you and Eva free to emigrate."

"Don't contemplate buying my visa at the cost of your life, Jonas!" her mother cried. "I won't even *think* of it—no more than you would have done in my place!" She sat down on the edge of his bed and took his hand between her two. "We'll leave together, we three. Or send Eva off on her own, if we must, to save her."

And Eva, who had been standing unnoticed in the doorway, slipped away, feeling guilty for having heard things that had not been intended for her ears but would reverberate in them forever.

■

Dr. Heilinger, Eva's mother told Aunt Hanni, had been "impersonal but correct" during the consultation. He had set the date of the operation for the end of September, her mother added, concerned about putting it off that long. "But what could we say?" she asked Aunt Hanni with a shrug. "Most of these doctors no longer even admit Jewish patients to their operating rooms. And he *is* an excellent surgeon, Dr. Neuburger assures us," she finished resolutely, to buoy up their courage.

And so, on September 29, while her father was fighting for his life on the operating table at Königin Luise Hospital, Eva and her mother sat in the waiting room, waiting, worrying, and waiting some more. Later, Arno came by and, when there was still no word, stayed on to wait with them. At last they saw the surgeon coming down the corridor, looking grave and noncommittal, but with an affirmative nod in their direction. They jumped to their feet and her mother gave Eva a quick, fierce hug. "Let Arno see you home, Eva—I'll get there later," she called over her shoulder and followed the doctor down the corridor toward the patients' rooms.

Outside, in the cool September evening, Arno put his arm around Eva. "Your father seems to be out of immediate danger, Eva. So *something* good has happened on this awful day."

She looked at him numbly. She had been too involved with her father's operation these last few days to be aware of much else.

But he had already guessed that she hadn't heard. "They had their 'conference' in Munich today, Eva—on the fate of Czechoslovakia. Two delegates from Prague were made to wait in another room while their country's allies caved in to Hitler's terms. On Saturday, Nazi troops will occupy the Sudetenland, 'liberating' the ethnic Germans there, as the radio puts it. And gobbling up the Czech border fortifications and heavy industries for their *next* move!"

She felt a slight shiver, as of the first grip of frost. They glanced at one another, each seeing the fear in the other's eyes, and quickly looked away.

At her door, he folded her into his arms and she clung to him for long minutes, until Arno gently took the key from Eva's hand, opened the door behind her, and with a light and final kiss turned and hurried down the stairs.

■

After school the next day, Eva took the shortcut to the hospital and stood at the foot of her father's bed, gazing at his face anxiously as he drifted in and out of sleep. Dr. Neuburger stopped by, a mere visitor where he had once been an attending physician, and drew up a chair at her father's bedside.

"You were lucky, my friend," he said, when Eva's father opened his eyes. "The other patient didn't fare so well yesterday."

"The *other* patient?" Eva's father asked, groggy and heavy-tongued.

"The one on the conference table in Munich. Who had his western flank severed by Hitler's knife, leaving the patient exposed and powerless against future attack."

Her father nodded. "It's Czechoslovakia's death knell," he said, his speech still struggling with the aftereffects of the anesthesia.

"Oh yes," the doctor agreed. "And the pallbearers are the governments of Britain and France who capitulated to Hitler's threats and guile, as they did when he remilitarized the Rhineland and seized Austria."

In school that morning, Eva's classmates—gleeful over another bloodless victory conjured up by their Führer—had made amiable fun of the British Prime Minister and his umbrella. Her father, speaking softly with Dr. Neuburger, saw Chamberlain as a duped and tragic figure, willingly deceived into believing he was buying "peace for our time" at the expense of the abandoned ally slowly bleeding to death on the conference table in Munich. War, her father was saying—engulfing Europe and maybe the world—was now merely a matter of time.

■

Her father was making progress from bed to chair to first walks down the corridor on the steadying arm of her mother. Eva came after school to keep him company and spell her mother for some fresh air or a quick errand nearby. Aunt Hanni, too, came and sat at her brother's bedside as he alternately napped and made quiet conversation, and shook her head at the sad turn things had taken: her brother's operation and Stefan stranded in Paris, barely able to subsist. One afternoon Eva walked in with an armful of purple dahlias, fresh from a greenhouse she had discovered not far from the roadside; and her father encircled the tall rough stems with his slender hands, peered nearsightedly into the glowing deep colors of the flowers, and drew in their pungent autumnal scent. Now and then, during Eva's visits, Dr. Heilinger stopped by, impersonal though correct in his white coat, just as her mother had described him. While Eva waited outside the door, he examined her father and shrugged when her mother, walking him from the room, asked in a low voice how his patient was coming along. ". . . must wait," Eva heard him murmur. ". . . previous operations . . . scar tissue . . . adhesions . . ." And he glanced at his watch, offered some perfunctory advice, and strode down the corridor.

In mid-October, her father came home and, soon after, began to spend some time in the store again. Uncle Ludwig, who had been writing ever more urgent letters to the cousins in America, had at long last obtained Arthur's promise of affidavits for himself and his family. Eva's father, too, was writing for help again: he had undergone surgery, was once more active in the business, and felt confident that he would soon be well enough to obtain a visa and provide for his family in America. All they needed—"urgently, in view of the disquieting situation here, of which you are no doubt aware"—was the formality of affidavits to satisfy immigration requirements. He wrote eloquently in his fine hand and excellent English, and Eva felt sure that *she* would be sending affidavits if she lived in America and received such a letter from Thalstadt. But when she walked to the Central Post Office with her father to mail the letter to New York and saw his pallor in the daylight and the slow, painful way he moved his frail body, she was overcome with fear.

Still, even if the affidavits were to arrive tomorrow, there would be time for her father to recuperate before being called to the consulate. Because the flood of immigration applications now exceeded the yearly places under the American quota for Germany, there was a long wait. "*Our* numbers," Uschi had told her glumly, "won't be called until next summer, they said at the consulate!" And when Eva's mother, alarmed, had rushed to the consulate for *their* numbers, two thousand more had been assigned in little more than a week, and she was told not to expect to be "called" until the spring of 1940. "Who knows what might happen by *then*, Eva," her mother had said with a worried headshake. "If Father hadn't been in the hospital, I would have become aware of these things sooner, and we could have gotten much lower numbers!" Eva waited for her to add that, of course, it had all been worthwhile, anyway, since her father's health was improving, would continue to improve. But her mother said nothing more.

FOURTEEN OCTOBER–NOVEMBER 1938

There was a sudden turn in the weather the last week of October, fall veering sharply toward winter as Eva and Thea, bundled up in sweaters and scarves, walked briskly toward the Community House for their Jewish history class. The cantor, peering at them over his glasses as they made a hasty last-minute entrance, was already beginning to prepare for Hanukkah, still weeks away. Each student, he announced, was invited to bring in a poem or song for the Oneg Shabbat observation of the holiday. It would take place at the Lehrhaus for adult Jewish education, he reminded them, where Martin Buber, the eminent philosopher, had lectured on the essence of Judaism "in earlier days," and engaged in dialogue with those few Christian theologians and secular scholars who shared with Jews concern about the tide of nationalism and anti-Semitism in the years before Hitler. The cantor's shrug conveyed better than words that, needless to say, such dialogues had long been verboten.

Eva and Thea, settling in on the bench they had been sharing forever, jotted down some poem titles and passed them to each other. It was their last year of formal Jewish studies; there had been many changes since the days when they had learned their first Bible stories and clumsily copied their Hebrew letters into their notebooks. Many of their classmates had left Germany; others had arrived from smaller towns and villages, where centuries-old Jewish communities were in the process of dissolution through emigration or flight to the city from violence and betrayal at the hands of once-trusted neighbors. On Lilo Levi's bench now sat two of these "new" girls, Ruth and Hannele Bloch, whose dark eyes and black braids had marked them as outcasts in their village, in spite of their broad Swabian country speech. A spirit of dejection, in contrast to its former air of exuberance, hung over the classroom, which the cantor did his best to dispel by making the glory of their history come alive for them, with its unending pilgrimage from persecution to spiritual resurgence. He spoke about those who had kept the flame of faith and freedom alight in the time of the first Hanukkah, like a beacon for those to follow. And resistance to tyranny need not be on a grand scale, he added. The small, brave gesture of unknown human beings asserting their humanity against oppression was significant in Judaism, just as it was written in the Talmud that "whoever saves one life saves the whole world."

Then the cantor asked Thea if she would "give an encore" of the poem she had recited the year before, after the lighting of the Hanukkah candles at the Lehrhaus. It had been a traditional poem written in Yiddish, Eva remembered at once. The language Thea's Polish-born parents had grown up with and often spoke with their children, Thea had told the class. To Eva's delight, she had understood the poem quite easily, so close to their regional German were most of the words. "O, ir kleyne lichtelech . . ." "Oh, you lovely little lights / telling stories dark and bright / Wonders without count . . ." And she remembered how Thea's eyes shone in the glow of the candle-light with the wonder of it all—the ancient story of redemption transcending oppression. Evidently the others remembered, too, for when Thea responded to the cantor's request for an encore by saying, *"ken"*—meaning "yes" in Hebrew—everyone applauded.

■

They had almost reached Wielandplatz on the way home when Eva, keeping her voice carefully even, asked if Thea had heard anything more about making Aliyah. Thea shook her head. "Maybe in the spring, Eva. In time for Passover." And catching the look in Eva's eyes, mingling hope for Thea with fear of separation, she added softly, "We'll always be best friends, you know that, Eva. No matter where life takes us."

She drew a deep breath. "We've had to say farewell so often, we Jews—wherever we lived, wherever we were driven out and dispersed. That's why we need a homeland of our own, Eva, where no one can force us to flee anymore, and part from the ones we love."

And she threw her arm about Eva quickly, almost roughly, and walked on toward Verastrasse without looking back.

■

Early the next morning, Eva discovered Thea's *Maccabi Song-book* among her own things: a slim, paperbound book chockful of songs in German, Hebrew, and Yiddish, from which Thea and she often sang together for the sheer love of melody, rhythm, and the often fervent poetry of the texts. But the song on the page where Thea had stuck a bookmark was a quiet one—one they would sing sitting in the Rubins' city garden on a summer afternoon, or giving the younger children a turn on the swing, their laughter ringing with the thrill of their airborne ride. "Tru-ue friendship sha-all not wa-aver," she read, hearing the tune in her ear, Thea's mezzo supporting her own voice in harmony. "Though we ma-ay be fa-ar apart, / You'll live on in my tho-o-oughts for-e-ever, / And you'll always keep *me* in your heart!"

Quickly she dialed the familiar number, in case Thea wondered about her book; but no one answered. She tried several times more with mounting uneasiness: even if Herr Rubin had left for work and the older children for school, where were Thea's mother and baby Ury at this early hour? She glanced at the clock on her bookcase: if she rushed off this moment, skipping breakfast, she could pass by Thea's place to make sure all was well and still get to school on time. She hurried down the stairs, running across Wielandplatz, through the narrow streets of the Old City, and up the steps toward Verastrasse, not pausing until she stood at the door to the Rubins' apartment building, her finger on their bell, catching her breath.

No one answered upstairs. At the Rubins' fourth-floor windows, the curtains were still pulled shut. A jolt of fear shook Eva. She ran around the corner of the house to the familiar garden, willing herself to find Frau Rubin standing by the swing, giving Ury an early morning ride in the brisk air. But the swing stood motionless, deserted—the gnarled trees, in whose sparse shade Eva had so often sat with Thea, bereft of leaves, the bare branches thrust accusingly toward the bleak October sky.

She felt a timid yet insistent tug at her sleeve. It was Lydia, the pale little blond girl from the basement apartment, whose parents had long ago forbidden her to play with the Rubin children. "Because you are Jewish," she had confided to Thea in tears. "But I'll tell the Führer not to let anything bad happen to *you!*" she had whispered and hugged Thea with her spindly arms before she abruptly ran off at her mother's sharp call. Thea had told Eva about it with an exasperated shake of her head and a catch of sympathy in her voice for the lonely small girl; and they had shared a scornful grownup laugh at Lydia's confused trust in her "Führer."

"Thea isn't *here* anymore, Eva," Lydia was saying, with the sniffle in her voice she had all year long. "A police car took them away in the night. Frau Rubin was carrying Ury, and Thea was carrying Miriam's doll, and Miriam was crying when the men made them all get into the car—Martin, too, and their father.

"I saw it from my bed, peeking from under the curtain!" Lydia persisted in a trembling voice. "The men woke me up thumping down the steps, and my father was out there with them, and when I asked him when Miriam and Ury would come back, he said to shut my mouth or he'd shut it for me, and now there would be *German* children for me to play with."

■

At home, Eva's parents seemed unsurprised to see her when she burst into the room in the middle of a schoolday and sobbed out her story. Sadly, their own voices breaking in the telling, they supplied the missing pieces. During the night, the radio had reported glibly, Jews with Polish passports had been rounded up throughout the Reich and taken to local police stations. From there, in the early morning hours, they were put on trains and deported in the direction of Poland.

"*Deported?*" Eva cried out the terrifying word. "But not the *Rubins*—not *Thea*! I have her *Maccabi Songbook*—see?" It was the only thing that seemed to be real, the well-worn little gray book she thrust at her parents, with the bookmark still sticking out where Thea had placed it, perhaps only the afternoon before. But her parents said nothing, gazing back at her wordlessly from harrowed eyes. "But *why?*" Eva whispered at last. "Thea's parents came here as children, they have always lived in Thalstadt, they don't even *speak* Polish!"

Her father nodded. "As usual, Eva, not only are the Nazis unashamed of what they are doing, they actually brag about it. They say that Poland has revoked the passports of Polish Jews living in Germany, effective tomorrow. So the Nazis decided to 'get rid of them before the Poles close the border and drop tens of thousands of stateless, formerly Polish Jews permanently into our lap,' as the radio put it."

"But maybe Thea *isn't* on that train!" Eva cried, clinging to a last shred of hope. "Thea was *born* here—*all* the children were!"

Her mother drew Eva into her arms. "I rushed over to the Community House after hearing that announcement, Eva, to see if I could help. I'm afraid I have sad news for you, for all of us. The Rubins were taken to the train early this morning. The community tried hard to gain the release of as many people as possible, but only a very few were let go on some technicality the Gestapo chose to observe. We were allowed to provide food for the others, at least, and warm clothing for those who hadn't even been given time to get adequately dressed."

They were both crying. "Let's hope we'll have word from the

Rubins soon, Eva," her mother said through her tears. "I remember Thea's mother speaking of relatives in Warsaw. Perhaps they will be able to help the family when they arrive in Poland."

■

Four fear-filled days later, Arno brought in a newspaper article that Professor Zeller had carried hidden between his music sheets from a brief trip to Switzerland. It told of the ordeal of a group of deportees, unloaded from their packed, sealed trains "somewhere at the rain-swept Polish border," and driven across a no-man's-land under the blows of the SS toward a line of Polish soldiers barring entrance into Poland with drawn guns, while armed guards on the German side barred their return. In the end, the Polish government relented, putting up the deportees in horse stables and barracks on condition that Germany cease further expulsions.

Arno gently retrieved the paper from Eva's horrified stare. "Zeller cursed under his breath when he showed me the article. And what about his own government, he muttered, which was just as heartless in turning back Jewish refugees at its borders, only a bit more discreet. And he named several friends, musicians of world renown, for whom Zeller had been unable to obtain asylum in Switzerland; others in desperation had gone across the 'green border'—meaning illegally—and ended up in Swiss internment camps."

But Eva didn't know any world-renowned musicians. Her thoughts were of Ury being carried in his mother's arms across a rain-swept no-man's-land, of Miriam crying herself to sleep in a dank, straw-strewn stable, of Thea and Martin and their quiet father. Where *are* you, Thea? she asked of the November dusk sinking over the rooftops beyond the window. *How* are you? Please find a way to let me know!

●

And then, miraculously, there was a letter from Thea! They had found temporary refuge with her mother's elderly cousins in their tiny apartment in Warsaw, she wrote, from where she hoped to join the Youth Aliyah at last and make her way to Eretz Yisrael. "More than ever now, Eva," she added, alluding, no doubt, to what they must have been made to endure along with the others. "Martin will try to come with me, and I pray we'll be able to let our parents and the children follow us. If you have my *Maccabi Songbook,* as I think you may, Eva, keep it for me till we meet again. And let me be in your thoughts as you are in mine."

The letter, flooding Eva's heart with such relief and gratitude she felt it would burst, reached her on the seventh of November. That morning in Paris, a seventeen-year-old refugee, whose Polish-born family in Germany had suffered the fate of the deportees, walked into the German Embassy and shot down a legation official, Ernst vom Rath. Arrested by French police and held on murder charges, Herschel Grynszpan with his desperate act became the pretext for a fury of anti-Semitic venom and cries for vengeance by Nazi leaders and in the Nazi press. And the Jews, defenseless hostages against the threatened reprisals in Thalstadt and throughout Hitler's Reich, listened to the hate-ridden voices on the radio and feared the worst.

FIFTEEN THE NINTH OF NOVEMBER

But nothing happened until the third night.

Getting off the streetcar that afternoon, Eva saw her father waiting for her at his accustomed corner. It was the first time he had come to meet her after school since his release from the hospital. He was glancing over the displays behind the showcase windows of the House of Germans Abroad. She noticed with a pang how frail he looked in his street clothes. She came up next to him and he hugged her close, without looking up. Behind the glass, on glossy life-size photographs, Sudetenland women showered flowers and smiles on a triumphant Führer at the Czech border; *Volksdeutsche* in Romania whirled their bright peasant skirts around a ribboned harvest wreath; a pamphlet, propped open at a conveniently lurid page, railed against "the ordeal of ethnic Germans in Yugoslavia." Perhaps to snare an indifferent passerby, there was also a current popular favorite: a novel by an American writer, Margaret Mitchell: *Vom Winde Verweht. Gone With the Wind*—somehow the title seemed to have been chosen with this bleak, windblown afternoon in mind.

They linked arms and walked down the Hofstrasse, where the first lights went on in the early November dusk.

"I'm relieved to see you all in one piece, Eva," her father said, giving her arm a squeeze. "They've been hammering at the assassination all day, the papers and the radio from Goebbels on down. Placing responsibility on our collective heads, threatening 'retribution.' " He paused to catch his breath and gave her a searching look. "Did anything happen at school?"

She shook her head. What good would it do to tell her father about the hastily called assembly, from which she had been pointedly excused by her teacher, Herr Voss, to the accompaniment of snickers from the boys' rows and blank stares from the girls'? Headshaking was a technique she had newly mastered; it spared her father from learning painful truths and herself from speaking lies. A detestable but, she told herself, necessary compromise. Compromising was a cowardly act, but more and more these days, it seemed the only way of staying alive.

At the store, Uncle Ludwig stood white-faced behind a counter.

"No one's been through the door, except for a gang of Hitler Youth boys shouting they'd come and get us later!" Behind his round glasses, his owlish eyes peered anxiously at Eva's father. "Something's in the wind—people are afraid to set foot in the store—they have been *told*!" he whispered. "I'd close up now and go upstairs, but maybe that would only call attention to ourselves—and what have we to hide?"

He spread his hands in a gesture of helplessness.

"What do they want from us? What has Bentheim & Sons got to do with Herschel Grynszpan? Are *we* assassins? Are *we* Poles?"

Her father shook his head wearily. "We are Jews, Ludwig."

He touched his brother's narrow shoulder. "Go on up, Ludwig. Eva and I will close the store in a little while. Go and bring Gustl and the girls downstairs. We may as well spend the night together—I doubt any of us will get much sleep."

For a moment, his brother stared at him irresolutely. Then he turned and walked heavily toward the door.

It was suddenly very quiet in the store. Eva watched her father gaze with unseeing eyes toward the windows. His face was drawn with exhaustion; the brief walk in the chill air had sapped what little strength he had regained since his operation. She saw him look up and quickly bent her head over a schoolbook, pretending to read. From outside, the sounds of the city filtered in: the screech of streetcar wheels on the curving tracks, voices of women shoppers, children at play in the alley. There was a soothing quality to the familiar cadence of sounds, erasing, for a swift, seductive moment, the mounting fear of the past days. Then it came back: the screaming red headlines on the *N.S. Banner*, the snide voice over the radio the evening before. And this morning, after the assembly, not even Anton had spoken to her; not even Renate. Perhaps they, too, had been "told"—knew that something was "in the wind."

"What is it, Eva?" her father asked, reaching out a wan hand to test the warmth of her own. "Are you cold?"

She shrugged. "Just tired. We have a French exam coming up. *The Fables of La Fontaine.*"

Her father glanced at his watch. "I think we have kept shop long enough," he said with a faint smile. "Let's go and close up."

∎

Evening had come. Around the square, shop windows shone through a thin mist. The massive structure of the new Hallenbeck building loomed starkly against the sky, the bright lights from its soaring stories piercing the night.

Her father touched a switch, plunging the store into darkness. He locked the door behind them and with an effort pulled down the iron screen across the entranceway between the showcase windows.

They turned the corner into the sparsely lit alley toward the door to the house, her father dragging his steps. Eva watched him in alarm: had he injured himself pulling down the gate? Dr. Neuburger had strictly forbidden any lifting or straining; she should have remembered. She wondered uneasily what she would tell her mother.

But after one look at her father's face, her mother made him stretch out on his bed and spread a light blanket over him. The bedside lamp cast a faint glow over his gaunt cheeks and the slender hands folded across his chest. He lay very still, his breath barely moving, looking at once vulnerable and in some way invincible. Suddenly, in a fierce, guilt-tinged way, Eva was grateful that her father was ill. Whatever might happen tonight, no one would dare touch him—not even *they*!

She tilted the lampshade away from his face and tiptoed into the living room, leaving the door ajar.

■

The Upstairs had already arrived.

Someone had turned on the radio and the lilting strains of a Strauss waltz came softly over the airwaves. Uncle Ludwig was pacing the floor, his shoulders hunched as if he were trying to make himself even smaller, perhaps to shrink away entirely.

Eva's mother was slicing a round loaf of bread with unsteady hands; she had put a spread of cold cuts on the table, but it had scarcely been touched. At the window overlooking the square, Ella was cautiously parting the curtains and peering into the darkness. Uschi huddled on the window seat, her freckles standing out sharply against the pallor of her cheeks. Only Aunt Gustl sat stolidly on a chair, bent over her knitting; her stubby fingers moved the swift needles with a rhythmic click.

"I don't know what everyone's so wrought up about," she murmured. "It will all blow over. Nothing is eaten as hot as it is cooked."

Eva felt a wild giggle rise in her throat, burst out between the fingers hastily clapped over her mouth—and suddenly she was laughing, laughing helplessly into her mother's shocked face, her uncle's disapproving one.

Into the abrupt silence that followed, the telephone rang shrilly. It was Lena Ullmann, a cousin of her mother's—a chatty, scatterbrained woman whom Eva had always secretly disliked for her rouged cheeks and the flirtatious way she had of "borrowing" cigarettes from her father.

The voice was breathless, words tumbling from the receiver. "Quick, Eva—your *mother!*"

"Yes, Lena," her mother said tersely, gripping the phone. "Yes . . . I'm so sorry . . . and thank you, dear Lena . . ."

She hung up quickly and nodded at Uncle Ludwig.

"It has begun. They've picked up Lena's husband. She ran to a phone booth down the street to warn us, brave soul—I shall never forget that. She saw them put Kurt on a big truck at the end of the block. It was packed full with men."

With a strangled cry, Uschi slumped against her father's

chest. "I won't let them take you, Papa—they'll hurt you, they'll beat Papa the way they beat Günther's father . . ." Her body grew rigid and her eyes, green as a kitten's, protruded beneath the soft sweep of her lashes. "They—stomped . . . Günther said . . . blood . . . so much blood—"

"*Don't*, Uschi!" Eva begged, hiding her face in the crook of her elbow to shut out the scene, willing herself to see the quiet room next door instead, her father's face against the smooth white linen.

Ella's broad hand covered her sister's mouth.

"Hush, Uschi—don't you dare frighten us like that! We need our wits about us now!"

She looked at her father with level eyes.

"You must leave, Father. They'll be here soon enough. They mustn't find you."

Her father stared at her. "*Leave*, Ella? But where would I go? Who would take me in?"

"Go *any*where, Father," Ella said in a quaking, shaking voice. "Walk the dark streets—all night, if you must. Hide in the woods on the Buchberg—it doesn't matter!"

"Hide in the *woods*, Ella—your father? Like a gonif, a criminal? Why should I hide, Ella—what have I done? Have I committed a crime, a single dishonorable act in all my life? I've been a law-abiding citizen, Ella . . ."

A thought crossed his face.

He turned and picked up the telephone. His fingers scurried across the dial.

"Whom are you calling, Ludwig?" Aunt Gustl asked fearfully, clasping her knitting to her chest, the needles trembling in her chubby hands.

"Friedlaender, who else? I can expect to be represented by my attorney on a night like this, can't I? Protect myself against unlawful entry, illegal arrest?"

He wiped his forehead with the back of his sleeve and stared into the receiver. In the hushed room, a distant ringing reached Eva's ear.

"He doesn't *answer!*" Uncle Ludwig said in disbelief. "Friedlaender has run out on me—on all of his clients!"

His eyes darted about the room. "What right does he have to desert us without a word of advice?" he cried out bitterly. "A trusted friend, a man of the law— "

"The law is dead, Ludwig," his brother said from the door. "Friedlaender's lawbooks can't save his own skin tonight—can you expect him to save yours?"

He took the receiver from his brother's hand and placed it back on its cradle.

"Friedlaender has given you his advice, Ludwig. Can't you accept it? Take your life into your hands, as he has done, and go into hiding. *I* would, if I had the strength."

"Go, Papa, go!" Uschi moaned softly.

Uncle Ludwig's face crumpled with fear.

"They'll recognize me for what I am, Jonas!" He wheeled and stared at his reflection in the glass doors of the china cabinet. Behind the pane, the silver bowls and Sabbath candlesticks shone in the lamplight, and the Dresden goose girl kept watch over her porcelain flock.

Uncle Ludwig clapped his hands over his ears as if to drown out a many-throated shout.

"My face will give me away, Jonas! They've made it a caricature, my face, an abomination: the face of an animal, a devil!"

"The face of a *man*, Ludwig," his brother said urgently. "It is a mitzvah to save the human face, it is becoming extinct. In the KZ, on either side of the barracks wall, it is hardly recognizable any longer . . ."

Aunt Gustl, her pudgy cheeks beaded with perspiration, padded across the room, the red knot of wool trailing behind her. The fuzzy yarn coiled about her thick ankles.

"Hide at the Ullmanns', Ludwig!" she whispered. "Go through the back streets: the alley behind the old post office and up the steps to Schifferstrasse. They've been that way already tonight—they won't be back!"

"Go, Papa!" Uschi moaned.

Ella threw her father's coat over his shoulders and pressed his hat into his unwilling hands. He peered into the deserted stairwell and drew back quickly. Behind the round glasses, his eyes were blank and bewildered, like those of a child.

"And you, Jonas?" he asked, white-lipped. "Won't you come with me?"

His brother hesitated for the merest moment. "I'd only be holding you back, Ludwig. Don't miss your chance."

Gently, implacably, Ella urged her father through the door and pulled it shut behind him. After a moment, Eva became aware of the pealing tones of a Mozart sonata over the radio and, like a ghostly counterpoint, Uschi's fitful sobbing from the window seat, piteously broken, ludicrously off-key.

"But you can't *stay* here, Jonas!" her mother cried suddenly. "Let me take you to Lena's myself! Or perhaps Anna—yes, Anna would let us spend the night in that little vegetable store of theirs. She has always kept faith with us! Let me take you to Anna's," she begged. "Think of Eva, Jonas—of me!"

Eva reached for her father's hand and felt it close about her own. "And Anna and Karl?" he said softly. "They would be risking their lives."

"They'd be saving their *souls!*" her mother cried. "*Someone* has to, on a night like this—'Do right and fear no one'—the way they told us in school. Or were they just fairy tales, the proverbs, the poems? Were we the only ones who thought they were for real, we German Jews?"

A rumble of footsteps shattered the silence.

Ella drew back from the window.

"They're coming into the square!"

With a sudden click, the piano sonata broke off. A voice cut in, crisply, efficiently: ". . . throughout Germany tonight . . . wrath of the people . . . avenging dastardly crime . . . henchmen of International Jewry . . . black night for those who persist in opposing . . ."

Aunt Gustl lifted an edge of the curtain.

"They're smashing the showcase windows! They're breaking into the store!"

"L-l-look!" Uschi stammered, her eyes dark with terror. "L-look, Eva, l-l-look, oh, l-l-look!"

The square was black with the frenzied, jeering crowd. Like a many-tentacled beast moving under a single will, it surged against Grandfather's house. It kicked its hooves against the sturdy walls; it burst into the store under a shower of splintering glass. Chairs smashed against pavement; drawers shattered on cobblestones; books—last remains of her father's bookshop long stored away—hurtled through the air like footballs, were ripped apart between fists, and expired beneath grinding boots. And there, under the streetlamp, beyond the tip of Uschi's pointing finger, a city police car idled against the curb; from time to time the policeman in the back waved his stick playfully, as if in some secret code of fellowship with the ringleaders. The driver's square hand rested on the wheel.

Then Eva saw the other car.

It came up the Marktstrasse, inching its way along the edge of the crowd, two uniformed men on the running boards. It was a black car and Eva had seen it before, gliding sleekly through the once tranquil streets, a tiger on the prowl. Now and then, on her way to school, she had seen its tiger eyes glint through the gray winter dawn as it pulled to a jolting stop— watched furtively as the black uniforms jumped to the sidewalk and ran up the stairs of some drab tenement or tree-shaded townhouse. And she had seen them return, minutes later, dragging some pale, mutely resistant woman or man on shaky legs to the car. Perhaps a small knot of onlookers had gathered by then, curious and awed; but always, at the flick of those kid-gloved wrists, they would disperse, going their own silent ways, shrugging their shoulders, shutting their eyes.

Now the car stopped under their own windows. The black boots gleamed in the streetlight. The car doors slammed shut.

"I won't let them *in!*" her mother whispered, drawing Eva close.

The doorbell rang piercingly, on and on.

"Open up, or we'll smash in the door!"

The crash of boots reverberated through Eva's body, set it atremble against her mother's, stifled her breath.

"Noooo . . ." Was it Uschi crying—or was it herself?

Her father went to the hall closet and pulled on his coat.

"It's better this way, Martha. You wouldn't want them—in front of the child . . ."

He walked out to meet them.

Staring at the black uniforms in the doorway, her mother's eyes turned to stone.

"Don't take my husband!" she pleaded. "He is a sick man— for God's sake, don't take him!"

Hands seized him roughly.

Her mother ran after them out on the landing.

"A sick man, I tell you! He's just come out of the hospital— the Königin Luise Hospital! Ask Dr. Heilinger, the surgeon!"

They were pushing her father down the stairs.

"*Bitte, bitte!*" her mother cried, crumpling over the banister. "A sick man—he needs rest, care, special food—he must have his bandages changed—ask Dr. Neuburger, our family doctor!"

Eva flung her arms about her mother's waist. Below them, cupping his hands to light a cigarette in the doorway, one of the uniforms laughed curtly.

"We take our orders from the Führer, not from the medical profession." He tossed the match to the ground.

They were pushing her father into the street. Silence closed over them, like a blanket of snow.

Someone came trudging up the stairs. A city policeman, boards creaking under his heavy tread. He ran up the last few steps and reached out a square hand to steady her mother's arm. It was the driver of the police car at the curb whom Eva had seen from the window.

He glanced about quickly. "Get a medical certificate, Frau Bentheim—*tonight*! They're keeping them at the city jail till morning—I'll see if the chief will put in a word for your husband with the Gestapo, if he gets the certificate before sunrise."

He shook his head.

"I used to deliver books for a publisher—I've known your husband for years! He often gave me picture books for my sick little boy."

He turned to leave. "Get that certificate, Frau Bentheim. Without a certificate, it's Dachau for your husband as for the rest of them."

■

The wind had shifted.

A thin flurry of snow was drifting from the low sky. Her mother tossed a scarf over her hair and with an absent flick of her hand flipped Eva's coat collar up. Stealthily, along the walls of the houses, they picked their way over the shambles that littered the silent square. In front of Hedy's House of Fashion, mannequins lay trampled in the gutter, their nakedness covered only with the soil of the street, their stiff hands stretched out as if in a last, futile gesture of pleading. The mob had moved on; from somewhere in the darkened heart of the city came the sporadic clang and clash of glass, the night air muting sound, as if the splinters were falling on velvet.

A streetcar, lights bright—a curious face pressed against the fogged windows—rounded the corner out of the dark and slowed to a stop at the end of the square.

"The streetcar, Mother—shall we run for it?"

Her mother turned into the deserted Hofstrasse.

"No, we must walk. Someone might recognize us—perhaps have us picked up. We cannot take the chance."

■

It was a long way to Dr. Neuburger's house. He lived in a workers' settlement at the outskirts of town; as a doctor for the old national health insurance, he had always felt that he wanted to stay close to the lives of his patients. And though he was no longer permitted to accept insurance cases—or, for that matter, treat any non-Jewish patients at all—he stayed on at the settlement: a neat row of three-story houses with modest, carefully tended patches of garden in front. The houses, replacing decaying tenements of the previous century, had been built by the Weimar government in the 1920s, the doctor was fond of pointing out; and the residents, with good reason, had been staunch supporters of the Weimar coalition. When the Nazis took over, more than a few of the doctor's neighbors paid dearly for their support of the democratic government: men, women, too, who were beaten, jailed, even murdered during that first wave of brutality which had left Alfred, Aunt Cora's husband, crippled for life. It was of these—trade unionists, Social Democrats, Catholics—"working people steeled in the forge of embattled lives"—that the doctor had spoken the night he had hurried to Alfred's side.

"Dr. Neuburger will be safe, Mother," Eva said, wanting to pierce the cocoon of silence her mother had spun about herself. "His neighbors won't let him be taken away!"

"Because they call him 'our Herr Doktor'? People forget

quickly, Eva, when their bread and butter is threatened—even more quickly when life and limb are in danger . . ."

Eva thought of the telephone calls her mother had desperately tried to place to the doctor's house before leaving, and of the operator's flat voice, cutting in time after time: "The number is busy." What could that mean? A deluge of frantic callers? A disconnected phone? And if the phone was disconnected— by whom? The doctor himself, fleeing his home perhaps on a whispered tip from a neighbor? Or the SS, making its round of arrests? In the end, her mother, unable to hold out another moment, had let it mean only one thing: "He is *home*, Eva—I know it. How else could his telephone be busy?" And she had reached for their coats. "If you are coming along, Eva—we must be on our way."

It was hard to walk against the driving wind, but her mother allowed her no pause. From time to time she drew a heavy breath that was less a sigh than a stifled sob. Eva knew she was thinking of her father in a crowded cell at the police station, and of that other, never-to-be-mentioned place—Dachau, from which only a few short hours separated him now. Holding on to her mother's unyielding arm, Eva barely kept up with her; but her mother wasted no sidelong glance on her, no word of encouragement or concern. It was as if in the entire city only two people existed for her: Eva's father and the physician whose word must save his life.

At last, around the bend of the street, the settlement was before them, the darkened houses scarcely visible against the night. A lone light shone through a drawn curtain and the shadow of a man was dimly outlined behind it. Was it the doctor preparing his instruments for an emergency call—or perhaps a worker come home from the night shift at the Dietz works outside the town? "They make autos by *day* and armored trucks by *night*," Anton had whispered once in the schoolyard. She wondered why she remembered it suddenly, now. There seemed no connection between that whispered, one-sided conversation and the happenings of this night—or perhaps, in some yet inexplicable way, there was. Perhaps she was only too wearied to get to the truth.

Her mother pushed open the door and drew her into the narrow hall. The odor of cooked cabbage hung over the stairwell and, mingled with it, faint traces of another, a vaguely familiar, disquieting scent. Her mother hurriedly scanned the names under the shining row of doorbells and was about to press a button when suddenly, out of the shadows of the hall, a woman appeared and laid a restraining hand on her arm.

"If it's our Herr Doktor you want, *Fraule*," the woman said slowly, in a hushed voice almost eerily calm, "you are too late."

"Too late?" Eva's mother whispered uncomprehendingly. She leaned against the doorpost, passing a fumbling hand over her face; exhaustion had finally, irresistibly, caught up with her.

"Too late?" she repeated dully. "Then they have come for him, too?"

The woman, a wispy wraith against the hall light, shook her head fiercely, almost triumphantly.

"They didn't *get* him! He always *said* they'd never lay their hands on him or her!"

Her eyes narrowed, flitted over their faces.

"I can talk openly with you—politicals, Jews: we're one and

the same to them. *Ja, ja,* they were here, all right—two car-loads of them, but the Herr Doktor had beaten them to it, and his good missus with him. A fine lady she was, from a doctor's family in Ludwigsburg—but never one for airs and graces: did her own marketing, in good days or bad, along with the rest of us at the old co-op store, until the Nazis closed it down."

Her worn, thin-lipped face thrust closer.

"*Gas!*" she hissed. "It's gas they took, the both of them, may God forgive them. Early this evening we found them, my old man and me. It was the note he'd stuck under the hall bell, not to *ring*—to keep the place from blowing up, you see. A thorough one he was, our Herr Doktor, thorough and thoughtful. They'll never see another one like him around here again, for all the *Sieg Heil*-ing they do."

Next to Eva, in the silent hallway, her mother drew in her breath. The brass bells in three shiny rows gleamed in the dim light. Beneath the third bell in the bottom row, a little white card inserted slightly askew bore the inscription DR. M. NEUBURGER, MED. PRACTITIONER RESTRICTED TO THE TREATMENT OF JEWS. The new designation stripping the doctor and his Jewish colleagues of their Physician status, though, as he had told Eva's father with a shrug, not of their skills. Eva thought of the doctor's shuffling, round-shouldered walk, his leathery face perpetually folded in lines of kindly pessimism, his small-town Bavarian speech in a voice always raspy from too much cigar smoke and, maybe, too many bedside talks. She thought of the blunt fingers that had eased so many hurts with such surprising gentleness, and which would never do so again. Of all this she thought, staring at the little white card tucked beneath the bell, and yet it all seemed curiously remote: as if it were no more than a tale told and dimly remembered through a cloud of tobacco smoke—as if it were not really she, Eva Bentheim, standing in the strange hallway between the two hollow-eyed women, but someone else, someone she hardly knew.

The woman followed them outside and along the dark path between the hedges.

"They won't last forever," she said in her eerily calm voice. "Someday it will all be over and people will look at each other and wonder how they could have let it happen. Maybe they'll remember the doctor then, a few of them, and be sorry for the way it went with him and his wife. And maybe, to show how sorry they are, they'll want to do something for him, like putting up a plaque for him or having the settlement bear his name. And it will be good, the plaques and the flowers—like purges are good for the body and fasting is good for the soul. Only it will be too late. The dead can't smell flowers."

■

From a telephone booth at the Central Railroad Station, her mother called Dr. Heilinger, the surgeon.

"If only we had a little more time, Eva," she whispered, listening to the distant ring. "To get him out of bed in the middle of the night—an eminent doctor . . ."

"He's a *physician*, Mother. Saving lives is his work."

Her mother's hand tightened about the receiver.

"Frau Doktor Heilinger?" she asked in a timid voice. "This is Martha Bentheim. Please forgive me for disturbing you, but . . ."

She shut her eyes and pressed her lips together.

"*Ja, ja,* Frau Doktor, I know the Herr Doktor needs his sleep, but it is an emergency—no, not a clinical emergency, but . . . *Bitte,* Frau Doktor, if you would only . . ."

Eva could hear the sharp, final click at the other end. Her mother stared at the receiver in her hand, at the smooth, pitiless instrument that would no longer speak, no longer be implored. Her face was very pale, and Eva, grabbing her sleeve with a cry of fear, drew her out of that closed, airless little space and made her sit down on a bench.

She rubbed her mother's chilled hands between her own. There was an all-night milk bar at the other end of the station, almost deserted, its counter lights dimmed except for one corner. With a practiced eye, Eva scanned the glass door for the JUDEN VERBOTEN sign; but there was none. Perhaps train station milk bars were not yet on the verboten list for Jews, to keep foreign visitors from knowing too much, too soon.

"Can you make it down there, Mother? You need something to give you strength—a cup of coffee, something to eat . . ."

Her mother slowly reached up and smoothed a strand of hair off Eva's forehead.

"You are cold, child," she said softly. "We cannot afford to get sick, you and I—Father depends on us." She glanced at her wristwatch. "Yes, we will take a minute for a warm drink. Then we will do whatever it is we must do next."

They sat down at the far corner of the counter.

A grizzled old man, indifferent eyes heavy with sleep, handed them their cups. They drank greedily, leaning their faces into the warming steam.

"If only she had listened, had let me explain . . ." her mother said, swallowing with effort the piece of buttered roll Eva put on her plate.

"She must have known why you called, Mother. They have a radio, too."

"Dr. Reissmann would have helped with the certificate, but he is in Palestine," her mother said. "Also Dr. Tannheimer, if he were still allowed to practice . . ."

She pushed back her cup.

"Someday, Eva, we shall be able to mourn the Neuburgers as they deserve to be mourned. They were unusual people, who not only held firm convictions but *lived* their ideals as few of us do. As for myself, I was always content to be a mother to you and a good wife to your father. That was my world, and still is. Even tonight I cannot weep over our good friends or worry about Uncle Ludwig until your father is safe."

She put some bills on the counter and got up.

"Perhaps an idea will come to us as we start walking."

■

The Königstrasse was cloaked in darkness.

Windows gaped jaggedly open at some of the elegant shops, and glass shards splintered beneath their cautious steps; but the crowd had gone home to bed, the day's "work" done. Against the shifting sky, the round clock in the station tower shone brightly, like a false moon. "The golden moon has risen . . ." Fragments of a song drifted through Eva's mind: "Lord, spare us retribution / Send sleep's calm absolution / To us and our sick neighbor, too . . ." It seemed long years since they had walked and sung together, her mother and she. Whatever had happened the day before yesterday was long ago.

Her mother suddenly clasped her arm. "Dr. *Kober*, Eva! We shall ask Dr. *Kober*, of course! Why haven't we thought of him before!"

Dr. Kober lived on Hofstrasse, not far from the Bentheims. It did seem strange that neither of them had thought of calling on him before now. And then, perhaps, it was not strange at all.

For Dr. Kober's father had been the grandson of a baptized Jew. Even before the Nazis, a tacit distance had been observed between his family and the Thalstadt Jews. One sensed, or perhaps merely suspected, that, having chosen their separate path, the Kobers had no desire for a meeting of the ways—and one wished to make it plain in turn that nobody intended to press the ancient bond. Four generations of Kobers had worshipped at the Memorial Church; a nephew of the doctor was studying for the ministry at the seminary in Düningen. And yet people in town still recalled the background of the family, whose name had not always been Kober but had once been Jacobi. The Nazis, too, must know. Would Dr. Kober risk calling further attention to his family tree by writing a certificate to protect a Jewish neighbor?

But her mother gave Eva no chance to voice her doubts, and Eva did not have the heart to make her listen. "If he writes the certificate, I shall go straight to the police chief," her mother said, hurrying Eva across the Schlossplatz with its barren chestnut trees and desolate flower beds. "If only Dr. Kober won't fail us!"

Bracing their shoulders against the sharp wind, they passed their own house. The windows of the Upstairs were dark, but Eva imagined her cousins lying open-eyed on their beds, worrying if their father had found a hiding place for the night. She thought of her uncle climbing the steep flight of stone steps to Schifferstrasse, goaded on by his fears—and suddenly recalled that afternoon in spring when she and Arno had run down the steps by the fountain, looking for rainbows in puddles, touching hands. It was the first time, she realized, that her thoughts were turning to Arno on this night and she forced them back quickly. Her father needed her more.

The hands of the clock above the Roeblin watch store pointed toward two. It would soon be morning.

At the Kobers' door, her mother knocked softly. They waited for a long moment, then Eva rang the bell.

Steps came swiftly down the hall and the door opened. It was the doctor himself, clad in a fine woolen robe, his expression alert as if it were the middle of the day.

"*Ja?* What is it you wish?" His voice was cool, professionally polite, with a hint of impatience; he did not recognize them at once.

Her mother held out a beseeching hand.

"*Ach, bitte,* Herr Doktor—may we come in and speak to you? I am sorry to disturb you at this hour, but . . ."

"Ah, it is you, Frau Bentheim—do come in!" the doctor said quickly, shutting the door behind them without a sound.

He walked ahead of them down a long hall into the front room and with a brisk wave of his hand motioned them into two deep leather armchairs. He sat down at his desk and lit his pipe.

"I saw what went on in the street last evening." He pointed his pipe stem in the direction of their house. "Has anyone in the family been hurt? Herr Bentheim, I'm told, has been quite ill; I hope he has not been mistreated by these people."

Eva's mother fumbled for a handkerchief in her coat pocket and, failing to find one, began to cry without it, tears running down her cheeks unchecked.

From somewhere within the recesses of his desk, the doctor brought out a bottle of brandy, half-empty, and two small glasses. He filled one and pressed it into his visitor's hand, his fingers slipping to her left wrist, his eyes on his watch.

"Suppose you tell me what happened, Fräulein Bentheim," he said to Eva, over his shoulder.

The formal address took her aback. But she began, groping for words at first, then stumbling over them, the events of the night played back before her eyes as on the screen of the Ufa Palace, at once with heightened clarity and with a sense of unreality, of make-believe.

"And Dr. Neuburger . . ." She suddenly felt her throat constrict, robbing her of breath. "Dr. Neuburger—and the Frau Doktor . . ."

Her mother's arm enfolded her and over the sobs that finally came Eva heard her repeat the word the woman had hissed at them in the hallway outside the Neuburgers' apartment: "*Gas! It's gas they took, the both of them . . .*"

Dr. Kober had walked to the window and back to his desk. When he spoke at last, he hardly seemed to speak to them at all.

"How heedless we are of a human life, we Germans, when we can barter it for glory on foreign battlefields! How we can make the words 'freedom' and 'justice' ring when we consider ourselves threatened from with*out!* But when the adversary is with*in*: when it is not Germany against the world but Germany against her homegrown tyrants—*ja*, that's an altogether different case!"

He had poured himself a glass of brandy and, having drained it, was now refilling and draining it again.

"*Zivilcourage!*" he muttered, waving the empty glass as if he were offering a toast. He gave a dry laugh. "The courage of one's convictions—that is what has been wanting in Germany since the time of the peasant wars, four centuries ago. Even my own Protestant Church has never done much protesting, finding more salvation in being a pillar of the State than in serving as the handmaiden of Our Lord. When conscience subordinates itself to authority"—he pointed a warning finger toward the ceiling, perhaps to the sky—"it renders unto Caesar its right to protest. Now that the State wants to turn us into *Deutsche Christen*—worshippers at the shrine of Hitler's Berchtesgaden in place of the manger of the Hebrew Child—Pastor Niemoller and others have spoken out, and paid a heavy price for their delayed opposition. But it is too late; we put our heads on the block a long time ago. Along with coins for the Nazi 'Winter Relief,' we have thrown our right to protest into the passing plate."

Eva's mother rose heavily.

"Herr Doktor, please write me the certificate. I cannot follow the things you are saying: just tell us, now, can you help us or not? My husband cannot survive the *Konzentrationslager*. I must find a way to save him before the sun comes up and I don't know where else to turn."

"*Bitte, bitte,*" the doctor said, swaying the least bit as he made a vague bow. "Please do me the honor of listening for another moment; it isn't every day I have the opportunity of talking to someone about such delicate matters."

He drew an unsteady hand across his throat.

"Did you know, for instance, that a whisper can be quite as deadly as a shout? Especially a whisper one is not used to, for—our new scientific theorists notwithstanding—there is really no such thing as a racial memory, take it from one who ought to qualify as an expert!"

He wheeled and pointed to a spot above the grand piano: a faint square outline on the wallpaper, a mere shade deeper than the surrounding area with its fading green pattern of leaves.

"Until a few years ago, Frau Bentheim, a painting used to hang there—a portrait of Raphael Jacobi, cardiologist, professor at Jena University. You have heard of my eminent forebear? His wife was a Laurentzius: the old Prussian officers' family, quite impoverished by then, gave its belated blessing to the couple when the bride persuaded her fiancé to submit to baptism and bring up their future children in the established Lutheran Church. Old Jacobi was the last Jew in the Kober family—and he has been dead for almost eighty years. But you see, this only makes us doubly vulnerable today. We have been brought into line, we Kobers: Protestant without protest, born soldiers and born subjects—with just enough 'non-Aryan' ancestry to provoke those whispers behind our backs. It may take only a small thing—a decent deed for a sick neighbor, an act of mercy in keeping with my Hippocratic oath—and my own windows will be shattered, my own life destroyed, my own children hunted on the streets of their town."

Her mother bowed her head. Eva followed her to the door, along the dimly lit hall with its faintly medicinal air. As in a dream, the hall stretched before them: interminably at first, so that there seemed time enough for a voice to call them back. A light seeped out under one of the closed doors; perhaps the talking had wakened the doctor's elegant wife. Somewhere a clock struck the hour, its timbre frail and tinkly, like the sound of a harpsichord.

Turning to let her mother pass before her, Eva saw the doctor hurry after them past the many doors.

"Give me half an hour, Frau Benthcim, to talk with my wife. I must not take a decision of this gravity upon myself alone. I will send word to you in half an hour."

The door shut behind them. They went down the carpeted stairway, her mother very slowly, her hand clinging to the banister.

The night wind was brisk and clean, with a sharp autumnal quality, like that of burning wood. Across the dark square, the solitary figure of a young man came swiftly toward them. His footsteps rang on the cobblestones.

"Quickly, Eva!" her mother murmured, seizing her sleeve.

The boy, breaking into a run, was waving his arms. In the periphery of the streetlamp, his features momentarily defined themselves against the dark.

It was Arno.

※

They said nothing. He held out his hand and she took it, and for an instant they stood gazing at each other and feeling warmth and life flow from their touch. There was nothing to be said. She needed him and he had come. He had sought her and she was there. They were no longer alone. It was almost like saying they were no longer afraid.

Upstairs, Arno helped Eva's mother out of her coat and made her lie down on the sofa. He heated up some coffee and brought it to the table.

"Arno—my father . . ."

He nodded. "I know, Eva. I've been here twice before—I spoke with Ella, upstairs. I've been looking for you for hours."

She told him the rest, quickly.

"And you, Arno—you were safe at the school, weren't you?"

Arno smiled. "Professor Zeller held them at bay, single-handedly, with his usual threat to call the Swiss Consulate. They demanded through the keyhole that he hand over his Jewish students, including his 'half-Aryans'; but he refused. They left, finally, with some ominous remarks about the vulnerability of mountain passes to modern warfare. An hour later some Gestapo bigwig rang up and told the professor that his residence permit was canceled and that he was ordered to leave the country within twenty-four hours. 'Resistance against the power of the National Socialist State,' or some such picturesque phrase!"

"And the music school?"

Arno shrugged. "They'll close it, of course. Zeller no longer cares. I think he would have gone home long ago if it weren't for us—his 'problem students,' as he calls us."

Time ticked away on the tall clock in the hall. At last, when Dr. Kober's half hour was nearly gone, there was a muffled knock at the apartment door. "It's the Kobers' Gretle," a hushed voice called out.

A young girl stood in the hallway, round cheeks flushed from the cold, the hem of her nightgown trailing beneath her hastily buttoned coat.

She thrust a letter into Eva's hand.

"The Herr Doktor asked me to give you this," she whispered, peering furtively over her shoulder. She held up her hand as if to ward off some evil—some insidious contamination. "I only *work* for them—I do as I'm told."

"No one will know," Arno said quietly, his arm around Eva's shoulder.

He shut the door.

Eva, ignoring her mother's outstretched hand, ripped open the envelope.

The lines, some words crossed out and hastily rewritten, flickered before her eyes.

". . . however, I regret . . . If I can be of service in other ways . . ."

Arno picked up his jacket and held up Eva's coat.

"I'm going to see Hans Valtary, Frau Bentheim—will you let Eva come with me? I'm going to ask my uncle to intercede on behalf of an old friend. With Eva there, it might be worth a try."

■

Outside, the black sky had already begun to fade and the streetlights shone dully in the impending dawn. Somewhere, a milk wagon rattled through the sleepy streets, and beyond the huddled rooftops of the Old City a streak of red tinged the horizon.

"Look, Arno—is it the sun?" She drew her breath in sharply,

the cold air with its faint substance of smoke stinging her throat.

He shook his head.

"The synagogue is burning, Eva. They put the torch to it soon after midnight."

She stared at him, horror and disbelief strangling speech.

He nodded gravely. "Not only in Thalstadt, Eva—everywhere in the Reich. 'The spontaneous outrage of the people,' Goebbels is calling it. And the fire hoses are 'spontaneously' trained only on the surrounding houses."

He put his arm around her, urging her on through the silent streets.

She matched her steps to his stride, averting her eyes from the eerie glow that whipped and flickered above the rooftops. "I cannot mourn the death of our dear friends," her mother had said, "until your father is safe." Now *she* had to turn away from a death of another kind, to help save her father.

■

Herr Valtary had moved. He no longer lived in the cluttered bachelor apartment in the reflected glow of the copper cupola over the Art Museum, where Eva and her father had once taken tea with him. His present quarters denoted the change in Herr Valtary's affairs, which had catapulted him from moderately successful art dealer to Official Consultant to the Reich Chamber of Culture and party authority on Degenerate Art. He now rented a suite in an apartment house on the Lindenstrasse—a dignified building with vine-colored stucco walls set back behind an iron fence and framed by the branches of stately trees. It seemed a suitable setting for a man of Herr Valtary's present responsibilities, combining a certain romantic flavor with the decorum called for by his official connections.

Arno drew Eva past the entrance to the discreetly lighted lobby, toward the garden in back. He lifted a rusty latch, opening a gate in the fence. A rainy week had turned the earth to mud; it clung to their feet like quicksand, tugging at their steps as if to drag them down.

Eva glanced at their shoes. "Your uncle won't like this, Arno—we should have come in by the street."

He shrugged. "How do you think I *knew* about this door? Who do you suppose told me to *use* it, on the rare occasions when he would have reason to summon me into his presence?"

They scurried up the drafty backstairs, soundless as mice from the fields. Below, in the paneled lobby glowing with warmth and soft lights, a doorman dozed over the N.S. *Banner.*

Arno rang the bell. They looked at each other, waiting. There was no sound.

"He is *home!*" Arno muttered. "His Mercedes was parked at the curb."

He rang again, leaning against the bell, the shrill sound piercing the silence.

"I *know* his car!" Arno repeated fiercely, his finger jabbing the button. "He's in there all right!"

His face was a blurred mask against the mahogany door.

When it opened suddenly, he stumbled, scrambling to his feet just as the door was slamming shut again. With a stifled cry he threw himself against it and pulled Eva inside with him.

Herr Valtary stared at his unbidden guests, his suave face flushed with embarrassment and ill-concealed rage. His feet were slippered in soft beige leather, and he wore a brightly figured silk pajama top over his flannel trousers. His eyes darted from the dirt marks their shoes had left on his cream-colored rug to a door just behind him. It had been shut, but evidently in great haste; now, under his startled gaze, it slowly, irresistibly gaped open, making a tiny squeaking sound like a scarcely suppressed yawn. A corner of the next room stood flagrantly revealed: the bed with a wine-red satin eiderdown, and the bare arm of a sleeping woman under a gleaming tumble of auburn hair.

Herr Valtary, rubbing his hands as if he were rapidly weighing and discarding a sequence of alternatives, finally pointed to the curved black couch and tiptoed across the room.

Arno pulled Eva down beside him on the couch, slipping one of the bright silk pillows behind her back. She leaned her head against his shoulder; a radio was playing softly in the next room: a popular Zarah Leander hit, with the singer's sultry, Swedish-accented voice dark against the sensuous piano beat: "Can love be sin . . . To forget everything once / For bliss . . ."

Herr Valtary shut the door to the bedroom, giving the knob a reassuring final twist.

"Highly incorrect of you, Arno, to burst in here like this," he blurted out, pacing nervously across the rug. "I've told you to stay away from this place—in your own and your father's interest as much as in mine. And at an hour like this . . ."

Arno bit his lip, staring past his uncle's sweat-beaded forehead, past the empty glasses on the low, curved table, the crumpled pillows strewn about the floor. Whatever bitter and painful words were on his tongue, he managed not to say them.

Their eyes locked: the man's smooth face strained and furtive, the boy's pale, haggard with fatigue.

"Eva's father was picked up last night," Arno said quietly. "He'll be sent to Dachau in the morning. So we came here."

For the first time, Herr Valtary looked at Eva, almost with relief that he had been forced to acknowledge her presence. There was no sense in ignoring her any longer; he must have known all along what brought them here.

He put his fingers to his lips and cocked his head to listen. There was no sound from the other room.

Lighting a cigarette, Herr Valtary sat down and crossed his legs.

"It's a bad business," he said, leaning toward them. "Bad all around. Bad for us abroad—the foreign press will tear us to pieces for it."

He shrugged.

"Of course, it's completely outside my own sphere of activities, you understand. I have absolutely nothing to do with political matters." He gestured with his cigarette. "My own pursuits are purely on the cultural side," he added with a deprecatory smile.

Eva stared at the floor.

"My father is very ill, Herr Valtary. He has just had another operation. If he is sent to Dachau . . ."

It could not be true, could it: this room thick with smoke and a musky perfume, the tall, tilted glasses and disarrayed pillows, and the sleeping woman beyond the door? And in this most unlikely of places, she, pleading for her father's life with this man who had once called himself his friend? It could not be true—but if it were not, why were her teeth chattering so loudly, why was Arno putting his arm about her shoulders and rubbing her cheeks?

The room, blurred and redefined, had stopped whirling.

Herr Valtary rose abruptly, indicating that the bizarre encounter had come to an end.

"I sympathize with you," he said, avoiding Eva's name as he had all along. "But believe me, I am quite powerless to act except . . ."

"In cultural affairs," Arno said evenly. He gripped her hand tightly, urging her to hold on, not to give up.

"Eva and I saw the exhibit on Degenerate Art at the Gallery last year. It's the only place left to see the Expressionist paintings—of course, you must train yourself to ignore the official commentary. Supplied by *you*, I suppose."

Herr Valtary's eyes shifted.

"I fail to see, Arno—"

"Alex Valtary would be insulted to know *his* paintings hadn't been included," Arno said dryly, his voice rising the least bit.

His uncle held up his hand. "Shshsh—I must ask you to leave. You are putting me in a most awkward position. You are no longer so young, Arno, as not to understand."

He motioned toward the bedroom, managing a half-smile of man-to-man confidentiality.

Arno ignored it. "You told me the paintings were confiscated when my father's studio was closed. Why didn't your friends in the Chamber of Culture put them on public display? Surely they were 'degenerate' enough—the work of an 'insane' painter, an enemy of the official 'aesthetic.' It should have been good for a lead article in *Volk und Kunst.*"

Herr Valtary glanced at his polished fingernails.

"You are being very difficult, Arno, I must say. Well now, I will tell you something I had not intended to tell. Number one, because I did not wish to boast of my continued efforts to protect your father. Number two, because it was carried out at such great personal risk as to be kept absolutely secret. The paintings were never confiscated because I took them from your father's studio before it was shut down. I knew the Degenerate Art exhibit was to be held, and I wanted to spare Alex the humiliation. The pictures are entirely worthless, of course. No dealer in all of Germany would dare to give you a pfennig for them."

"In *Germany*," Arno repeated, staring at the door. Next to it, against the wall, stood a stylish pigskin case, snapped shut and pasted with foreign stickers; and over the back of an armchair hung Herr Valtary's tan trench coat, freshly cleaned and pressed.

"In Germany, yes," Arno said. "But, fortunately for you, Uncle, your Strength Through Joy trips frequently take you abroad, where art dealers are free to ignore the official line from Berlin when they buy paintings."

Arno's hands were shaking and he stumbled over his words. But as he looked into his uncle's chalky face, his dark eyes shone with a faint, cold glimmer of amusement.

"What has come into your head, Arno?" Herr Valtary whispered hoarsely. "I absolutely forbid you to voice such things— and I must ask you to leave, this very moment! You are not only compromising me with your presence, you are impugning my honor as a German officer and Party official. I will not stand for this."

Arno took a deep breath. "In Switzerland last year a confiscated Klee is said to have brought a small fortune at private auction. A highly secretive affair, of course, this selling of stolen paintings for foreign currency abroad. A highly lucrative one, too. I doubt that the authorities—Göring among them, one hears—would tolerate competition."

Something stirred in the next room. A soft, petulant voice, like that of a pampered child, came through the shut door.

"What are you doing up, Schatzi? Come back to bed—the train leaves in four hours . . ."

"Does she *know*?" Arno whispered, pulling Eva to her feet. "Did you take her along on those other trips, too?"

Grotesquely, because it had been conjured up only with a supreme effort of will, a smile spread over Herr Valtary's face.

"Go back to sleep, Nannerl!" he called back with forced heartiness. "Gustav dropped in for a moment. He thinks his boys have turned up some degenerate paintings during the raids and wants my professional opinion. This won't take long—go back to sleep."

For a moment he studied his manicured hands, his face taut with concentration. Abruptly, he picked up the phone and dialed, his fingertips moving as if by rote.

"Listen, Gustav," he called in a muffled voice. "Do you have a Jew there at the station, name of Bentheim? It happens that a friend of mine wants to relieve him of his business worries—

wants the store for himself, in other words, not for some old veteran of the Beer Hall days, to whom the Party might let it go if the cure at the KZ proves too strong for him. What you can *do*? Well, you can hold him at the jail for a few days, so my friend can take care of the matter—with lawyers—to observe all the legal niceties, as usual! Can be arranged? Well, much obliged, Gustav. Heil Hitler!"

Herr Valtary, an obsequious grin still pasted on his dead-white face, put back the receiver and passed a trembling hand over his thinning hair.

"You've put me in a ticklish situation, you two. Let's hope nothing goes wrong!"

He walked his unwelcome visitors to the door, dragging his feet on the lush carpet. "If one syllable of this gets out," he said, staring hard at them, "then we're *all* lost!"

"No one will know," Arno said, for the second time that night.

Herr Valtary wagged an avuncular finger at him.

"Of course, your little friend may tell her father—someday, when the world is back on track," he added, suddenly clasping Eva's hand. "Jail is no place for a man like him—a cultured, sensitive man. I think it will please him to know his life was saved by an old friend from his student days."

He pressed her fingers, waiting for her to say something—her hand, caught tightly within the soft, insinuating clasp of his moist palm, recoiling from the touch.

"*Danke schön*, Herr Valtary," she whispered, forcing the words through her clenched teeth.

Her face was hot with shame. Of all the terrible things of

this long, terrible night, speaking these words of thanks was suddenly the hardest.

For a moment, following Arno down the stairs, she wondered if her father would have thought it worth doing at all.

SIXTEEN THE TENTH OF NOVEMBER—AND AFTER

Through some of his fellow prisoners at the city jail—as Eva was to learn afterward—her father had heard that his brother had been caught in the net during the early morning hours, put on a truck where he stood ashen-faced with others seized in the roundup, and sent to Dachau. Through the small window of his cell high overhead, Eva's father heard the sounds of blows, screams, and curses: "Get up on that truck, you . . . !" as endless rows of prisoners were taken away. When steps approached down the corridor, he steeled himself for the moment the guards would come for him. Instead, a thickset, red-faced man came puffing into his cell, followed by a flustered-looking older one who introduced himself as an attorney and demanded Jonas Bentheim's signature on a contract that would turn over the family store to his client for a fraction of its worth and an implied promise to be let go.

Fearful for his brother and aware of numerous such "Aryanization proceedings" against Jewish-owned businesses under Gestapo threats to "sign or take the consequences," Eva's father played the one card left in his hand. "As you see, J. Bentheim & Sons is jointly owned. You will need to bring my brother here so that his signature can be affixed as well."

The flush-faced man began to rant that a prisoner, a Jew, was in no position to set conditions for "Aryanizing" his business. But the lawyer, perhaps leery of legal loopholes that could cost the client his booty at some unforeseeable future date, conferred with him in a corner and hastily stepped outside to talk with an official briefly glimpsed in the corridor by Eva's father.

Shortly, the lawyer returned. "Your brother is in the KZ, in *Schutzhaft*—protective custody from the just wrath of the people. To be freed, a KZ prisoner must sign a statement that he will leave Germany within three weeks. Can your brother do so?"

Yes, Eva's father said quickly—the necessary affidavits were being readied for his brother and his family by American relatives.

◼

And so Uncle Ludwig came home, his gray hair shorn close to his head, his newly weather-beaten skin stretched taut over his haggard face, and so shaken by what he had seen and suffered in Dachau that he was scarcely able to speak—even if he had not been made to sign a pledge of silence about conditions at the KZ, as everyone lucky enough to get out was made to do. He was brought to the city jail for his signature on the contract next to his brother's. Ella had already cabled a frantic plea to Arthur Bentheim, their cousin in New York. Obviously shocked by what overseas papers were reporting on the mass arrests in Germany, Arthur sent back a terse message announcing that affidavits for Ludwig, Gustl, and "the girls" were being airmailed. His brother Richard, in England, would put the family up in London under a temporary British transit visa, until they could obtain their immigration visas at the American Consulate there and sail for the United States.

As for Eva—for whom her cousins would never be "the girls" but always *Ella*, who had lent her own eiderdown to Eva whenever she slept upstairs, and *Uschi*, from whom she had learned her first French poem—she tried very hard to be happy for them. But when she told them so, her face suddenly crumpled, and it was Ella who pulled out her big wrinkled handkerchief to wipe Eva's cheeks. "We'll see each other again, Eva—in America!" Ella said softly, and Eva nodded.

But she knew that even if they did, things would never be the same again.

■

Eva's father, too, was let go, coming home to learn the full extent of the violent happenings: the suicide of his close friends; the burning of hundreds of synagogues; the tens of thousands thrown into the camps; the beatings and murders. In Ettingen, Grandfather Weil had walked the high road through the long night under a relentless drizzle of rain, until he crept home ill and feverish before dawn and fell into bed. He had missed his nocturnal visitors, Grandmother told him in a trembling voice, by an hour.

With all that had happened, Eva and her mother spoke little about the night of her father's arrest. If he suspected his former classmate to have been behind the forced sale of the store and his release from jail, he asked nothing, enabling Eva to shield him from the sordid chain of events at Hans Valtary's posh new quarters. Nor, as if all of them were in a tacit conspiracy of silence, did Arno speak of it. However contemptible he judged his uncle to be for enriching himself from the clandestine sale of his brother's paintings and for belatedly playing the hero in "saving the life of an old friend," Arno knew that he held his father's fate in his smooth hands. It was for his father's sake as much as for Eva's, she sensed, that he had told his uncle, "No one will know." In Nazi Germany, where a slip of the tongue or the flick of an eyelid might betray oneself or others into the Gestapo cellars, the less known by even a trusted few, the better for all.

■

One afternoon—Eva's mother having gone to Ettingen overnight to be at her mother's side during Grandfather's illness—Eva and her father went for a walk, his first since his release from prison. Skirting the main streets with their demolished store windows hastily boarded up like their own, they suddenly—yet with a sense of inevitability, it seemed to Eva—found themselves approaching the torched synagogue. From the opposite sidewalk, where families would cluster after services to wish one another Sabbath peace, they gazed at the charred ruin and small, trampled garden behind the wrought-iron fence that had been so easily breached by those sent to ignite the fires. Inside, beyond the shattered windows and gutted walls, beneath the blue and golden cupola now soot-streaked and smashed, Eva had stood on the women's balcony next to her mother, their voices merging with those of the congregation in the familiar melodies of praise and devotion. From there she would see the velvet-clad Torah scrolls brought from the ornamented Ark like precious children, enveloped in the glow of the Eternal Light. Here she would listen to Rabbi

Gideon's scholarly sermons, to the cantor's fervent chant, his voice dark as the wine shimmering in the silver cup upraised in his hand.

Beside her now, her father stood motionless, his eyes reddened by something beyond the sting of the encroaching November night. He who had rarely come to services and, when called to the Torah, read from it self-consciously—he who perceived himself as Jewish in spirit, way of life, and from a bond of ancient connectedness more than from unassailable faith—grieved over the desecration of the sanctuary, the torching of the sacred scrolls, the blasphemous flames searing the skies of his native town.

He drew in a sharp breath of air, still tinged with traces of smoke and a telltale whiff of benzine. When he spoke, he seemed to be scarcely aware of her.

"We came to seek the peace of the city, we Swabian Jews— as Jeremiah once bade us do, in Babylon. We worked and raised families and were neighbors and citizens. But in the end, the peace of the city has eluded us, our dreams gone up in flames, our hopes turned to ashes . . ."

Her eyes moved from his distraught face to the ravaged sanctuary across Asylstrasse. There, at the apex of the gently curved roof line, below the fallen cupola, something held fast: the twin stone Tablets etched with Hebrew lettering, the Ten Commandments. Foundations beyond destruction, beyond extinction.

Her father had followed her gaze and reached for her hand. Then they walked down the darkening street toward home.

Soon after, the skeletal walls of the sanctuary were razed to the ground by a group of Jewish prisoners ordered back from Dachau for that purpose. The Thalstadt synagogue, almost a century old, was no more.

■

But in time, over the weeks and months that followed, a whisper was heard within the bereaved community, a whisper exchanged only between a few here and there, yet refusing to die: that the stone Tablets had been secretly saved and whisked into safekeeping, at great danger to their rescuer. Was it one of the prisoners? The aging architect forced into overseeing the demolition? The Christian custodian who had vainly sought to intervene when the SA men—in civilian clothes but wearing their notorious boots—had burst into his apartment next to the synagogue and bullied him into submission? No one knew, no one dared to probe further, for fear of imperiling others. But the whisper would not be stilled: that the Tablets were in hiding, biding their time for some future, as yet unimaginable resurrection.

■

There had been a letter waiting for Eva when she and her father returned that evening—a letter slipped under her door without address or sender or even a signature. But she recognized the precisely looped handwriting at a glance—and the delicate drawing of a blossoming cherry branch as only Renate could draw it. They hadn't seen each other for more than a week: Eva had stayed away from school since the afternoon when it all began; she knew she would not be missed.

"Don't come back to class tomorrow, Eva," Renate wrote. "Diete's father told her that all Jewish students still in German schools will be expelled on Monday on orders from the Education Minister. I don't want you to be there when it gets announced, Eva—to be made to leave that way, in front of everybody, to get hurt."

There was a big space, as if Renate had been uncertain whether to go on or not. But then she did.

"A young friend of my parents came to see us today, filled with shame over what was done to the synagogues. He said that the Church needs to stand with her violated sister, to comfort and defend her. Or are we too faint of heart to bear witness when we are called, he asked.

"Dear Eva," Renate's letter concluded, "I share your sorrow over your House of God and pray for you and all your loved ones. May God grant us a *Wiedersehen*—soon, if I am not one of those faint of heart our visitor spoke of. Or in a better time, if you can forgive me."

■

One night soon after, Eva heard muffled sounds on the staircase and recognized Uncle Ludwig's dragging steps, followed by Uschi's hurried ones, by Ella's and Aunt Gustl's. Through the crack under her door, she watched the gleam of her father's bedside lamp come on; he must have heard, too.

In her mind's eye she saw her uncle descend the stairs, the brim of his fedora shading his face with its deep, skeptical lines, saw him pass by his brother's door stealthily, without stepping inside for a last farewell. "We're taking the night train to Calais," Uschi had said a few days before without naming the date. Now Eva knew why her uncle had made this choice. The bond between the brothers had been an unusually close one, a lifetime of mutual loyalty and concern. Now Hitler had come between them, forcing the elder to flee for his life and leave the younger, ailing one behind. Anguish and despair drove Uncle Ludwig past his brother's door, to steal away in the night. And on the other side of the wall, her father stared into the small circle of light from his lamp, hearing his brother's steps on the stairs, approaching and receding—and yet perhaps knowing that it was better this way.

From the living room window, to which she ran barefoot for a last glimpse of her cousins, Eva saw them walk across the sparsely lit square between their parents, in their gray winter coats and matching berets, each carrying a small suitcase, a rain cape, and an umbrella—walking swiftly away from Grandfather's house, without looking back.

SEVENTEEN WINTER 1938-1939

Her schooldays were over. She thought of them, when at all, with relief outweighing regret. When she told Arno that—despite Nazi teachers and ostracism—it surprised her that she was taking expulsion from her old school so calmly, he shook his head. "It's called growing up, Eva. It comes to us all, sooner or later. Though some things speed up the process, I guess, like forcing a flower." He drew her into the crook of his arm. "We'll have more time to see each other. To work on the Schubert sonata—for the drawer, as Alex would say. Have you thought of that?"

She had, but her mind wasn't on music, either. Fräulein Lehmann had left, having both an affidavit and a luckily low quota number; and the Jewish Kulturbund was dissolved. Other things once taken for granted were no longer open to Jews: swimming pools, concert halls, cinemas, sports. It was all part of the *Sühneleistung:* crushing fines placed collectively on the Jewish communities in "expiation" for the individual act of a seventeen-year-old student in Paris. And this in addition to being forced to bear the costs of the very destruction inflicted on the synagogues and Jewish property.

Eva saw the worries these cynical measures caused her parents: fears about what there was left for them all to live on after their household's part of the "expiation" fines were paid. Fears regarding their dwindling possibilities for emigration. Arthur, in New York, had written regretfully that "having helped Ludwig and his family, as well as several relatives on my wife's side," he could not vouch for any other immigrants—nor, on the basis of his income and resources, would Immigration policy permit him to write further affidavits. And Jonas's ill health, he was sorry to add, made "a successful adjustment to the American workplace difficult to anticipate." Even Eva, with her schoolgirl English, knew it all added up to *no*.

Then, literally out of the blue, there was an airmail letter from Celia! Arthur's daughter, whom Eva remembered so fondly from the *Amerikaners'* visit to Germany the fall before Hitler took over. The bright, perceptive college student who'd already then urged them to leave, to come to her country. Now Celia wrote that with her residency behind her, she had recently opened a practice with another young woman doctor, so that she was finally in a position to "offer Jonas and his very nice family" the affidavits she knew were so urgently needed. "I remember all of you with affection and look forward to showing you *my* hometown, New York, with the same cousinly hospitality you extended to *me*." When the papers were joyfully received a few weeks later, they were put away toward the day when they could be presented at the consulate—the day their own magic numbers would be called. It was more than a year off, and, as her mother once said, a lot could happen before then. But it was a beginning, a slender lifeline to hold on to. Meanwhile, with a few other girls waiting for magic numbers and opening doors, Eva went on with English lessons from Dr. Tiefental where she had left off the day her classroom door had shut her out.

Her mother, too, was learning English, from an elderly woman whose apartment was crowded with birdcages in which countless birds whirred about, sometimes even *outside* their bars! She learned to handsew elegant leather gloves and to fashion fine Continental chocolate confections—all this in preparation for the "American workplace" where she and Eva would hold "jobs" (another new American word), if her father was not well enough to work. Toward that end, Eva took lessons in typing, which she loved, and in shorthand, which she disliked and which, being *German* stenography, seemed of questionable value for America. But, as her mother said, it might come in handy, after all—and it helped pass the days.

For a new, unsuspected enemy had made its appearance: Time. It hung over their lives, Arno's and Eva's, with a relentless, amorphous presence, each day scarcely different from the one that had preceded or was to follow it: days strung like gray beads into endless weeks of unalleviated sameness. With Thea and Eva's cousins gone, with more and more of her friends and Arno's fellow music students leaving, and with their own lives increasingly restricted by Nazi regulations, they had only each other now—and strangely, though neither would have admitted it, it was not enough. Their very closeness had lost some of its savor and secret joy; and if their feelings for each other continued to grow, even this seemed too precious, too untested a thing, nurtured in the claustrophobic languor of a hothouse. ·

■

One early evening in February, as they walked through the dusk settling on Königstrasse, the electric signs on the Ufa Palace were just beginning to glow. The doors stood open: the afternoon performance had ended and people were streaming out of the brightly lit lobby of the movie theater, chatting about the film they had seen. It was a story set in Vienna; the Strauss waltz was already drifting through the open door, coaxing the passersby inside for the next performance: a romance set in Austria—or Ostmark, as it was called since its annexation into the Reich. One could tell at a glance what it was from the glossy photos in the Palace windows: brawny young men in lederhosen; apple-cheeked girls in dirndl costumes, with blond braids circling their comely heads. Without setting foot inside, Eva knew this film was everything she detested: sentimentality, mediocrity, and that peculiarly Third Reich distortion of reality she remembered only too well from propaganda lectures and film programs at school. It was only when Arno's gently prodding arm had brought her to the next corner that she also realized she would have given anything to go inside. It meant so much, suddenly: the simple act of walking up to the window and asking the cashier for tickets; the musty warmth of the lobby; the velvety feel of the red carpet under one's chilled toes; the expectant wait in the darkness with her head against Arno's shoulder—even the organ's gushy rendition of the Strauss waltz as the first image of the film took shape on the screen . . .

"Let's go back, Arno!" she blurted out. "Look at that stream of people—who'd notice us?"

Arno laughed, a bit too contemptuously. "For *that*, Eva? Take risks for that concoction of edelweiss and kitsch?"

"But it doesn't *matter*, Arno!" She heard herself yelling at him, unable to stop. "It isn't the *film* I want to see—not *any* film! It's just that I want to go to the movies—like everyone else!"

Arno shifted his violin case to his other arm and brushed a windblown strand of hair from her angry eyes. "If it means so much to you, Eva, I think I have a better idea."

Arno's "better idea," after a last moment of hesitation, turned out to be the Botenstrasse Cinema, a run-down movie house that even in its best times could hardly have been considered plush and that had become so dilapidated that it was called, with unadorned Thalstadt bluntness, the Fleapit. Because of her parents' strict orders, Eva had never been given an opportunity to find out if the Fleapit actually lived up to its popular name. But the perpetually deserted look of its ticket window suggested that it played host to few cinemagoers of any species. Even the films advertised in broken letters on its crumbling marquee seemed dated, like the lost souls that shambled through its door, perhaps as much in search of a warm, dry place to sit out the weather as on a quest for entertainment. A far cry from the sumptuous setting of the new Ufa Palace, Eva had to admit; yet everything about the Fleapit suddenly seemed to be an asset: its location in a less central, largely industrial part of town; its condition of decay and questionable repute, which would make it unlikely that they would run into someone who might recognize them; its very dearth of customers, which might even induce the ticket taker to look the other way . . .

It was this latter fact, on second thought, that made Eva hold back. "Crowds are safer, Arno. Better to hide in."

Besides, she went on, hadn't there been rumors some time ago? Something about the Fleapit being in trouble the year before: a picture on the verboten list it had dared to run, an early Chaplin silent film, for which audacity or foolhardiness the Nazis had confiscated its box office receipts and shut it down under "temporary *Spielverbot*." She was not sure if it had ever been permitted to reopen.

It *had*, Arno said. He knew because a friend of his was a kind of jack-of-all-trades there. "Sells tickets, you know, what there is of them. Plays an ancient organ, old enough to have been Buxtehude's practice instrument, then runs upstairs to splice the film together when it comes apart at the seams."

Eva, following him through the early evening throng without acknowledging that they were walking in the direction of the Fleapit, burst out laughing. "And who runs the projector? Your friend, when he isn't playing the organ or patching up the film?"

"The owner, usually. An old man who doesn't seem to have a soul in the world, and no other goal in his life than to keep the Fleapit going and look at his collection of silent films, pre-Nazi, on the screen."

"And your friend? Is he a music student?"

Arno steered her across the traffic into a side street running west. "A pianist, you guessed right. Plays the rickety upright at the Fleapit when the old American silents call for jazz. And looks out for the old man, keeps him out of trouble, if he can."

He shrugged. "They're birds of a feather, you see. A boy and an old man who don't fit into the machinery, don't *want* to, either. It isn't that they're politicals, or Jews, or Jehovah's Witnesses. They simply don't want to be co-opted into marching with the Hitler Youth or into showing kitsch films made by the Nazis. Willi is a working-class kid who happens to be crazy about the American jazz the Nazis call 'animalistic'—and about the black jazz musicians they ban and revile. The old man tries his best to keep the Little Tramp out of the clutches of our cultural storm troopers."

He glanced at his watch. "We might just make the next film, whatever it is. The old man—Willi always calls him *der Alte*, I don't even know his name—the old man had to sign away his rights to screen Chaplin films before they let him reopen the Fleapit, but whatever he shows is good stuff: films of the Weimar cinema pioneers the Nazis have declared 'decadent' because they didn't show society through a rose-colored lens; because they took stands, told the truth."

He smiled his wry smile. "Willi can let us in through the projection room in back, you see. My usual way!"

Catching her questioning look, he added with a dry laugh, "I've never told you about my escapades, Eva—I'm crazy taking you *now*, putting you in danger. Are you *sure* you want to do this?"

She nodded, more eagerly than she felt, with her heart hammering in sudden fear.

They were passing a phone booth. "Do you want to call your parents?" Arno asked. "They must be expecting you home about now."

She shook her head. "They're having dinner at Aunt Hanni's. I'll be home before they get back. We're in luck!" she added brightly, tightening her hand on Arno's arm as he quickened his steps.

At the corner of Botenstrasse, Arno hurried Eva past the bleak entrance to the Fleapit under the battered, still-unlit marquee and toward the iron steps in back that led upstairs to the projection room. But Arno's swift taps against its door brought no reply, no answering voice, no light promptly switched on. Twice more Arno knocked, three sharp raps followed by a legato one; then he shook his head and hurried Eva back down the steps. Only when they had rounded the corner and, passing the entrance, took a closer look at the ticket window, reflecting the dim light of the streetlamp in the dusk, did they realize that there was no one behind the glass. The darkened theater was closed.

■

The next day, Arno put his finger to his lips and then to a page of the *N.S. Banner* he had smuggled into the Bentheims' living room inside his music score. It was a very small item on a back page of the Nazi paper, dealing with a matter of scant importance in the Nazi scheme of things, not worth sensationalizing. The Botenstrasse Cinema had been closed indefinitely. The owner, who had persisted in showing films "unworthy of National Socialist cultural standards," had been given an indeterminate jail sentence, having been spared more severe punishment only because of his age.

There was no mention of Willi. But Arno told Eva what the newspaper omitted. He'd gone back to the shuttered theater later the previous night and, under the pretense of wanting a beer, he'd stopped by the ramshackle old tavern across the street, where the bartender had told him more than he wanted to hear. When they'd arrested the old man and searched the

Fleapit for more "un-German" Charlie Chaplin films, they'd discovered Willi's photos of black jazz musicians on the walls of the projection room and his collection of jazz music on the shelves. This much the bartender had pieced together from their clipped conversation as they waited at the bar, keeping an unswerving eye out for Willi through the grimy window of the tavern. When they finally saw him coming up the street and pulling a key from his pocket to open up the theater, they pounced.

"Shot out of here without paying for their drinks and grabbed the kid before he knew what was happening to him. Worked him over pretty badly with their fists and boots and threw him into the car . . ."

The bartender fixed Arno's face and lowered his voice. "I've seen you over there before—lucky for you it's only me who's seen you." He shrugged. "Your friend's on the Heuberg—or in some other KZ. Maybe they'll let him go in a few months—just in time to fight their war, the way things look. Maybe they'll even let him join the band, being a musician, I mean. If he isn't too far gone, that is—after what they did to him across the street . . ."

■

Eva's mother came into the room to spread the table with a linen cloth. "Not playing this afternoon, Eva? Arno?" she asked, aware of their silence.

They shook their heads, averting their stricken faces.

"Not today, Mother," Eva said in a small voice, closing the pages of Arno's music score and handing it to him. "Maybe later. Maybe some other time."

She got her coat from her closet next door. "Arno and I are going for a walk, Mother."

"But it's almost suppertime," her mother said, instantly alarmed. "Where are you going so late? What for?"

"Just out, Mother," Eva said from the door. "Just to talk."

But they *didn't* talk. Just walked the busy, indifferent streets through the gathering darkness, her hand in Arno's, her head tilted against his shoulder, walking, walking.

There was no place to go.

■

Soon after, under a new decree, all Jewish residents were required to obtain a *Kennkarte*—an identity card, complete with fingerprints, photo, and a black letter "J" stamped on its muddy gray cover. The photo was to show the face in profile, exposing the left ear—which, by the lights of Nazi science, revealed "typically Jewish physiological traits." In their signatures, Jewish males were to take on the middle name "Israel"; Jewish women and girls that of "Sara": two honorable biblical names usurped by the Nazis in a cynical game intended to brand and debase those forced to adopt them. The *Kennkarte* was to be carried at all times and produced for anyone demanding to see it.

Eva and Arno tried their best to trade flippant remarks over this latest brew of racist venom mixed with a class bully's spitefulness. But they knew it was no laughing matter. It was another step in isolating Jews from the general population, in identifying and ostracizing them, making them objects of suspicion, ridicule, and contempt. "*Now* try to get into the Ufa Palace for edelweiss and kitsch!" Eva said, flippancy tinged with self-pity despite herself.

Arno shrugged. "This isn't just about getting into a movie, Eva. It's another bureaucratic 'legality' paving the way to whatever hell they're devising for us."

He went with her to have her picture taken, her fingerprints made; she had wanted to spare her parents the embarrassment of her presence when they had *theirs* done—and herself the pain of seeing them processed like criminals, two people who hadn't committed an illegal or even unkindly act in their lives. Pushing her hair behind her left ear, she looked blankly past the photographer, felt some official hand enclose hers with impersonal roughness to press her fingers against the inked pad.

Later, in the photo inserted next to her fingerprints, her face looked at once impassive and defiant, her eyes staring glumly, like those of a trapped creature. Looking at those deadened, furtively watchful eyes, she felt violated, robbed of her real self, transformed into a figment of someone else's twisted perception of her.

Over her shoulder, Arno studied the photo and shook his head. "All right, Eva, so it's a bad picture! What did you expect under those conditions—Mata Hari?"

She tried to join in his mocking laughter, summoned up for her sake, she knew. But she didn't succeed. Instead, she buried her face in the crook of his sheltering arm and let her tears, of rage, of frustration and fear, flow against his sleeve.

EIGHTEEN   AUGUST 1939–MAY 1940

Suddenly everything seemed to happen in a kind of blur—a newsreel flitting past her eyes so swiftly she felt like a numbed spectator, even though the events were rushing in on *her*.

At the end of August, Hitler's threats against neighboring Poland rose to a shrill pitch with the claim that Poles were violating the border and "massacring *Auslandsdeutsche*"—ethnic Germans living in Poland. Similar unfounded charges had preceded Hitler's invasions of other places; Austria, the Sudetenland, the rest of Czechoslovakia. But now, Herr Gerber said on one of his weekly visits with Eva's father, the British and French could no longer delude themselves that appeasement would buy them "peace for our time."

"They'll have to put a stop to him, Bentheim, or turn all of Europe over to him! It'll mean a second World War."

Her father put his frail hand over his forehead. "And with more terrible bloodshed now for having been deferred."

"It will be the end of him," Herr Gerber said grimly. " 'Better an ending with horror than a horror without end.' "

Her father shrugged. "And when the end comes—years from now, who knows?—it may come too late for most of us."

He glanced in Eva's direction and added, barely above a whisper, "I could face it better, if only my wife, my child . . ." His voice faltered, and Eva, hearing the desperate love and fear for her in that voice, suddenly needed to escape from that burden of love and despair placed on her shoulders, at times more heavily than she could bear.

She mumbled something under her breath that her father evidently chose to accept as she had intended him to—that she had to leave on a quick errand—and hurried down the stairs into the late August afternoon.

■

Arno stood at the entrance to Professor Zeller's house, as if expecting her, and quickly drew her inside. "Inside" was the deserted parlor, its draperies drawn, its ancient Steinway mutely folded in on itself under a light film of dust. She followed him up a narrow staircase into a small, cluttered room, with a sofa bed beneath a blue-and-brown surrealist cityscape by Arno's father; bookshelves lining the opposite wall; his violin leaning against a music stand in the corner; a table doubling as a makeshift desk under the window. Professor Zeller, dispatched across the border to his native Switzerland for his refusal to hand over his students, was in no hurry to sell his graceful old house on Wertherstrasse, despite persistent pressure by the Nazis. And though the music school had been closed down by them, Arno and the last of his former fellow students were able to stay on for the time being—"to show the house to prospective buyers," as the professor let it be known through his intermediary, the Swiss Consulate. A *business* arrangement, the professor insisted, so both the consulate and the German authorities went along with it—though it was anyone's guess for how long.

"I saw you coming up the street," Arno said, surprise and

pleasure mingling in his voice. He shuffled some musical scores strewn over the sofa to make room for her and gestured toward the window. "I was putting up the blackout blinds—block warden's orders," he added with a shrug. "In case the Führer's patience ran out and the Poles would need to be given a taste of the German fist."

He leaned against his bookshelves and gave her a curious glance. "You haven't been here since Zeller's last student concert more than a year ago. And then no farther than the music room," he added pointedly. "Despite my passionate pleas."

She smiled bleakly. Ordinarily, she liked being teased by Arno and teasing back, playing at flirtation from a safe distance, a threshold that neither of them felt ready to cross, perhaps because they also knew how easily they could have let themselves do so. But her heart was too heavy now to respond to the lightness in his voice, the mocking glance of his eyes.

"I'm scared, Arno!" she blurted out, feeling a chill seep through her body despite the sultriness of the spent day. "What's going to happen to us once the war breaks out? When we're totally cut off, totally in their power . . ."

He sat down next to her on the sofa and put his arms around her. They huddled close, seeking strength and comfort from each other where there were no words left to say. After a while, Arno got up, put his finger to his lips, and pulled her to her feet.

"You've come at the right time!" he said in a near whisper, though the house seemed empty except for themselves. He glanced at the battered alarm clock next to his bed. "Radio Luxembourg—two minutes from now! Or Strasbourg *Deutsche Welle*—whichever comes in on that antique set Zeller bequeathed to me before he left!"

He stretched out on the floor, flat on his stomach, and reached for something under his bed: a scruffy old shoe box, mercifully hidden from view by the fringes of his spread. Inside, revealed a moment later to Eva's shocked eyes, was a tiny short-wave radio. Arno fumbled with buttons and knobs and after some futile attempts tuned in to a woman's voice asserting in a French-accented German that the Nazi accusations were false—that the border violations had in fact been staged by Nazi troops disguised in stolen Polish army uniforms.

It was, of course, verboten to listen to foreign radio broadcasts, and Eva fought down a tremor of fear at the thought of being caught. And yet there was something deliciously conspiratorial about it: lying on her stomach next to Arno on the threadbare old carpet beside his bed, listening to the distant voice above the high-pitched warbles and ear-splitting beeps of the static. It was, they both knew, their last tenuous link with the world beyond their Nazi prison—a world that shut them out and granted them nothing more than the winged sound of a woman's voice drifting over the airwaves; but they were grateful even for that. "Will Monsieur Daladier and Lord Halifax allow Herr Hitler's next aggression against an ally whose territorial integrity their governments have guaranteed?" the cultivated voice wondered, winding up the broadcast. "The next days and hours will provide the fateful answer . . ." There was a murmured *"Bonsoir"* over the station's Brahms Symphony theme, followed, abruptly and incongruously, by a popular French hit, sung by a cabaret singer's throaty voice.

Arno switched off the receiver and pushed the shoe box with its dangerous secret back under the bed, letting the fringed hem of the spread drop into place. *"J'attendrai . . .* By night and by day / I am waiting for / Your return . . ." he sang softly under his breath, parodying the sensuous voice of the French singer and gazing into Eva's eyes with a look to match the performance. She scrambled to her feet, at once flustered and flattered, and let him draw her into his arms. They danced, swaying to the rhythm of the song, his voice humming close to her ear, her eyes shut against the waning August sun that streamed through the flimsy curtains at Arno's window.

"*J'attendrai* / For the bird far astray / will return someday / here to stay . . ."

"Arno, I . . ." she whispered out of the urgent rush of confused feelings, at once soothed and disturbed by his nearness, the ebb and flow of his breath against her cheek. She let her eyes open up wide enough to catch the tender, troubled, dark-eyed gaze of his.

He smiled and lightly touched his finger to her lips, shifting his shoulder to let her head rest in the crook of his arm. "Time flows swiftly by / We're apart and my heart / beats its silent cry / So by night and by day / *J'attendrai* . . ."

Less than a week later, on the first day of September, Hitler's troops and tanks poured across the Polish border.

■

In little more than a month, Poland had been crushed, its cities pounded into destruction. Blitzkrieg, the Thalstadt newspapers called this overpowering, lightning-speed assault on a small, ill-prepared country. And already there were ominous hints of the maltreatment of civilians, Poles and Jews, at the hands of the occupiers.

Walking through the flag-festooned streets of Thalstadt among faces jubilant over the swift and easy victory, Eva blinked back her tears and hurried home in waning expectations of a letter from Thea. It had been weeks since Eva had heard from her. Had she survived the bombing of Warsaw? Or had she been able to leave for Palestine with Martin, perhaps had already arrived? There were so many fearful questions these days, and so few answers. Aunt Hanni was ill with anxiety for Stefan in Paris; since France and Britain had declared war over the invasion of their Polish ally, all contact between these countries and Germany had been suspended. Eva's father, hoping for some word about the situation of refugees in France at the Community House, came back shaken. There were reports that internment camps had been set up for soldiers of the defeated Spanish Republican Army who had fled across the Pyrenees for asylum in France. These camps were now rumored to detain "alien Jews" and other refugees as well—under conditions suspected to be poor, or worse. It frightened Eva to think that Stefan might be in such a place, and her father could not bring himself to give his sister the fragments of information he had received.

Otherwise, as Arno said dryly, the French seemed to feel secure behind their "unbreachable Maginot Line." And the Nazis were in no hurry to attack it, having perhaps their own plans, he added cryptically.

"Such as?" Eva prompted anxiously.

"Well, Belgium, next door to France, doesn't *have* a Maginot Line, right? And once you're in Belgium, all roads lead to Paris."

"But you can't just march into a neutral country! It's international law, signed by Germany, too!"

He shrugged. "Worth no more than a scrap of paper, the

Kaiser's Chancellor said in 1914, as the German army marched into Belgium."

"Stop it, Arno!" Eva cried, clapping her hands over her ears. Sabine was in neutral Holland: at least there still was mail from there! And Grandmother had just confided to Eva's mother that there would "soon be a new arrival in the Hartog family," as she had delicately put it for Eva's ears. It was the first time in months that Eva had seen her smile. Grandfather was failing; he had never regained his health since the cold November night when he had fled from his nocturnal visitors.

Her parents had phoned Amsterdam to congratulate Sabine and Jozeph, and Eva had heard her father ask if Jozeph was making plans "for some travel south, considering the shift in the weather." But Jozeph had laughed his good-natured laugh, her father said afterward, and told him that the weather was beautiful where they were and where his family had been for three hundred years—and he and *his* would be fine, even if there *should* be some clouds on the horizon for a while . . .

His answer had soothed Eva's fears for Sabine and for the baby soon to be born into a perilous world. Now she was angry at Arno for making her face fear again. Until he held her close, and told her that he was sorry he'd upset her. Just then her mother's quick steps came down the hall and they flew apart guiltily, burying their flushed faces in the English grammar Eva was studying for Dr. Tiefental's weekly test.

■

In midwinter, soon after Sabine called home to tell her parents that she was "beginning to feel life," Grandfather died in his sleep. Only a remnant of mostly older people still in Ettingen attended his funeral, and of his four children only his eldest daughter could be there with her family to join in the Kaddish. Eva remembered her walks with Grandfather, her hand in the cool hollow of his palm; his looming presence at the head of the Seder table, his brooding patriarch's eyes. At the end of the week of mourning, Eva's parents urged Grandmother to give up the old house with its vast, echoing rooms and move in with them in Thalstadt; and Grandmother, gazing through the frosted panes into her little garden, nodded a tentative yes. But later that evening, there was another call from Amsterdam: Jozeph, announcing that he was able to arrange for a visitors' visa for his wife's mother, to be at Sabine's side during her pregnancy and confinement and for the first year of the baby's life—with Sabine interrupting tearfully to plead with her mother to come.

Not long after, Eva and her mother took Grandmother to the train station in Thalstadt, and Eva stood on the platform once more to wave her handkerchief at the departing train. "When will we see each other again, daughter?" Grandmother had whispered the last moment at the window, as the wheels slowly began to roll. And Eva's mother, her arm around Eva, had called back softly, "You stay well, Mama—and take good care of Sabine and her baby . . ."

And then the train was gone.

■

In April, the *Sitzkrieg*, as the Thalstadt papers called it, abruptly came to an end when German forces struck again, invading Norway and Denmark by land, sea, and air. It seemed only a matter of time before they would strike next.

A month later, just before Nazi armies thrust across the borders of neutral Holland and Belgium, Eva's mother frantically tried to put through what she feared might be a last call to Sabine—and reached Jozeph as soon as the operator had made the connection! "I've just come in from the hospital, Martha," Eva, her ear close to the receiver, heard him say in his booming voice. "Sabine is fine and we have a beautiful little girl—named Simone, after her Grandfather Simon, of course! Mother is still at the hospital with the two ladies, but I rushed back to give you the good news!"

"Mazel tov!" Eva's mother called out in relief, tears rolling down her cheeks. Eva's father came to the phone, too, wondering anxiously if there might still be a way for Jozeph to take his family "south."

"Some people are trying just that, Jonas—but how can I move Sabine and the baby at this time?" Jozeph said, his voice suddenly faltering. "But all is not over yet!" he went on resolutely. "And we Hartogs have reliable friends in Amsterdam and the countryside. Whatever happens, we'll be all right!"

Eva reached for the receiver to send her love to Sabine and Grandmother, but there was only the crackle of static and the intangible sense of distance rushing past her ear. The connection was broken.

Three days later, the Germans unleashed a terror bombing on Rotterdam to force the overwhelmed Dutch Army into surrender and turn the land "that has been a place of refuge to many over the centuries," as Rabbi Gideon had said at Sabine's wedding, into Nazi-occupied territory.

■

Late in May, just before their quota numbers came up at the American Consulate, Eva's parents told her over her favorite ersatz dessert during Friday night dinner that she must go to the consulate alone. It was her father's illness, they explained in careful, reasonable voices: it was the consulate's policy not to separate families who applied for immigration; if one member was turned down because ill health might make him a "burden on the state," the others were refused visas as well. Because of the possibility—even the likelihood—that her father would not receive his visa, they went on in the same carefully detached tone, gazing at her intently over their scantily filled glasses of rationed wine, they did not dare jeopardize Eva's chances to immigrate. They had decided to wait for now, let Eva go ahead without them. Perhaps later, when she was safely in America . . .

She was so stunned, so overcome, she could hardly speak.

"How can you be so sure of this? It's only a rumor—like all the other things people 'know' . . ."

"There have been several such cases, Eva, unfortunately," her father said quietly. "You know the Bamberger girls, Trude and Liesl . . ."

She did, of course. Everybody knew Liesl, the red-haired younger sister, a small, solidly built girl, one of the best athletes on the Maccabi girls' team. Then there was Liesl's sister, Trude, whose lips were always blue as if she had perpetual chills, and who could not take part in sports at all.

"You know that Trude has a heart condition, Eva—she's had it from birth," her mother said softly. "And now, you see—Trude didn't pass her physical at the consulate—and all four Bambergers were turned down."

"Well, I'm not going without you!" Eva cried in a choked voice. "I'm sorry the Bambergers didn't get visas—but that's just *one* case! It doesn't mean—"

"I wish that were so, Eva," her father said. "But there are others. Herr Fromm, who used to run the pharmacy on Bahnhofstrasse . . ."

Herr Fromm, a large-faced man whose dark-rimmed glasses emphasized the somber look of his heavy eyes, came by sometimes to visit her father and to exchange bleak comments about the times. Herr Fromm had a pretty blond wife and twin sons, of whom he always spoke admiringly with his slow, melancholy smile. "My Manfred and my Peter," he would begin, telling of some childish prank they had played on him, or of some artwork they were doing at kindergarten. In time, Eva began to realize that only Manfred could have been doing any of the things their father spoke of with such aching love and pride. For though the twins, with their father's dark eyes and their mother's soft blond hair, looked so much alike it was difficult to tell them apart at first glance, they were not identical. Peter was retarded. He would never be able to take care of himself, she had heard Herr Fromm say to her parents one evening, adding how worried they were already, he and his wife, about the time when they would no longer be "there" for him.

"Peter was denied a visa yesterday," her father said sadly. And that meant that his brother and parents were turned down as well, her mother added with a sigh: that was the policy.

"His parents wouldn't have left without Peter, anyhow," Eva cried. "They should have let *all* of them go—the Fromms and the Bambergers—they would have found a way so no one would become a 'burden on the State.' Just as *we* will!

"I'm not going alone!" she said fiercely, as they looked down on their plates without meeting her eyes. "We'll go to the consulate together and get our visas. Maybe they won't even find out that Father is sick," she added hopefully.

"You know there are medical records to bring, Eva," her mother said, shaking her head. "And a physical examination to pass, you know all that." Her voice faltered. "This may be your very last chance, Eva, please! Who can tell what's ahead of us yet—you're too young to . . ."

". . . live on my own in a strange country, yes, worrying about you two!"

"You may be able to do more for us from there than we can do from here, Eva," her father said quietly. "And whatever happens, we will feel better once you are safe. I could not bear seeing harm come to you because of my illness—"

"But you are asking the same thing of *me*, don't you see! You're asking me to run out on you, desert you . . ."

Her father took off his pince-nez and rubbed his eyes.

"I keep thinking of the Kyber story you recited in Dr. Brachmann's class, Eva. The small bird waiting for the door of his cage to open just once—to let him fly beyond the blue mountains . . ."

She shrugged. " 'The Great Moment,' " she said indifferently, through the wad of tears squeezing her throat. It was a long time ago—when she was still in school. Before the night of smashed windows, shattered lives . . .

Her father nodded. "But when that moment came, he found that he could no longer fly," he said softly, groping for the lines she had rehearsed with him endlessly that spring two years ago. " 'Had the wings withered in the long years behind the bars . . . ?' " He paused and looked at her questioningly, waiting for her to continue.

" '. . . or was it something else that had withered inside him . . . ?' " she went on for him, in her thick, tear-choked voice.

Her father reached for her hand.

"Don't be that caged bird, Eva! Don't let fear fetter your wings—not even love. Let love set you *free*—for us, for you. For *life*, Eva," he added, and with his fine-boned hand lifted his wineglass from the white linen cloth and held it out toward her. "L'chayim!"

"L'chayim!" her mother said, so softly it barely hid the tremor in her voice, and gently closed Eva's fingers around the stem of her glass. "To life!"

Over the dark red pool of wine in their raised glasses, her parents gazed at her with eyes filled with love, pain, and expectancy, waiting for her decision.

"L'chayim," she whispered at last, looking from one to the other with brimming eyes.

It was a pledge of some kind, she knew. One she would need to redeem all the years of her life.

NINETEEN JUNE 1940

To carry an American visa stamped into one's passport, as Eva now did, was in the late spring of 1940 in Germany nothing less than a miracle. But in this wartime spring-into-summer, a second miracle was needed: a way of leaving Germany and reaching the United States. The war had put an end to transatlantic travel from the ports of Northern Europe. Only Genoa remained a last possibility; and Eva's parents were at the Italian travel agency on Ulrichstrasse to buy her ticket when Mussolini—not to be outdone by his Axis partner, Hitler—belatedly declared war on France. The ship leaving Genoa that morning, the man at the ticket window told her mother sympathetically, would be the last to cross the Atlantic "for the duration."

Looking out from her window over Wielandplatz, where the flags of imminent victory over France already fluttered in the breeze, Eva nonetheless felt a weight lifting from her heart: she wouldn't have to leave her parents, after all, wouldn't have to part from Arno, to brave the scary unknown world on her own. But a smaller yet insistent voice spoke up in her as well: now she would never see the *Freiheitsstatue* in the harbor of New York: the Statue of Liberty with the torch held high, which friends had described almost reverently on their picture postcards, because the torch stood for freedom, and that mighty maternal figure for at least a *promise* of justice and equality. In a land to which Eva might yet have brought her parents, too, if only she had found a way to reach it.

Her parents, clinging to a last shred of hope, conferred with Herr Rothschild, a onetime travel agent who now was advising desperate emigrants on the ever-dwindling routes of exit, with the help of an outsize map spread against the peeling wall of his "office" at the Community House. It was to this map that Herr Rothschild was pointing with a long and practiced ruler one afternoon to explain to Eva and her parents "something that might be of interest to them all."

The Russians, he began, who had so shockingly signed a Nonaggression Pact with Nazi Germany last year, were willing to let small groups of refugees pass through their country on the way to Japan and places beyond to which they had visas. Eva could join the next refugee transport put together by the Jewish Aid Committee in Berlin. His ruler traced the route: Berlin to Moscow, via Lithuania and Latvia; from Moscow by the Trans-Siberian Railroad clear across Russia and Central Asia to Manchouli, a mere dot on the border of Manchuria. (Renamed Manchukuo by its current Japanese masters, he added under his breath, in case their own "masters," Japan's Axis partners, were listening in.) Eva's head swam, but the ruler swept on: through Manchukuo, via the old Manchurian city of Harbin—through "scenic Korea" to its southern port city Pusan; by boat across the Korea Strait to Japan, and by train to Kobe. There they would be sheltered by the Jewish community, themselves immigrants from Russia, for perhaps a week. As soon as their ship was ready (the *Yawata Maru*, a sleek white boat on its maiden voyage), the refugees would sail from Yokohama across the Pacific to an American West Coast city called Seattle. "From there you'll go by bus or train to New York, Eva," her father said reassuringly. "Where Celia will put you up until you find your first American 'job.'" And noting her look of panic at the thought of this impossible journey, he added quickly, "You'll simply travel east instead of west to reach America—and see a lot of interesting things on the way." (She who had never been farther from home than to Lake Constance or the Black Forest!)

Her mother, looking up from a murmured conversation with Herr Rothschild, nodded eagerly: she herself would be able to go to the consulates in Berlin beforehand to get Eva's passport stamped with all the transit visas needed, except the Russian. "That one you'll have to get in person just before you leave from Berlin toward the end of July, Eva. I'll come with you to the consulate, of course," she added hastily. "Meanwhile Herr Rothschild will make all the arrangements with the Jewish Aid Committee in Berlin to get you on the transport."

It was all settled then; her parents had seized the chance without hesitation. They shook Herr Rothschild's hand in a mute gesture of thanks, admonished Eva to do the same, and made her precede them down the narrow dark staircase into the blindingly sun-flooded street.

A few days later, the German Army—having outflanked Belgian and French forces and put France's British ally to flight across the Channel at Dunkirk—marched into Paris.

■

While her mother was in Berlin to obtain the transit visas, Eva's father stood shakily but staunchly in the long lines at a string of government offices with her. From each of these she required an *Unbedenklichkeitserklärung*—a document confirming that her emigration complied with their regulations and that her parents were paying her *Reichsfluchtsteuer,* a crushing "tax" imposed on all those forced to flee the Reich for their lives.

The last of her clearances had to be obtained from the Gestapo itself, and Herr Rothschild had told Eva with a regretful shrug that "the applicant" must appear unaccompanied at its headquarters on Theodorastrasse. It was a building Eva had passed hundreds of times, unremarkable in itself yet emanating a sense of dread as if the smooth gray stones were stifling the cries of those who had been interrogated behind them or left their names scratched on the cellar walls in final witness.

Yet once her legs had carried her past the entrance, the ordinariness of the ground-floor office, with its rows of desks and clacking typewriters overseen by an outsized framed photograph of the Führer, seemed little different from those of the other government agencies she had been to. Someone took her completed application and motioned to have Eva follow her to one of the cubicles in the back of the room. There a Gestapo official, silver swastika pin in the lapel of his gray suit, impassively glanced over the form and without wasting a look in her direction put his signature to it. It was not so much hatred or contempt she sensed in his attitude as utter indifference. As if he were dispatching a piece of baggage toward its destination, or a case of nails.

Then he leaned back in his chair, lit a cigarette, reached for the *N.S. Banner,* and with a tilt of his chin motioned to her to pick up the signed paper and get out.

■

She called her father from the nearest phone booth to give him her news. Arno was sitting on the window seat halfway up the staircase when she came back. He'd spent some time in Weissendorf, and she scrambled into the spot next to him, trading hugs. He had already learned her news. "Your father told me. I rang the bell just now and he said your mother had phoned from Berlin since your call. She got all your visas!"

He kissed her cheek lightly. "So you'll be leaving soon!" he said in a tone to match his kiss. "The next chapter of your life will be *Eva in Amerika!*"

She did not return his smile. There was no rejoicing about leaving, the way things stood.

"And *you*, Arno? What will *your* life be like here? And mine *there*—without you?" They had talked little about it before; it hurt too much.

He shook his head. "I'll be leaving, too, Eva. I didn't want to tell you until you had all your papers."

It was wonderful, unbelievable news!

"You're leaving, Arno?! Where to? With your father?" He had always made it clear that he could not run out on his father, left on his own inside the walls of the sanatorium.

He put a silencing finger to his lips and scanned the stairwell, listening for footsteps. It was Gertrud, the drab, aging daughter of the Haeberles upstairs, of whom they were most wary when they sat talking on their window seat. Gertrud, who back in the time of the Republic used to hanker after the old, "romantic" days under the monarchy, as irretrievably lost as Gertrud's faded youth. But the Nazis had provided an ersatz kind of glory. Gertrud had become a block warden, passing down the regulations and, people suspected, reporting back on her neighbors on Wielandplatz. She was given a uniform and put in charge of firefighting equipment in case of air raids. Though her family had lived in Grandfather's house all her life, she no longer rang the Bentheims' bell, or even acknowledged their presence when they met in the hallway. The Nazis had many ways of ensnaring souls in their net: a step up the ladder at the factory; a posh position and the apartment to go with it; being allowed to carry the flag as one's HJ troop marched singing down the road. A scrap of authority and an ill-fitting uniform over her shapeless body had done it for Gertrud.

But all was quiet on the stairs for now. Arno stuck his hand inside his light jacket and brought out a folded piece of paper. He spread it apart and smoothed it out against the top of the window seat. On it, as Eva could tell at a glance, was a drawing by Alex Valtary. A black-and-white pencil sketch, not an oil painting in vivid colors and shapes, like the half-finished one Eva had seen in his room. In this picture, done in large strokes conveying urgency and haste, children were being herded toward a waiting truck. Children with sightless eyes or gaping mouths, children with stunted feet, hobbling on crutches or strapped into wheelchairs. Children crying in mute accusation as they were put on the truck by their guards: men and women in white uniforms and with the set faces and mechanical motions of robots. Children screaming some unheard but piercingly felt cry of pain or terror: sick children, stricken in body or mind, but children no less, holding up their small hands beseechingly, thrusting their arms out toward the beholder in a last plea for succor, for pity, for rescue, for love.

Eva, shaken, wanted to thrust out her own hand to ward off the terrifying spell of the drawing.

"Who *are* these children, Arno?" she whispered.

Arno refolded the paper and slipped it back into his pocket.

"Alex saw them from the pantry in back of the sanatorium, where the cook took him secretly one evening last week. The cook is a half-mute himself, you know—can barely make himself understood. But Alex made out that these children were being taken away, to a 'home in the mountains.' " He bit his lip.

"And *there*?" Eva whispered.

" 'Kaputt . . .' the cook stammered out, and burst into sobs. Führer's orders—no useless mouths to feed in wartime." Arno shrugged. "That and, I suppose, simply the Nazi view of 'inferior beings' not having the right to live. Life unworthy of living, I think they call it."

She thought of the parents who had placed their children in care for healing, for whatever could be done for them—not death. "My Manfred and my Peter," Herr Fromm had said, loving one as much as the other—without condition.

Arno took her hand. "Alex wants me to get the picture across the border—to where it can sound the alarm before more innocents are killed. If they can do this to their 'own' children—sick *German* children, 'Aryan' children—they'll do it to *other* children, sick or well."

She nodded. "But where will you *go*? How will you get out?"

"Before Zeller left, he showed me a pass on a detailed map where I can get over the green border and be helped by a friend of his on the Swiss side. Zeller and his wife would gladly put me up in Zurich—even without official permission! But I must get to the South of France, before the 'Unoccupied Zone' gets flooded with Gestapo agents. There are rumors of a small band of Americans helping refugee writers and artists trapped near Marseilles to escape across the Pyrenees through Spain and Portugal, for emergency rescue in the United States—"

"Then you'll try to get your father there? And go with him to America?"

"Alex won't leave, Eva—even if I could get him out of Weissendorf and across the border. He says there are many kinds of soldiers in this war and *his* battlefield is a white rectangle of paper. That he has to stay at his post until there is nothing left to be drawn.

"And I won't leave Europe without him," Arno added. "I'll search for those Americans and hand them my father's drawing to 'alert the world,' as Alex wants me to. I'm not sure I have as much faith in the power of art to persuade and transform. But it's *his* decision, and if his message might speed the allied invasion and save even one child one day sooner, I have to try."

"And then . . . ?" Eva asked, fearful for him.

"Then I'll find the French Resistance and become *their* kind of soldier for a while! Don't look so scared, Eva—I'm lucky I had a Jewish mother, or the Nazis would have made me fight *their* war against you and your parents. Against the children on that drawing and those in Warsaw and Rotterdam."

He tried for a smile. "Instead I may be able to fight my way back here and bring Alex home and tell him that his drawing has helped to carry victory and humanity to the world."

"Are you sure you'll still find him there, Arno?" Eva asked softly.

His eyes clouded. "I've pleaded with him to let me try to take him along with me: clearly the 'mercy killing' of the *children* is only the beginning. But Alex insists it's too dangerous for me to do. He thinks Hans Valtary will shield him from the worst—that he is an opportunist, probably a thief, but that he has no stomach for murder, his brother's murder." He swallowed hard. "Sometimes I wonder if smuggling the drawing out of the country is partly my father's way of getting me to leave Germany."

He drew a deep breath and pulled her into his arms, his eyes meeting hers with the old tender, caring gaze of his.

"Someday the war will be over and I'll come and look for you in America!"

"And *then* . . . ?" She felt as if all the improbable things he had told her were no more than a dream—and the most improbable was its happy ending.

"Then we'll be old enough to decide."

"Decide . . . ?"

"What to do with our lives. I think I'll go to Budapest and find out more about my mother's family: my aunt who taught the violin, my grandfather the cantor. Alex spoke to me about them; it will be the homecoming my mother never had—and a beginning for *me*." He pressed her hand. "For *us*, Eva. With Alex safe after the war, I can become who I've always *known* myself to be—without having to watch my step for his sake. And I'll work on my music again . . ."

". . . and give concerts at Carnegie Hall and marry me!"

He smiled. "Of course. If you haven't fallen in love with an American by then!"

"I won't, Arno. Could *you* fall in love with someone?"

He shook his head. "But I already did, don't you know? Love in time of war. *J'attendrai*—remember?"

He tilted her face to kiss her and she clung to him, the peppermint scent of his breath mingling with the taste of her tears.

Then she let him lift her from the window seat and slowly take her to her door; she followed him with her eyes as he quickly walked down the stairs and into the street.

■

Several things happened over the next few days. Her mother came back, exhausted from her rounds of foreign consulates in the Berlin heat, and returned Eva's passport stamped with the five transit visas to her as proudly as if they were trophies. A few days later, Eva noticed a white envelope that had been slipped under their door. As once before, there was no name or return address on the envelope, and when she hastily tore it open, a small sheet of paper fluttered into her palm: a watercolor painting of delicately drawn light blue flowers. Forget-me-nots . . . Her eyes welled up: could Renate have sensed that Eva was about to leave Thalstadt?

The next day, her father wordlessly passed the *Mittagsblatt* to her and pointed to a notice on one of the back pages. The once very popular Pastor R. in one of the southern suburbs, she read, had taken it upon himself to question government policy regarding the racial health and strength of the nation by citing Scripture in a recent sermon, "Suffer the little children to come unto me . . . ." The pastor had been dismissed and warned that any further offense would lead to his incarceration and to *Sippenhaft* for his family.

It was the first time Eva had come across the term "detention of kin" in the Nazi vocabulary. A chilling new concept: holding family members hostage to someone's act of conscience, of courage. And the threat of prison it spelled now hung over Renate—over all the Reinhardts.

■

"You'll find her greatly changed," her father warned Eva when she told him she was going to see his sister to say goodbye. Aunt Hanni hadn't been over in weeks. "Stefan might call," she'd say when they phoned. "I'm waiting to hear from Stefan—I must get off the line!"

They'd shake their heads. With the fall of Paris and the German occupation of much of France, it was unlikely that Stefan would risk calling attention to his whereabouts—if indeed he wasn't already in a French internment camp.

On a sudden impulse, Eva took her old roller skates out of the closet, to clatter down the alley on them as she used to years ago when visiting her aunt. Later she had gone on her blue-and-silver bicycle—her "reward" for having her tonsils out—learning to steer through the traffic on Hauptstrasse, letting the brisk wind ruffle her hair. Until one late afternoon when boys had suddenly darted around the corner of the alley just doors from her own, seized the bicycle's handlebars, and pushed her to the cobblestones. Her knees bleeding, she'd sobbed out her story to her mother—except for the names they had called her. What good would it have done to tell? No court would have sided against them on behalf of a Jewish girl. Nor did she ask her parents for a new bicycle. She didn't want so much as to *look* at another one, and their powerlessness to protect her must have weighed as heavily on her parents. Then Arno had come into her life, and their long walks together had helped her break free of the memory.

■

It took barely a moment for the apartment door to open when Eva rang. Aunt Hanni stood on the threshold, her face expectantly tilted up. "Ah, it's you, Eva," she said absently. "Excuse me, my phone is ringing!" Leaving the door ajar, she hurried back into the apartment without asking Eva to step inside.

She did so anyway, following her aunt into the living room with the green plush sofa and letting herself sink into its billowing cushions. At the small table with the telephone, Aunt Hanni was calling into the receiver, "Hanna Strauss here—is anyone *there*? Stefan?" Her hair was no longer well coiffed and white but hung in yellowing strands, and the bows of her high-heeled shoes were flecked with dust, like the frames of the family photos on the mauve wallpaper. Even the fur of Hexie, the calico cat resting next to Eva on the cushion, seemed to have lost its sheen. Aunt Hanni hung up and asked Eva if she hadn't heard the ring. Eva, who had not, managed a noncommittal shrug.

Aunt Hanni sat down beside Eva and halfheartedly offered her something cold to drink, her mind elsewhere. "What's *happened* to the boy?" she whispered. "Does he have a roof over his head? Even enough to eat?"

Eva, not knowing what to say, smoothed Hexie's fur. "I've come to say goodbye, Aunt Hanni," she said after a while. "Mother is taking me to Berlin next week and . . ."

Aunt Hanni nodded. "Your father told me on the phone, Eva. I'll miss your visits, but I'm glad for you. Do you know that I'll be staying with your father until your mother returns?" She took a deep breath. "And next month I'll be moving in with your parents permanently—as permanent as anything can be these days! Jews are no longer permitted in 'Aryan' houses, did you know?" Her glance lingered on her polished mahogany chairs—the corner desk where she had done French translations to "keep her independence"—the miniature ivory furniture in the alcove that Eva had been allowed to play with, gingerly, as a special treat. "I have to leave here, Eva, and find space with a Jewish family. I'm fortunate that your parents can take me in."

Aunt Hanni rose and reached for a book on the shelf above her desk.

"It's a gift for you, Eva—from Stefan, one of the last Jewish books published in Germany, by Jacob Picard. Stefan sent it from Paris just before the war broke out, and I want you to have it now, to take on your journey."

Eva was already leafing through the pages of the linen-bound book. A collection of stories, each with an inviting title of its own. From Stefan!

"It came with his last letter, Eva—I've read it so often I almost know it by heart. 'Eva will love these elegiac tales about village Jews in a corner of southwest Germany in the last century. Rural Jews as devout as those in the shtetls of Eastern Europe, speaking the regional dialects, yet versed, as well, in the holy tongue of their country synagogues—at home in their landscape, among Gentile neighbors who respected their customs and faith. A brief interval, perhaps in part only imagined, on the dark road of our history.' "

Aunt Hanni dabbed at her eyes. " 'Tell Eva to read this book,'

Stefan wrote in closing. 'Eva and the other young people growing up in a world that defames them and their heritage. It will help them affirm their dignity as human beings, as Jews—and yes, as Jews of Germany, last leaves on the old tree.' "

"Thank you, Aunt Hanni," Eva said in a whisper, not trusting her voice, hugging the small woman close to her. But suddenly the diminutive body stiffened against her. "Did you hear the *phone*? Excuse me, Eva!" Aunt Hanni jumped to her feet and lunged for the mute receiver. "Hanna Strauss here—is anyone *there*? Stefan . . . ?"

Eva, waved away by Aunt Hanni from where she stood rooted by the telephone, picked up her skates with trembling hands and walked shakily down the stairs, carrying Stefan's book with her into the late sunlight.

■

At dusk the next evening, Eva's parents had a visitor of their own. Her mother answered the doorbell, her voice instantly apprehensive. "Lisbeth—come in! Is anything wrong at home?"

"Herr Gerber's daughter is here to see you, Jonas," she called out, leading the young woman into the living room.

Eva's father rose from his chair and Lisbeth took his hand in hers, struggling for speech. "My father won't be here for the chess game this week, Herr Bentheim. He was arrested again, sent to Mauthausen this time . . ."

"*Mauthausen* . . ." Eva's father gasped. "Gerber—in Mauthausen?" The very name of the camp struck terror, even in Eva's ears.

"It's because they're extending the war, Herr Bentheim. They don't want anyone around who might 'stir up the populace,' as they call it, against the war. But my father is strong—my mother and I have hopes he'll survive."

Lisbeth drew a small object from her pocket. A hand-carved chessman, still not quite finished. "For the game when it's all over with the Nazis, my father said. Tell Bentheim to hold on to his king. No checkmate!"

They shook hands in silence, beyond speaking or tears. Then Eva's mother led the visitor to the door and they embraced briefly. "You hold on, too, Frau Bentheim," Lisbeth said. And with a nod for Eva: "My father's thoughts are with all of you—for good reason."

"And ours with him," Eva's mother said with a sigh, as Lisbeth closed the door behind her.

■

Among the things that remained to be done was a last visit with Anna. She had not come to see them for a long time; with Gertrud's sharp block-warden eyes keeping close watch on everyone's comings and goings, it was better that Anna not be seen entering their door. But she had insisted that Eva's mother stop by her little store as often as possible to bring her news of the family; and on those occasions Anna never let her leave without a precious pat of butter or a tiny bag of coffee beans hidden beneath the carrots or potatoes her mother's Jewish ration book would allow. At first Eva's mother had protested: what if they were found out? The very least that would happen to Anna was that the Nazis would close her store.

But Anna would not listen. "It's the only thing I can do for you now, Frau Bentheim, and you mustn't stop me from doing it," she said, and said it so firmly, so insistently, as if much more were involved than a scarce item of food. And perhaps to Anna it was; perhaps for her what was involved was even more than a gesture of kindness to those who had been kind to her. Perhaps what she had to do was to make a chink, however feeble, however minuscule, in a seemingly impenetrable armor.

It was of this and many other things that Eva thought as she was walking toward Anna's house that late June afternoon, with the heat of the passing day beating up from the pavement. She walked slowly, as one does at the end of a sultry summer afternoon, on a walk that was also a leave-taking. Shops and offices were beginning to close, and at the streetcar stops, workers in small silent knots were waiting for their ride home after an exhausting day's labor. They were older men, for the most part: the young ones no longer ran machines in Thalstadt; those who had once duped them with the promise of work and bread had found bloodier uses for their hands. On the tower of the City Hall the Nazi flag hung limply in the listless air, running red as if liquefied. There was a languor, too, it seemed to Eva, in the passing faces—a furtive wariness, as if the lull in the giddying succession of easy victories had given them pause to think. But perhaps it was only the heat.

A little farther out, the linden trees still spread their pristine green over the dusty streets, fragrant of other summers, granting shade. There was the house where Thea had lived, and the steep, wooded patch behind it where they had often played and talked before that chilly October morning when Eva had looked in vain for her in the deserted garden. No word had come from Thea since the invasion of Poland, and now it seemed hardly more than a dream that they had ever walked these streets with their arms around each other and with their schoolgirl secrets and childish hopes, the sun on their faces and death a stranger nobody knew . . .

■

Eva waited across the street from Karl and Anna's store until she saw Anna draw the shades at the narrow windows flanking the entrance steps. The door, just below street level, flew open under her merest touch, as if it had been waiting for her to arrive. Anna was sorting apples into a shallow bin and called back over her shoulder at the sound of the door, "We're just closing."

"It's *me*, Anna."

Anna turned around quickly and drew her inside.

"Eva—so late?" She scanned her face anxiously. "Has anything happened to you—or at home?"

"I've come to say goodbye, Anna. I wanted to wait until everyone was gone."

Anna nodded and absently began to polish an apple against her apron, turning it round and round until it shone. It lay in her hand, a small, perfect globe.

"I've never liked to *peel* an apple," Anna said, twirling the stem slowly between her fingers in the dim light. "It always seemed wasteful, sinful almost, to tamper with something so beautiful and whole."

She placed the fruit in Eva's hand and pulled a piece of sackcloth over the bin.

"Come upstairs for a little while, Eva. Karl left for work just before you came—he'll be sorry he missed you. But let's sit down for a cup of tea together and talk."

Eva followed Anna up the few steps to the little apartment

in back of the store. In the kitchen, already tidied and closed down for the night, Anna opened the window to the evening air and drew up a chair for Eva at the table. When she had brewed the tea, she brought the pot to the table and sat down.

It was cool in Anna's shaded kitchen—or perhaps the temperature had dropped quite steeply, for children were pouring into the alley beyond the window for a late game of hopscotch or ball. Their voices rang in the dusk.

"Maybe you'd rather have had a *cold* drink, Eva—a little sweet cider, or ice water with raspberry syrup?" Anna said, stirring her tea. "But, you know, a warm drink is better for your stomach in hot weather, and . . . I once heard that . . . in the tropics—the English—and they ought to know . . ."

Her spoon clinked against the saucer.

"*Ach*, Eva, why did it all happen? How could we *let* it happen?"

Eva looked at the tiles that covered the kitchen floor. If one saw the black tiles from a particular angle, they formed a pattern of diamonds against a white ground; from another, they made up a checkerboard. And yet it was the same design, either way. The difference was in the looking. Anna had never learned to look at the world upside down, as everyone else had. She had never learned that although Eva was the same person she had always been, she was to be hated and despised.

"We had a house full of children, back home in the village," Anna said with a catch in her voice. "I was the oldest, and I often chafed at the mothering I had to do of those little ones—the noses that needed blowing and the skinned knees that had to be scrubbed. But you know, Eva, I missed them later, when I came to live in Thalstadt. If it hadn't been for you, I would have been really homesick, I guess. But there you were: someone to look after, to scold and to fuss over—though I'm afraid I was always stronger on the scolding, eh?"

"And I deserved every bit of it," Eva said, magnanimously from the vantage point of her teenage years. It seemed a long time ago.

"You were a *child*," Anna said, almost angrily, as if children were inviolate, or ought to be, simply for being children.

Outside, the children were bouncing their ball against the house. It made a sharp thud as it glanced off the wall, and the sound reverberated in Eva's heart. Once she, too, had played the game—with Uschi, with Renate. But now, in a world filled with the crash of guns and bombs, the sound of a ball had no meaning except one of accusation.

The children's voices echoed in the yard. "Polen—Dänemark—Norwegen . . ."

You picked the name of a country and when its name was called, it was your turn to run forward and try to catch the ball.

"Holland—Belgien—Luxemburg . . ." Their childhood game had become a roll call of Hitler's invasions.

Anna hung her head. "A woman next door, Eva—her son was thrown into the KZ—another soldier had seen him pass a crust of bread to a homeless boy somewhere in Poland. And in France—Karl heard at work that we're shooting *schoolchildren* for refusing to tell on their parents!

"They say it's the *Nazis*, those who will talk about such things at all. But the sin is on *us*, I tell them, on *all* of us, because we let it happen long ago, right here—because we didn't speak up when the *first* children were made to suffer, in Thalstadt . . ."

Eva reached for her hand. "I must go, Anna. I have to get home before the blackout, or Mother worries."

Anna rose tiredly. "How will they bear your leaving them, your mother and father? And you them?"

"They want me to live, Anna. I want to bring them out." Her voice sounded flat to her ears, as if she were reciting by rote. It was what her parents had told her, over and over.

Anna nodded. "Your mother says that it's the only way. She's very proud of you for being so brave—and I am, too. Do you know that I once thought of going to America myself, Eva—but then I got scared . . ."

"You didn't *have* to go, Anna. When you *have* to, you're too scared to be scared." She tried to say it flippantly, flinging it over her shoulder on her way to the door, but Anna would not play.

"There is something you must tell your parents for me, Eva," she said in a suddenly changed voice, her hand fingering the doorknob. "I don't like to worry you, Eva—and maybe it's no more than a rumor. But I want you to know that whatever happens, as long as Karl and I have a scrap of food, your parents . . ."

"What *is* it, Anna?" Eva cried, trying to read Anna's angry eyes, the steely tone in her voice.

Anna drew a deep breath. "From what we hear around the market, Eva—from some who're in with the Nazi big shots—the stores in town won't be allowed to serve Jewish customers much longer. They'll have to go to some out-of-the-way little hole-in-the-wall to shop for their bit of food, whatever their rations will allow." She managed a wry smile. "Karl and I figure stores don't come much smaller and out of the way than our place here—and with a bit of grease in the right palm at the right time, huh, Eva . . . ?"

She gave a brisk tap to Eva's shoulder, and for the ghost of a moment, there was her old, quick laugh.

"It's *one* way to get away from hearing Heil Hitler in the store all day, isn't it?"

Eva looked up at her, at the strong, still-handsome face, with the dark blond hair still braided tightly and coiled above her ears.

"You are so good, Anna . . ." It had suddenly become easy to say it, to her who had never uttered professions of love or expected to receive them. It was as if the small kitchen were lifted out of the boundaries of the shadowed streets and yards, as if the two of them were quite alone in a world of their own making—a world without guilt and therefore without shame.

Anna shrugged. "*Good*, Eva? For doing no more than is written for us in the Bible—the Jewish Bible, the old village teacher back home would remind us: to treat your neighbors as you would have them treat yourself?" She shook her head. "And we were *nearer* than neighbors, Eva, remember? I lived with you, broke bread with you, saw your family up closer than anyone else did in all of Germany, in sickness and in health . . ." She turned away and roughly wiped her eyes with the corner of her apron.

They walked down the few steps to the store. In the near darkness, passing the bin covered with sackcloth, Eva suddenly felt her mother's presence in the shadows, wearing her plain brown coat and carrying the familiar mesh shopping bag she used to take to the market when Eva was small. But when Eva looked closer, she saw that it hung empty.

Eva felt her heart contract. How could she leave her parents? What would happen to them? What should she *do*?

"Anna . . ."

"You're doing the right thing, Eva. It's what your parents *want*, for you and for themselves."

"*Auf Wiedersehen*, Anna. I'll never forget you—never."

She wanted to say, Thank you for looking after my parents when I'm gone, for promising you'll *try* . . . But suddenly her throat closed up and a hard stone sat on her chest, squeezing her breath.

Anna folded her into her arms, as she might once have done over a quarrel with Ella, or a failed arithmetic test. And as Eva hid her face against Anna's shoulder and the stone dissolved into tears, she felt that in taking leave from Anna she was taking leave from the Germany that might have been—a realm of childhood and innocence that had turned out to be an illusion, to be remembered always with longing and pain.

TWENTY   JULY 1940

Her mother moved about the kitchen, serving a hurried breakfast to the two of them, her hands performing accustomed tasks
with gestures so leaden and yet precise she might have been
moving in her sleep. She had slipped an apron over her traveling suit and already wore her hat. They spoke little, and then
only in whispers. It was too late to put on the kitchen lamp, and
yet not quite day: in the soft shadows, the unaccustomed hush,
the kitchen had lost its workaday face, had already turned into
a memory. Every corner had that quality, at once palpable and
remote, felt only in dreams. At times, Eva almost expected
Anna's brisk steps coming down the hall or Uschi's freckled
face at the door—or Ella's familiar frown: "Eva is making us late
for school, Aunt Martha . . ." But across the table, there were
only her mother's sleep-heavy eyes, silently pleading with her to
be brave, for Eva's sake as much as for her own. The muted peal
of the City Hall chimes drifted across the rooftops, a ghost
sound in keeping with the unseen faces present in the room.
Atlantis-like, the bells tolled from a sunken world—the lost
land of her childhood that had cast her out long before this
morning when she was about to leave it forever. The sound receded into the graying dawn. It was not quite five on the old

clock in the hall, still limping behind by a few minutes, as if its slowly gliding chains were trying to hold back time . . .

Her father sat in his armchair by the window of the living room, his eyes closed. Was he asleep, or did he merely pretend sleep to himself, to ward off the moment when he would have to open his eyes and see her standing at his side, for the last time?

Seeing him like this, his frailness pitifully plain in the pale early light, Eva felt a piercing shame for her own youthful strength, her own sound body, her fierce young need to live that had turned into a kind of betrayal. For was she not betraying him, too, as his homeland, his neighbors, his faith in humankind and human kindness had betrayed him? "I won't leave without you!" she had cried out to her parents; but in the end, it was her own life she had agreed to save; in the end, she had turned out no better than those who preached that only the strong had a right to live. And as she stood, not daring to call his name, with the minutes ticking away inexorably, she was overcome by an unutterable sense of sorrow and loss, as if in leaving her father she was also denying the very essence of his life.

At last he looked up, vainly seeking to force a smile to his eyes: those keen, pensive eyes that had so often opened the world to her own. He held out his arms and she went into their frail embrace, hiding her face against the gaunt cheek with the bristle of beard stinging her lids.

"I'll do all I can!" she sobbed. "Knock at doors and plead with them and make them listen. I'll find a way . . ."

She felt his hand on her hair in its old wordless gesture of comfort.

"Yes, Eva, you will find a way. If not a way to save our lives, then a way to live your own life not for yourself alone but for us as well. You must never take your life lightly again, nor take it for granted: you must make it count. For in a sense it is our legacy to you—the only thing that is still ours to give."

He cupped her chin to make her meet his gaze. "But it is not a gift that ends in the giving. It must be gained anew each day, as a field needs to be tended to bear its fruit. It is for this that you must leave, Eva: to live so that our own lives will always be contained in yours—to be our heir and witness to a world that must never again shut its eyes to suffering and inhumanity."

Her father's hand closed about hers with surprising strength: a strength born not of resignation to death but of a vindication of life—her life and theirs. Then she laid her cheek against his shirt with its familiar scents of linen and tobacco smoke, and they both wept.

■

The waiting room at the Berlin Jewish Aid Committee was full of desperate faces. Old people sat on the crowded benches; mothers with children in their arms had dragged their chairs near the windows to catch a breeze. Men stood together in haphazardly formed groups, picking up aimless snatches of conversation—waiting, their eyes empty, ears straining to hear their families' names called out. The low, insistent ripple of voices in a medley of regional tongues—the droll Bavarian and drawled Hessian, the clipped Prussian and singsong Saxon—had an almost ceremonial quality, like the murmured Hebrew incantations in the presence of death.

It was a motley company of mourners incongruously come together in this crammed, littered place of last resort. Scholars who might once have held lofty chairs of learning at the great universities; small-town matrons in dowdy small-town suits primly buttoned over their corseted waists; cosmopolitan Jewish artists and intellectuals rubbing shoulders with the no-longer-solid Jewish burghers they had always rejected and sometimes denied; bewildered village women wearing the stiffly waved wigs of Orthodox tradition. Last hunted stragglers of the German exodus, each of them mourning a private tragedy, a shattered way of life, and yet together mourning the end of a long and honorable shared journey: the twilight of the Jews of Germany.

Her mother added Eva's name to a long list of other names. They stood and waited. Next to Eva, in the back of the room, a thin, stoop-shouldered girl carefully flattened a sheet of paper against the wall. She drew a pencil stub from the pocket of her skirt and began to write, slowly, in a slant, childish hand, her face puckered in a scowl of concentration: *"Mein lieber* Helmuth . . ."

Someone jostled her arm and her pencil scratched a jagged black line across the empty sheet. The point snapped. She dropped her hand and looked at Eva with a shrug, speaking without preliminary, as if they had known each other all their lives.

"We were going to be married, in Amsterdam." Her voice had a child's petulance, and in truth she was scarcely more than a child, with a child's angular body and unfinished face. But then it was no longer unusual for people to be married before they had quite grown up: sometimes they married for the sake of an affidavit, or to get on a quota—or perhaps simply because no one knew any longer how much time there was left to grow up and live. Eva thought of Arno, and of the last time he had held her in his arms, and of the way his eyes had looked when he said, "But I already did fall in love, Eva . . ."

The girl was saying, "He wanted to *wait* for me, in Holland, so we could all go to America together. He's caught there now—the harbor of Rotterdam is blown off the map and They won't let him come back here—it's we who'll be leaving without him!"

But you can *write* to him, at least, Eva thought with a pang of envy: you know he is alive. And she wouldn't be alone; her parents were leaving with her: the pale lady watching her with a guarded look of concern from under the brim of her hat—and the much older man beside her, his head bent over a book, impervious to the din and bustle of the room. It was something her own father might have been doing, Eva thought, biting her lip: absorb himself in a book in this most improbable of places, as if books still mattered, in spite of everything . . .

"Do you think They'll put them in camps, the way They are doing in France?" the girl said, smoothing the unwritten letter against her flat hip.

Eva looked away. Stefan might be in one of those internment camps. And Arno? Perhaps by now Arno, too. And where in occupied Holland were Grandmother and Sabine and Jozeph and their child? What could she say?

But the girl wasn't waiting for an answer. She had crumpled her letter in her hand and buried her face in the crook of her arm propped against the wall. Her thin shoulders shook.

■

Eva's mother found a seat near the door and made her sit beside her on the edge of her chair. Next to them, a baby with dusty white booties on his plump feet squirmed restlessly on his older sister's lap. The girl, no more than eight or nine, was dangling her black, ribbon-tied braids before his clenched fists, as if he were a kitten to be distracted by a dancing ball of wool. But the baby stared up at her blankly, perspiration filming his round forehead.

Eva's mother laid her hand on the little girl's arm.

"Perhaps your brother is thirsty. Mother might have a bottle for him."

"Mama is up front, talking with the lady," she answered in a small voice, without turning her head.

"Then maybe you would let me hold your brother for a while," Eva's mother said gently, stretching out her hands. "He might be a bit more comfortable here, seeing my lap is larger," she added with a smile of reassurance.

The black braids trembled.

"Bubi is tired, and so am I." With a sigh of relief, she gave up the baby and shifted her legs. "We've been on the train all night, from Cologne. And now . . ." Her voice faltered. "Our papers may not be good!" she added in a whisper, as if a secret shame attached to the admission.

"Where are you going?" Eva's mother asked soothingly. "To America, like Eva here?"

"Papa is in Shanghai. He sent us our papers long ago, but Bubi was very sick, and when he got well again, all the ports had been closed and the Committee in Cologne said we would have to go through Siberia, and now the Berlin Committee says our

Shanghai *Zertifikat* will run out before we get there and we have to go back to Cologne and start all over again getting our papers . . ."

They sat and waited. After a while, the children's mother came back and picked up her baby without a word. Someone offered her a chair at one of the windows and she sat down, holding the little boy in her arms and staring vacantly out on the sunlit street. She was waiting; waiting to be called again; waiting for some magic word of hope; waiting as everyone else in the room was waiting.

It was better to keep on waiting than to give up.

"Eva Bentheim?"

A graying, harried-looking woman scanned the room, motioned them toward her desk.

She studied the papers Eva's mother placed before her.

"Eva will travel alone, Frau Bentheim?"

Her mother nodded, as if she could not trust her voice; but her eyes hung on Eva's passport.

The interviewer pushed back the papers. "Perhaps one of the families on the transport will agree to look after the girl," she said with a shrug.

"But first," she added quickly, "first I must tell you that there has been a slight change of plans. You will have to turn back Eva's railway ticket to Moscow and get her there by plane."

Eva, who would get airsick on Thea's backyard swing and panicked at the thought of heights, felt the room whirl around her.

"By *plane!*" her mother repeated in a shaken voice. "But Eva has all her *transit* visas—look!" She snatched up the passport, fingers flying through its pages. "Lithuania, Latvia—as well as Manchukuo, Korea, and Japan!" She took a deep breath, trying to put firmness into her voice. "They told us in Thalstadt all we needed was to get the *Russian* visa and Eva could travel through all the way from Berlin to Japan!"

"They told you in *Thalstadt!*" the interviewer scoffed. "Do they have any *idea* in Thalstadt what goes on in Berlin? Did *you?*" Her arm motioned haphazardly across the room. "See for yourself: hundreds scrambling for a way out each week—Shanghai, Curaçao, the Philippines—*any*place where there is a mousehole opening up to slip into, *any*where in the world! Do you know how many we have to turn back every day—for lack of papers, or visas, or transportation! And they keep coming, by the day, by the hour, from all over Germany!"

She shook her head and quietly retrieved Eva's passport.

"The fact is that the border with Lithuania has been *closed*, Frau Bentheim. Russian troop movements, it seems—not that we're being *told*—but it's just as *well* the trains aren't running. With all that turmoil, it would be dangerous for our transports to be caught in the middle."

Her voice was flat: she must have given the same explanation a dozen times over, and expected to give it a hundred times more.

"They're all afraid of each other—the Russians of German agents, despite the pact. The Baltic states of the Russians."

She pushed back her chair and deftly steered them through the swarm of anxious, defeated faces.

"Let's hope we can get plane space for your daughter, Frau Bentheim. It's a bad time for people," she added in her dry, flat voice. "For Jews."

"Eva . . . ?" her mother said, unable to articulate her question, her despair. It was the first time either of the two women had asked her anything at all.

There was no choice, Eva knew. "It will be faster by plane, Mother," she said quickly, before the knot of fear could rise from the pit of her stomach to her voice, her eyes. "It won't be so bad."

◼

A young woman, her bright red hair incongruous in this desolate makeshift place, was holding the door for a group of people going down the stairs.

"One more for you, Inge!" The interviewer pushed Eva's papers into her hand.

She turned to look at them, the flash of a smile fading into a puzzled look.

"*One*, Frau Gaertner?"

"*One, bitte*," the interviewer said tersely, with an almost imperceptible shake of her head. "The child has to catch the Trans-Siberian in Moscow on the fifth of August. She'll need her plane ticket, Russian visa—the usual last-minute things, like the rest of your group." She glanced at her wristwatch, waved a rushed goodbye to no one in particular, and strode back to her desk.

"*Wird jemacht!*" Inge called after her in purest Berlinese. "Will do, Frau Gaertner!"

The red head bent over the paper in her hand. Briskly, as she had spoken, her neatly pointed pencil checked off a name on a long list of others.

"Bentheim, *ja?*"

Eva nodded. She walked through the door held open for her

and down the stairs with the others. Behind her, her mother's steps followed heavily. Eva did not look back; they both knew that she no longer belonged to her mother. She had become one of the others now. A name on a piece of paper, to be processed, disposed of.

A refugee.

They took the U-Bahn rushing along its subterranean route beneath the vast city. Afterward, they walked down a broad, tree-lined avenue between looming Prussian office buildings, walking in small groups of two or three, as they had been cautioned to do. Around them, on the streets and squares, surged the life of the city: men and women going to work, policemen waving on a steady stream of cars, shops opening their doors to lines of women talking animatedly about a rumored shipment of silk stockings from Paris. An ordinary morning in Berlin—not so very different from mornings in the business section of Thalstadt. Here, too, the war seemed very far away—except in the tense faces of the refugees, the feigned casualness of their walk, as they strove too strenuously to become inconspicuous, to lose themselves in the crowd. It was their eyes that gave them away, anxious, guarded—that and the way they carried their coats and jackets over their arms, despite the gathering heat: the homeless, clinging to their last possessions as to a last, tenuous shred of respectability.

Their intermittent conversation, too, strove for a token of normalcy: the sultry weather, the lumpy mattresses in the pension, a child about to lose its first milk tooth. As if by secret agreement, none spoke their real thoughts; it was easier this way.

Safer, too. "No talk of politics, visas, consulates—nothing

that will call attention to us, *meine Damen und Herren,*" Inge had instructed them before they had stepped out on the street. Now, walking between Eva and her mother, she kept up a chatty stream of conversation, innocuous and breezy as if she were conducting visitors on a sightseeing tour.

"*Na,* what do you think of Berlin, Eva? First the U-Bahn, and now all these towering buildings—they must seem sky-high compared to Thalstadt, *ja?*"

Berliners—they were all alike!

"What do you mean, compared to Thalstadt? Thalstadt isn't exactly a village, you know!"

And then they stared at one another, not knowing whether to laugh or cry.

"*Lokalpatrioten,*" Inge said dryly. "To the bitter end."

She turned to scan the street for an elderly couple who had fallen behind.

"*Ja,* I suppose one might have spent a perfectly happy life in your Thalstadt, without ever giving a thought to transit visas or the Trans-Siberian Railroad," she muttered under her breath, ignoring her own advice. "Still, as for me, I could never have lived anywhere but in Berlin!"

She caught Eva's astonished glance.

"Oh, I'm not talking about Goebbels' phony Berlin," she went on quickly. "Or Göring's garrisons—or the Gestapo dungeon on Prinz Albrecht-Strasse. But you see, I'm just old enough to remember another Berlin—Max Reinhardt's and Käthe Kollwitz's Berlin. And Claire Waldoff's: she didn't know her Berlin had died till Göring threw her into jail for singing one of her biting Berlin cabaret songs about him!"

"*Ach ja,* Claire Waldoff," Eva's mother suddenly said. Eva

wasn't aware she'd been listening; she had walked beside Inge in such silence, almost as if resenting the intrusion. "We heard her sing in Thalstadt once, your Waldoff—long ago, Eva's father and I. We were young people then, happy with our new baby, full of wonderful plans. And now . . ."

"Oh, sure," Inge broke in smoothly. "But in those days there was nothing like Berlin! Maybe New York is a little the way Berlin once was: it sounds that way from letters my friends have sent from there. It's something I'd have liked to find out for myself. As things stand, I'll have to take their word for it."

"You don't have an affidavit, Inge?" Eva tried to keep her own voice as cool as hers had been, but she felt suddenly ashamed. "Hundreds scrambling for a way out each week . . ." the harried voice across the desk had said. And yet, in the midst of the scramble and the panic and the pain there were those who kept the door ajar for others, with perhaps no hope left for themselves . . .

"Oh, I have an affidavit all right," Inge said lightly. "But an affidavit is one thing and a visa's quite another!"

She tapped a slender finger against her chest.

"Lung spot. Caught it on the ward, nursing at the Municipal Hospital. So I saved Adolf the trouble of having to fire me along with the other Jewish nurses and doctors—I was in Davos, putting flesh on my ribs, when *that* order came out!"

"In Switzerland! Then why did you come back, Inge?"

She shrugged. "I got better, unfortunately. Now I'm too healthy for the Swiss to keep me and too sick for the Americans to let me in!"

She touched Eva's mother lightly on the sleeve and unexpectedly flashed her bright smile. "So here I am, back in good old Berlin. Mother cries and cries. Poor woman—I have spoiled all the glorious plans she had for me: head nurse at the Mayo Clinic—winters at Palm Beach wheeling sweet old Park Avenue ladies along the walks—moon over Miami, marriage, babies . . . You know the silly dreams you mothers have, *ja*, Frau Bentheim?"

And before Eva's mother could lower her eyes from those clear, unblinking ones, Inge stopped abruptly before the entrance to one of the faceless gray buildings and held up her hand.

"The Russian Consulate, *meine Damen und Herren*. Please have your papers ready and keep calm at all times, no matter what."

Again she held the door for them—opening doors shut to herself. When Eva passed her, she gave her a conspiratorial wink.

"I'm holding my thumb for you, *ja*?" she whispered, folding her fingers over her thumb for good luck, the way Renate used to do for them both before arithmetic exams. It was an old schoolgirl game, oddly out of place in the lobby of the foreign consulate—belonging to a time when figures could still be added and subtracted and come out in neat solutions, unalterably right. Three take away one leaves two.

"I *can't*, Mother! How can I leave you and Father?"

Gently, her mother's arm urged her toward the stairs.

"You *must*, Eva. There's a whole lifetime waiting for you. And, Eva—there is Arno."

Yes, there was Arno. Somewhere, waiting for her. *J'attendrai* . . . She *had* to believe that.

271 ▪

And on legs so strangely weighted that they seemed scarcely part of her at all, she walked up the stairs and stood with the others who had come to appeal for their right to live.

■

It was the *Russian* Consulate, but it might have been any other: the room and the desks and the aloof official faces, the questions answered abjectly and evasively, as if one tacitly acknowledged guilt hidden even to oneself. At the calling of a name, figures detached themselves from the knot of people lining the walls, moving forward at once eagerly and hesitantly, to be looked over by the men behind the desks: passport photographs compared with anxious faces—visas of countries of transit and destination—a few sharp questions—a shake of the head or a curt nod followed by a quick motion of gray-sleeved elbow as an official stamp clacked on the proffered page—a suppressed intake of breath while the passport moved to the next desk for the signature of the last official. But just as Eva saw her passport land faceup on the last desk, the man seated behind it looked up—a square, boyish face under a trim haircut that did not quite conceal a rebellious trace of curl. With a quick glance from Eva's photo to her face, he handed the passport back to her, unsigned, and jumped to his feet. "Consulate closed for rest of day. Important meeting. Tomorrow morning, nine o'clock . . ."

They shuffled back, stunned, toward the stairs, Inge's face pale under the flare of red hair. "*Tomorrow*, Eva," she whispered on the way down. "We'll get it tomorrow, I promise!"

"And the train ticket?" Eva's mother asked tonelessly. "And the Trans-Siberian Railroad waiting for Eva in Moscow? What if anything goes wrong tomorrow, too?" She took the passport from Eva and held on to it warily.

They walked through the lobby, those who had received their transit visas walking with quickened steps; the others, like Eva, lagging behind, as if waiting for a voice to summon them back up the stairs. At the door, with the sun streaming blindingly into the dark, cool interior of the building, Eva's mother suddenly leaned against the wall behind the stairs, her hand over her heart. "You go ahead, Inge. I need to catch my breath. Eva and I will be out in a moment."

Inge shrugged. "Don't be too long, Frau Bentheim!" she said with a shrewd, measuring glance, and followed the others into the street.

Above them a door slammed shut, footsteps clattered down the stairs, and in an instant a group of young men passed by them unaware, bantering noisily, the Russian voices bouncing back from the walls.

Suddenly Eva's mother stepped out of the shadowed corner and seized a passing gray sleeve. The official looked up, startled, the boyish face under the stubborn hint of curl clouding with anger.

"*Ach bitte, Herr Konsul!*" Eva's mother whispered, thrusting Eva's passport into his hand. She put a trembling arm around Eva and drew her close. "*Mein Kind, Herr Konsul*—my child! *Bitte den Pass unterschreiben!*" Her free hand vaguely described a writing motion in the air above the opened passport, beneath the Russian stamp already affixed.

"Come on, Boris!" one of the others called out impatiently from the door. The curly-haired man nodded and called back something in Russian, and they both laughed. But his eyes passed quickly from Eva's frightened face to her mother's anguished one. Abruptly he pulled a pen out of his shirt pocket, unscrewed it, and hastily scrawled his name beneath the stamp.

■

Outside, in the blazing afternoon sun, the world had that faintly unreal look as after a visit to the theater: it seemed to move languidly, slowed by the heat. One returned to it, but one could not quite bring oneself to believe that it was all over: the drama in which she had almost voicelessly played her allotted part; the passport with the signature her mother had wrested from the impersonal machinery of the consulate, and which she was now slipping into the innermost safety of her brown pocketbook under Inge's astonished eyes.

Out here, the air was laden with the smells of city summers: exhaust, hot asphalt, and somewhere on the lazy breeze the brackish tang of a river. It made Eva remember summer afternoons in Thalstadt, when she and her mother went swimming in the Neckar—days not so long ago if measured in years, and yet already so remote, so lost and gone, as to have scarcely happened at all.

"When we get back to the pension, Eva," her mother said tiredly, "We must phone home. Your father will be so happy to know you have all your visas now. So happy . . ." she repeated brokenly.

Inge, with one of her shrewd glances, insisted on putting Frau Bentheim on a bus going back to the Committee. If there were plane cancellations, she said firmly, they would be phoned in just about now; it was best to be there to arrange for Eva's ticket. "And as a token of Berlin hospitality," she added wryly, "our ladies still manage to keep a pot of genuine *Ersatz Malzkaffee* on the stove. Eva and the rest of us will join you after our next stop, the Reichsbank, where we are about to transact a small matter of international finance!"

And she said it so jauntily, in her slurred Berlinese, that she almost succeeded in bringing a fleeting smile to the straggle of haunted faces around her.

The international finance transaction was the exchange of ten Reichsmarks into dollars. It was all the refugees were permitted to take out of the country. At the day's exchange rate, it came to exactly $3.65.

Outside the Reichsbank, Inge handed Eva her American money with a flourish. "Your change, madam!" She wheeled Eva around and pointed toward the tall, sparkling windows of the building. "Take a good look at yourself—*du siehst schon ganz amerikanisch aus!*"

Looking like an American already? All Eva saw was a small girl with limp, disheveled hair and frightened eyes.

Inge was tucking something into the pocket of Eva's coat.

"It's nothing!" She shrugged and added jestingly, "I give it to all my young patients."

It was a little address book; on the cover, a white dove spread its wings against a painted blue sky.

"Thanks, Inge!" Eva leafed through the blank pages, trying to look pleased. What good was an address book to her now? To whom could she write? To Renate, the shy and vulnerable girl who was facing her own battles? To Thea, whose dream of Eretz

Yisrael might have turned to ashes? To Arno, lost in a world of violence and death, perhaps already lost to her forever . . . ?

"It's for *new* friends, Eva," Inge said softly. "For your new life. Don't look back too much."

Her eyes, without their saving pretense of flippancy, were startlingly gentle.

Impulsively, Eva thrust the little book into her hand.

"May I write to you, Inge? Please put down your address."

She shook her head. "What for, Eva? Remember me a little. Memories are more durable things than streets, nowadays."

Her eyes sought out the picture on the cover, glanced up toward the blue, unruffled sky.

"The dove no longer flies to this city, Eva. Berlin has sent its death birds over Warsaw and Rotterdam. Soon now, they're coming home to roost."

■

The long day was over.

They walked back with the people going home from work, the shoppers streaming out of the closing stores. A touch of evening thinned the air: the sun slanted lean shadows across the wide streets; the leaves swayed softly in the linden trees. An ordinary evening in Berlin: even with the foreign bills in her pocket, it did not seem real that it was to be Eva's last in Germany. It was as if she had only to blink her eyes and she would see the house in Thalstadt, her room with her books on the wall and on her bed the brown eiderdown quilt with the tiny pink rosebuds. The living room with her father's chair by the window. Her father's face . . .

On the crowded steps of the U-Bahn, Inge suddenly drew Eva's head against her shoulder.

"It's all right, Eva—go ahead and cry. Cry all you want—I'm used to it. But then, *Schluss—ja?* No more tears with your mother!"

And she held her tight, there in the dusty, noisy whirl of the U-Bahn station, held her for many long minutes while indifferent strangers hurried by and the trains whistled shrilly on the gleaming tracks below. And so she said goodbye.

Later, at the pension, her mother opened a small jewelry box drawn from her purse and brought out a slender chain and a heart-shaped pendant engraved with the Hebrew letter Shin. "It is a blessing, Eva," she said softly. "It's been in my family for generations, passed on from mother to daughter, and now it is yours." With her rough-gentle fingers she locked the clasp in back of Eva's neck. "May it protect you always," she said and rested her hand on Eva's hair. "May the One whose Name it bears bless and keep you wherever you go . . . ."

By nightfall, so many refugees had crowded into the small pension to which the Committee had assigned them that there were no longer enough beds. That night, Eva and her mother slept in one bed: together at the last as they had been in the very beginning, she in her mother's arms. Once more, now, Eva lay close to her mother-body, sheltered by its intimate softness and scent against the coming dawn.

"Don't forget to brush your shoes, Eva," her mother murmured once, rousing herself from her fitful moments of sleep. "And write every chance you have to send a postcard. And don't speak to strangers."

"Yes, Mother." It would be a world of strangers from tomorrow on.

It was a mild night for midsummer. Beneath the blackout blinds, the subdued hum of the city came through the open window on a cooling breeze. From somewhere beyond the rows of shades across the street, strains of a popular song drifted into the room: the high-pitched laughter of women, the husky, insinuating voice of a man. A party, perhaps for a soldier on leave from the cruelly fought war in Poland, or from the cheaply bought one in the West. Within the house, there was quiet—a restive quiet, in which beds creaked, throats cleared, voices whispered. A child whimpered behind one of the shut doors: a thin, forlorn whimper, less of protest than of abandonment. Perhaps it was the baby in the Cologne family, the one whose Shanghai certificate had run out.

"What will you do now?" her mother had asked the other woman, wanting to be of help.

"Go back to Cologne, what else? What does it matter where we go. We're *lost*, all of us—you know it as well as I!"

Her eyes darkened. "You're lucky—at least you're saving your child!"

And Eva's mother had turned away, hanging her head as if she knew hers was indeed a gift so rare and priceless as to be almost undeserved.

■

Her legs ached. They had walked so much during the hours past, knocking at reluctant official doors. It seemed to her now as if they had never stopped walking, her mother and she, since that November night in Thalstadt when they had walked the dark streets, pleading for her father's life. Now again she was walking, walking endlessly, chilled with exhaustion and fear. There were the gabled rooftops and the City Hall tower, silent of chimes. Silent, too, the square, with Grandfather's house felt, rather than seen—shadow without substance and even shadow submerged by night. But the moon pierced the clouds, and in its cold glare the naked store mannequins lay tossed across the cobblestones, their stiff hands held out as in a last futile gesture of pleading. So many of them, lying limb to lifeless limb, piled grotesquely one upon the other—overflowing the square and stretching across a vast and empty waste . . .

And then she saw the shoes: an endless row of shoes stacked neatly beneath the bitter sky. New shoes, as they would have been new on mannequins in a well-lit shop window—but, strangely, old shoes, too: worn, earth-caked shoes, muddy shoes with their toes split open, shoes that were only shells of shoes without laces or soles, flimsy summer sandals incongruously crusted with ice. There, too, were Aunt Hanni's high-heeled pumps with their outsized bows, and her father's sickroom slippers, her mother's sturdy brown walking shoes and the red velvets in which Sabine had gone dancing at the Maccabi Ball; the patent leather shoes of the members of the Jewish Children's Chorus; even the dusty white booties of the baby from Cologne . . .

A reek of ashes hung in the wind, fouling the air, erasing the feeble stars in a gust of smoke.

"They're burning the Synagogue, Arno!" she cried, remembering. She thought she saw his slim shoulders just ahead of her, his collar upturned against the icy wind.

"No, Eva, that was *another* night." His voice came from far away. "That night they tried to burn His spirit. They always try to kill the spirit first before they burn the flesh . . ."

"Don't leave me, Arno! Arno—I love you!"

". . . love you . . ." whistled the icy wind; ". . . love you . . ." echoed the bitter air.

The ground dropped away; the frozen earth, steeply aslant, tore the bare soles of her falling feet.

Something crashed down from above, heavy and black, filling the pit and sealing off the sky.

She struggled for air. "I can't *breathe*, Mother! We're *dying*, all of us!"

And then she was lying at her mother's side, in the calm of the small room, with the deceptive balm of the summer night cooling her face and the touch of her mother's hand soothing away the grasp of death.

"Not *you*, my child—you shall *live*!" she whispered, cradling Eva in her arms until she felt herself drift off to sleep, with her mother's tears stinging her cheek.

■

They woke into the gray dawn of the morning, their senses still dulled after the brief, restless night. Later, they stood in a thin drizzle of summer rain, among blurred faces and hushed voices speaking the hurried, half-formed phrases of last farewells. One moment Eva stood beside her mother in the rain—the next their fingers touched through the window of the moving airport bus, and for a few seconds she saw her mother walking alongside the turning wheels, neither smiling nor weeping: being with her till the very last, coming with her as far as the world had let her come.